ABOUT THE AUTHOR

Richard Cobourne writes with a production background in the broadcast, corporate, music and global events industries. Many well-known TV, radio and music friends have helped him with deep background to ensure the tittle-tattle of real-life show-business and the law are accurately portrayed – including Spice Girl, Melanie Chisholm; broadcaster and voice-artist, Alan Dedicoat; and former Police Superintendent Andy Pullan.

He sold his business four years ago to enable him to write full-time. He lives with his wife in the Wye Valley and Fuerteventura.

Richard Cobourne
Wye Valley, March 2020

BANDWAGON

RICHARD COBOURNE

Matador
9 Priory Business Park,
Wistow Road, Kibworth Beauchamp,
Leicestershire. LE8 0RX
Tel: 0116 279 2299
Email: books@troubador.co.uk
Web: www.troubador.co.uk/matador
Twitter: @matadorbooks

ISBN 978 183859 298 1

British Library Cataloguing in Publication Data.
A catalogue record for this book is available from the British Library.
Cover designed by Vikki Byrne

Printed and bound in the UK by TJ International, Padstow, Cornwall
Typeset in 16pt Minion Pro by Troubador Publishing Ltd, Leicester, UK

Matador is an imprint of Troubador Publishing Ltd

'What's past is prologue'
William Shakespeare, *The Tempest*, Act 2, Scene I

1
THURSDAY, ELSTREE STUDIOS

THE REHEARSALS HAD NOT BEEN GOING WELL. They had been at it from nine o'clock each morning until six in the evening for three weeks, six days a week. In the old days, two weeks together and the show would have been reasonably tight, leaving the remaining rehearsal time to polish and sprinkle on the fairy dust.

But today, tempers were frayed. They did not have a show that the paying public would feel justified the £95 upwards a ticket, never mind the grand or more for the VIP golden circle tickets that some were bidding for on secondary market websites.

One of the lifts that was to carry the thirty dancers high above the crowd had failed, jammed under the massive stage, spraying sticky hydraulic oil across the floor of Elstree Studios' George Lucas production space. The routine could not continue with a hole the size of an articulated trailer where the thrust stage should have been. The rigging team were on it. Everyone else waited, drinking tea, coffee, water and Coke. Some outside smoking.

Martha, the star of the show, dozed in her oversized custom trailer with the extended sides. She was bored. Stop. Start. Wait. Go again. She sipped still water directly from a glass bottle – especially imported from springs somewhere in west Wales.

The lighting designer, Andy, normally calm and who could be relied on to keep the rest of the crew together had had enough. 'We are all wasting our time and pissing away the rehearsal budget.'

James 'Jimmy' Patrick, the tour manager, privately agreed with his long-time friend. But Jimmy was being paid a premium to make this enormously complicated tour deliver not only a spectacular show but also return a big profit. 'Martha doesn't have her old spark back yet – but she does still have a massive loyal following. We'll make this work.'

They were joined by some of the other technical and creative crew. Andy spoke for them all: 'Let's have tomorrow as a day off. Today's Thursday – let's all start again on Monday.'

Jimmy thought about it – the idea had some appeal. It took the pressure off the hydraulics engineers and riggers, giving them three days to ensure everything was ready for the final push. The challenge would be persuading Stanislaw Nowak – who trebled as *The Management* and unusually also the producer and the promoter of the tour.

'I suppose Martha can rehearse to playback with the dancers on one of the empty stages,' mused Jimmy. 'Yvie, her vocal coach says she is nearly ready to go – just a bit of help to hit and hold the high notes is all that is needed. She could also use some extra sessions with her personal trainer, the choreography team don't think she is fit enough to make it to the end yet without losing her breath. There are some pretty vigorous dance moves during the encore.'

There was muted agreement. Criticising the star of the show isn't the accepted norm, but amongst friends, Jimmy thought it pointless hiding what everyone tacitly thought.

'I'll get back to you.' Jimmy went off to find a quiet spot in one of Elstree Studios' drab backstage corridors to call his boss, Stanislaw Nowak.

Martha – real name Jenny Johnson – hadn't had a song in the charts for over seven years. She hadn't had a number one for ten years. Sales had fallen off a cliff. At her height she was one of the world's biggest recording artistes. This forthcoming UK, European and North African comeback tour, announced just four months ago, had rekindled the madness, affection and emotion.

Back in the day just saying the name 'Martha' would have whipped up crowds into a frenzy, busied local police forces and had the media in a feeding pack that outclassed any famished piranhas. The paparazzi could sell a decent off-guard picture for several thousand. One lucky snapper had caught Martha topless on a private beach in Ibiza – the pictures made a major splash in virtually every UK and European tabloid, funding the photographer's forthcoming retirement. Some say he was tipped off. Martha had just had a boob job.

Danny Owen, celebrity and music reporter at Starshine 98.2 FM, arrived at Elstree's gatehouse twenty minutes early for his exclusive interview with Martha. He was shown up to the door of the studio by one of the show's runners – he passed through the maze of alleyways and corridors; the BBC's temporary production cabins; and avoided several stacked scenic flats and tables of props ready to take their own starring roles in the various film and TV productions in Elstree's other studios.

The PR, Daisy deVilliers, saw Danny waiting at the vast, open, soundproof door. She looked at her watch. *Bugger, he's bloody early,* she thought, but then brightened at the thought of seeing Danny again. Daisy had been told by Jimmy that Martha was 'resting', not to be disturbed until the riggers had fixed the faulty staging.

Daisy smiled brightly and waved for Danny to come on in.

Danny paddled through the sticky hydraulic oil without at first noticing. He cursed – his off-air language was legendary. His on-air language occasionally fell afoul of the regulators. His deck shoes were ruined – they weren't exactly pristine before he arrived. The walk from Elstree and Borehamwood station, along Elstree's high street with its kebab and greasy fast-food outlets was littered with the trappings and effluent of last night's excesses.

'Wardrobe will probably have some shoes your size?' offered Daisy. Danny and Daisy knew each other of old from the circuit, as many in the industry do. They kissed three times – once on each cheek and then a little more lingeringly on the lips. A few years ago, they enjoyed a bit-of-a-thing during the UK tour of *The Sound of Music*, sparked by Connie Fisher being told that she might never sing again. Danny was the first celebrity journalist to interview Kirsty Malpass who was deservedly thrust into the role of Maria.

Danny and Daisy didn't work out then, not for any real reason other than they both worked in the personally antisocial business of show. They had together struck up a working unholy alliance that marks the relationship between journalist and PR, PR and journalist – sometimes based on mutual respect, not always, but as in their case followed by exchanges of bodily fluid. They had got over that, mostly. It could start again in the right circumstances. Or maybe not. *There was certainly a latent chemistry between them*, Daisy silently admitted.

Daisy's long, dark hair tied in a loose ponytail swished as she turned. Her willowy frame made the best of her jeans and plain white blouse. She was one of those people who always managed to look perfect whatever the time of day – or whatever had happened the night before. She had made a little extra effort knowing that she was seeing Danny today – she kidded herself she wondered why. Had Danny noticed? *Probably not. Bloody men.* She humphed out loud.

Over the years they had worked and played together, Danny and Daisy had seen a parade of hot new things come and go, many dropped by their management and labels far more quickly than they had been wooed. A few survived – survived until they could no longer provide a lavish income for the varying-sized entourage that hang protectively on the tailcoats of *The Talent*.

Daisy led Danny to the wardrobe area. 'Daphne, have you got a spare pair of trainers please?'

Daphne ran the wardrobe and costume department like a military operation. She had to – after each show everyone's sweaty clothes had to be cleaned and pressed. On the forthcoming 'Martha Movin' Out' tour, she had five sets for everyone so she could leapfrog. With some of the dancers making five changes per show and Martha herself with eight, her empire was going to fill at least three articulated trailers, two for clothes neatly arranged on hanging rails and one for laundry and running repairs. The security on these trailers is always tight – some fans get very excited about dirty clothes.

'Don't talk to me about trainers, the whole front end is full.' Daisy wondered if Daphne was having a go at her. Daphne's role as tour costume designer and wardrobe mistress – *frocks and socks* – was sometimes eschewed by the rest of the crew, yet adored by fashionistas, gossip magazines and the artistes.

'Nike have donated a range of their latest products for the after-show parties,' Daisy explained to Danny. 'And for Martha and the band to wear during interviews.'

Daisy was proud of bringing in the lucrative Nike deal as part of her role generating sponsorship, however, she knew she trod on creative sensitivities and alleged integrity on the well-worn path between art and profit.

'Size elevens I reckon?' Daphne said, peering at Danny's oily deckies. She held up a sparkly multi-coloured pair embattled with purple sequins. They all grimaced. The Air Max black ones with the distinctive Nike tick fitted perfectly.

'Let's get a coffee. Martha won't be rehearsing again until the staging is fixed.' Daisy led Danny over to catering. 'I'll fill you in with the background.'

Danny knew he had to listen to the PR-spurt, it was part of both their jobs – and to be fair Danny knew he wouldn't be fed the bullshit that more inexperienced tour PRs would offer as the truth.

As they walked over, Danny marvelled at the location catering. 'Starring-Meals-on-Wheels' was up there with the best. Carbs for the stage crew. Protein for the performers. Haute cuisine for *The Management*. Salads. Wheat-free. Vegan. Vegetarian. All had to be given equal attention. *The Talent*, Martha, had her own special menu. All had to be ready within thirty minutes of arriving on site and capable of serving the entire touring crew and hangers-on of well over a hundred within forty minutes – all prepared and served from a modified 7.5 tonne van.

'Two cappuccinos please, Shirley.' Daisy ordered for Danny. Danny nodded with a smile.

The normal frothing and bubbling sounds could soon be heard. Decent coffee was important for cast and crew morale – no instant here.

'Do you want something to eat?' offered Daisy, hoping he would say yes. All helped to cover the delay whilst the technical problems, hopefully, were sorted. Danny had been promised that he could see the rehearsals of one song before he interviewed Martha.

The blackboard menu offered the obligatory bacon sandwiches, and halloumi for the non-meat eaters – the foundation of the morning ritual of any crew on the road, be it music, film or TV. 'Morning' always came late in the night-time focused world of performance.

Danny realised he was hungry. At just gone nine-thirty that morning, he had struggled from Leicester Square, central London against the last of the morning rush hour, then caught the Thameslink from London St Pancras to Elstree. He had finished his early shift on the Starshine Radio breakfast show – his alarm had 'exploded' earlier that morning at four-thirty. Danny wasn't the main DJ, but one of the regular on-air team that added extra sparkle acting as a foil, or fall guy, to the monstrous ego of the main man, Gordon.

Lynne (traffic), Phil (sport), Alan (news) and Danny shared a mutual loathing of Gordon – well hidden on-air. Sometimes it bubbled over off-air especially if anyone had, in Gordon's insecure mind, stolen the punch line or upstaged him. Gordon told anyone and everyone who would listen he was 'The Main Man' and the rest of his colleagues were just lucky to have a job on the radio.

'Location catering always amazes me.' Danny's coffee arrived across the high stainless-steel counter in the branded 'Martha Movin' Out' mug.

'You can keep the mug.' Shirley had two thousand. 'This is the easy bit.'

Shirley was happy to chatter as she grilled the bacon. 'During rehearsals only the odd visitor, the performers and tech crew to feed. Loads more when we get on the road – some days over two hundred I'm told. Never heard such a thing. No one will confirm how many. How am I expected to cater without knowing how many? No doubt, all starving and not much in the way of local supplies on some legs, so we'll have to take most with us. Lots of plant-only menus too – far more than normal. We'll be taking a self-powered refrigerator truck. Honestly, never heard such a thing. Bollocks to Greg Wallace – cooking really doesn't get tougher than this.' Shirley emphasised the word *'this'*.

They all laughed. Shirley continued, 'Now go and sit down in the sun and I'll bring the sarnies out to you.'

Daisy quickly ushered Danny away. They could both hear Shirley's repeated mantra over the sizzling, 'never heard such a thing'. She happily admitted she could talk the hind legs off a donkey; nevertheless, Shirley was a calming maternal influence for many of the cast and crew. She was told she had a 'bus-stop face' – people would tell her their innermost secrets. Shirley was very good at keeping secrets.

The production design team had set up some trendy sea-side deckchairs, comfortable polyrattan chairs, tables and umbrellas outside, behind Elstree's George Lucas production stage, to take full advantage of the early spring sunshine – and to get everyone out of the artificial indoor world, full of tension that was beginning to turn to frustration.

Danny munched the thick organic bacon in the soft, white crusty bloomer. Butter dribbled down his chin – without being asked, Daisy wiped it off with a paper serviette.

'Weren't you and Martha in school together?' Daisy enquired. *Jealous,* she wondered, *or professional interest?* She thought she knew the answer. *It was good to see Danny again.*

Danny was an attractive guy; tall, short blond hair, the heavy-rimmed glasses made him look studious – and although he didn't look as if he worked out, he was certainly fit enough. His piercing blue eyes had melted many a heart. Daisy wondered what he would look like walking out of the sea in her own personal Poldark moment. At thirty-eight he was still resolutely single after a failed marriage – his latest girlfriend had moved out a couple of months ago. Apparently, Danny wasn't home enough.

'Martha and I were in secondary school together near Birmingham. We helped each other out revising – we both took English, Art and Music. Although clearly Jenny, sorry Martha, was absolutely the best in music the school had ever had. We sort of went out together for a while. Nothing too serious then, just a bit of snogging and fumbling at the youth club. We met up again a few years ago and dated for a while.' Danny vacillated. 'But then things got in the way as they do. You know what it's like.'

Danny decided not to say more. The relationship had developed a sinister third partner as Martha's career declined – she had returned to booze and drugs. He had tried his best to get Martha to see someone, but in a massive state of self-denial she refused. They argued about it until Danny could take no more and he had ended it. They hadn't seen each other since.

Daisy nodded – she knew about some of Martha's problems.

'You were just starting in music and celebrity, weren't you?' She gently probed a bit further. 'You were less critical of Martha's later music than many others?'

'I actually liked it – it had a certain honesty. Probably too complex and self-indulgent for some of Martha's adolescent fan base. Made for good late-night radio play.' Danny sipped some of his coffee.

'It wasn't commercial.' Daisy paused, cup in mid-air. She hoped she wasn't obviously interrogating Danny. 'Did you know her brothers and sisters?'

'I knew her twin sister Vikki, but not as well as I knew Martha. I went to their house many times when we were in school. Homework. Shared love of music. But Vikki and I never really got on, nothing serious, just didn't click I suppose – she was a wild child. I didn't hang out with Martha's other brothers and sisters either, two sets of twins too – they were younger. The house was chaotic most of the time. Six children in three pairs all within four years of each other!'

'Wow!' Daisy looked askance. 'Were Vikki and Martha identical?'

'They looked similar without make-up when they were younger. But Vikki cut her hair short and dyed it as Martha became more known. She always tried to distance herself from Martha – jealousy, I guess? Must have been

11

difficult with a talented twin sister, even at school Martha was always the star, top of the bill at concerts and events. They were never that close, but when a few other kids tried to bully them both, they did stand up for each other. Only thing they did do together – if the going got tough they were a formidable pair supporting each other. Definitely a love-hate relationship. Vikki could be vicious and spiteful. Martha was always the more naïve and friendly of the two.'

Danny's mood changed and sadness spread across his face, the elephant in the room now released. 'The accident was terrible.'

'What was it, twelve, fifteen years ago?' asked Daisy.

'The minibus driver was stoned. He lost control in thick fog on the M1 north of Watford. They were all killed – the children, the parents, and the driver. It was an awful time for everyone. Neither Martha nor Vikki were on the bus.' Danny reflected on how that night changed his life. He was surprisingly more affected than he thought he would be – death and mourning takes everyone differently. Some of the emotion welled up now. Daisy reached across and gently held his hand in an unexpected moment of intimacy.

Neither knew what to do or say.

The moment passed.

Danny tried to pull himself together by engaging professional mode. 'Martha was clearly going to be a star even back then. The five of them in the group were just beginning their music careers as a family. They called themselves Solihull Soultrain. Naff name, but they had a couple of minor hits and a lot of determination. The parents were managing them – they were incredibly ambitious and controlling. Vikki wasn't in the band – she wasn't good enough. Probably that's what made her rebellious? Obviously both Vikki and Martha were devastated, to lose your parents and siblings in one go is unimaginable.'

Daisy nodded. 'I remember. The vultures circled – any number of allegedly *sympathetic* management companies offered to take Martha on, sensing a commercial opportunity based on the media potential of the accident. It did ensure a bit of airplay and led the news for a couple days. And it did launch Martha's stellar rise to the top. Her chosen management company, gone long ago, made a killing.'

Danny gave Daisy a wry smile at the accidental faux pas. They sat in silence for a while, reflecting, while finishing their coffees.

'Martha and I discussed whether we would bring the accident up again now. She said she would answer if anyone really pushed but we weren't to include anything in the press releases.' Daisy was insistent she controlled the message.

'Fair enough, I won't go there. I suppose it might reveal where Martha was – out of her skull at a party with Vikki. Martha always said it was Vikki who had introduced her to drugs?' Danny's unasked question was now out there, awaiting an answer.

'She's clean now,' Daisy obliged. Danny might be a trusted friend, but she still had her PR job to do. 'Martha told me she didn't know about the accident until the following morning. She switched on her phone – it didn't stop pinging. She had over two-hundred messages. Off the record she had several counselling sessions for PTSD. Couldn't shake off the guilt.'

'Probably the beginning of the end of the sisterly relationship too?' asked Danny.

'For a while neither Vikki nor Martha spoke to each other – I don't really know how their relationship stands now. Only hearsay.' Daisy made a note on her iPhone – possibly a loose end. 'I have been told they are back on reasonable speaking terms.'

Danny waited for Daisy to finish tapping away. 'It's an ill wind and all that. The deaths certainly did catapult Martha's solo career – didn't her first CD and single go straight to number one?'

'I wasn't working with her then – she had an uncompromising management company that pushed her too hard. They didn't give a toss about her emotions, just cynically leveraged every opportunity.' Daisy's freelance life hip-hopped between music and celebrity clients. 'Martha's "Missing You, Loving You" was the Christmas big one. Stayed at the top for seventeen weeks. You couldn't switch on daytime TV without finding Martha being interviewed and talking about the accident – and then shedding a tear, magnificently timed to coincide with the last fifteen seconds of the interview.'

They both laughed at the pre-planned machinations of the world of show business. The mood lifted.

'Even *Private Eye* had a front cover suggesting she cried because the interview was over, and she could see the floor manager winding them up. It was a miracle she managed to get it together when asked to sing.'

'You have to admire her – she knew how to work an audience.' Daisy put on a face. 'The last big close-up with a tear just beginning to form kept the emotional sell going.'

'I was surprised to get the email from Martha with the invitation to come up here for an exclusive one-to-one – especially after all this time...' Danny hesitated, 'and our past. I listened to some old tapes last night and to the documentary I made just after the release of her final album. Brought back memories.'

Danny omitted to mention the blazing row that was their final straw and the acrimonious split. Luckily for them both, their former relationship and Martha's recreational habits were overlooked by the media.

'I'm looking forward to seeing her again.' Danny was obviously not that enthusiastic – he was a professional and the interview would make good radio. 'I do wonder, why me? There seemed to be something more though. It was weird. Martha had emailed *"We NEED to speak. I MUST see you."* Need and must in capital letters.' Danny finished his bacon sandwich, wiped his hands on another recyclable paper serviette and threw it in the bin.

'Martha absolutely insisted you were the only person she would give an interview to during rehearsals. Helped me a load.' Daisy was curious, but Danny's loyal following on Starshine Radio did make PR sense. 'I've only been working on this tour for a few weeks.'

'Maybe I'm being paranoid? Reading more into the email than there is – celebrity histrionics?' Danny and Daisy had seen it all before. 'Attention seeking?'

They got up and walked back into the studio to somewhere quieter. Danny had pulled out from his tan Billingham bag, with the distinctive leather straps, the Yellowtec iXm recorder microphone, the staple of most radio reporters. He popped a single earpiece into his left ear and hit the red record button – a signal to them both that, from now on, it was on the record.

'So, tell me about the tour. You seem to have a sure-fire success.'

Daisy switched to work mode. 'The forthcoming world comeback tour has rekindled the madness, emotion and love for Martha. We're thrilled that CD re-issues and downloads are doing well. Tickets have already sold out for many of the gigs.'

'You left many fans disappointed when the web-site crashed,' Danny demanded.

'Martha is really sorry about that. The back-room team have increased the bandwidth and number of global servers, so it shouldn't happen again. The tour's initial ticket run was oversubscribed in just a few minutes – showing how much Martha is loved. For more tickets go to www.MarthaMovinOutTour.com. Remember no G.'

Daisy had persuaded the creative team to parody Steve Wright's Serious Jockin' as part of a strategy to win an invitation to appear on BBC Radio Two's influential afternoon show.

'We have already announced more dates,' she continued, getting into her stride. 'We will be releasing even more soon, and the tour is being extended across even more countries. Martha loves her fans and she wants to see as many as she can. Please keep visiting www. MarthaMovinOutTour.com. Remember no G.'

'Will Martha be singing new material or relying on her back catalogue?'

Daisy was about to pitch the story when she was interrupted by a carefully contrived verbal explosion from behind the massive stage.

'What the fuck do you mean, give the crew some fucking time off?' Stanislaw Nowak was not taking Jimmy's suggestion well. 'If they want some fucking time off, they can fucking fuck off for good. They are here to fucking well get this fucking show fucking perfect. If they can't hack it, fucking get in someone else. What the fuck do I pay them for?'

Stanislaw Nowak waddled across the studio floor as fast as his corpulent bulk would take him – his shirt untucked and already wet from the exertion.

Daisy ran over to the source of the outburst, hoping to prevent an incident in front of Danny. 'The music reporter from Starshine is here to interview Martha. I was just giving him some background while we were waiting for the stage to be fixed and Martha to restart rehearsals.'

Stanislaw Nowak knew Starshine Radio was important. His attitude changed instantly – as if he had never had the outburst. He tucked in his shirt, checked his hair in one of the many back-stage mirrors, and seemingly serene, walked around the corner. 'Mate, how are you...?'

Danny was utterly silent. The blood drained from his face. Shocked. The bile catapulted up into his throat.

Seeing Stanislaw Nowak again after all this time was an appalling surprise. He rushed outside where he explosively threw up onto one of Shirley's gaily striped deckchairs.

Memories of ten years ago flooded back.

Stanislaw Nowak left Daisy and Danny to it. *Fucking journos,* thought Nowak.

Daisy stood there, wondering what had just happened.

The smell was appalling.

The microphone continued recording.

2
TEN YEARS AGO

Danny was known as Dan ten years ago.

He looked up from his Mac, smiled and hit 'print'. Ten thousand words of pure gold – and he had pictures to bring the story to life.

Finished – ten weeks of deep cover, research, late night drinks in dodgy bars and too many bungs. Some people had more money than sense, with a decidedly variable moral compass.

The time was just gone ten in the evening on a wintry Friday night – maybe he'd have time for a quick one at the Dog and Duck. Dan's wife wouldn't be back from the community hall until later, and their six-year old twins were sleeping over with friends.

His editor wanted to run the story across three weekends, starting just after Christmas. He had pulled in three juniors to research and write the box-outs. There was excitement that this would be the scoop to start the year.

This was probably going to be Dan's big break too as an investigative journalist. He had worked at *The Weekend News* for three years with an increasingly successful run of exposés and by-lines, the currency by which journalists judged each other.

The catalyst for Dan's story had come after a very long lunch in the Drawing Room, the third-floor restaurant at The Ivy Club, followed by too many large glasses of Calvados in the second-floor Piano Bar. Joe Thompson's mellow cocktail piano arrangements had lulled Dan and 'an anonymous source' into a state of befuddlement. Dan's guest had left, but he had decided to stay on for just one more with a couple of friends who had recently arrived – which inevitably turned into a few more.

Dan was a founder member – he used to be a regular at The Ivy restaurant on the ground floor. After a full week of lunches, for which he was awarded a special plate as a prize, he was invited to join the exclusive Ivy Club – the invitation-only Willy Wonka of private members' clubs. The then newly opened club spans three floors, all with the Ivy's iconic diamond-shaped stained-glass windows keeping members safe from the prying eyes of the surrounding buildings in London's Soho. The club was proving extremely popular as a haven for the great and the good, the bad and the ugly of creativity and show business.

All stories must start somewhere – sometimes luck and sometimes judgement. This time luck.

Dan had staggered out of the glass elevator, nearly knocking over the arriving Stephen Fry and Hugh Laurie, through the club's camouflaged entrance, a florist's shop, and into the gloom of West Street.

The rush of fresh evening air temporarily confused him; he leant on the black Range Rover parked in the disabled parking bay. Two minutes later the famous footballer, Emanuele van Damm, equally tired and emotional, fell out of L'Atelier de Joël Robuchon, the very up-market restaurant next door to the club. Van Damm didn't like anyone touching his pride and joy, never mind using it to stay upright.

'Fuck off, twat.' He shoved Dan away from the car and leapt elegantly straight into the driving seat of his Range Rover. Van Damm clearly was far from disabled and had been celebrating signing for an as yet publicly unnamed premiership football club – personal terms to be agreed.

Dan was incensed, his sense of public duty exacerbated by the third bottle of an excellent Barolo, the Calvados, followed by the 'few more' with his mates.

'You're not bloody dishabled, you schit,' he slurred.

Van Damm smiled and waved his blue disabled parking badge at Dan as he accelerated off.

'Hope you geth breathily-lysed,' was the best Dan could manage, shouting at the rapidly disappearing car as it passed St Martin's Theatre, home of *The Mousetrap*, then in its fifty-seventh year.

The following day, with his head in recovery mode, Dan started wondering how van Damm had obtained a blue disabled badge. Half an hour later he found that Blue Badge fraud was a fifty-million-pound-a-year business in the UK. He was appalled – fraudulent badges meant disabled parking spaces were often full and with parking in London costing £40 a day or more, no wonder organised crime had muscled in.

Dan's headache disappeared as it dawned on him; he had the potential for a massive front-page campaigning story. *The Weekend News* loved a campaign that would excite middle Britain. This would lead the news agenda, be the talk of the Shires, and incite the Liberal Metropolitan Elite for weeks. And, of course, increase circulation and advertising revenue.

As luck would have it, a few days later, Dan walked past a Lamborghini with a Blue Badge on prominent display in a disabled parking bay. Opposite was the café that he and many other journalists used in the early mornings for a 'cheeky breakfast' – sometimes on the way home from a long night. But this late in the day it was not far off empty. Gianfranco, the owner, had bedecked his café with Società Sportiva Lazio posters in the hope that his extra support would take them to winning the Coppa Italia – and maybe more across Europe. Danny, a long-time Spurs supporter, ordered a pancetta ciabatta with a large cappuccino.

He took a seat by the window and waited. The red plastic bench hemmed in by the Formica table wasn't comfortable – sticky rings left evidence of the previous occupants' slovenly eating habits. At the next table the Italian version of a full English, with an extra fried slice, was being noisily scoffed by a group of what Dan assumed to be decorators by the state of their overalls. Dan acknowledged the arrival of his coffee and food without taking his eyes off the street.

Already buzzing from the caffeine, he was about to order his fourth cappuccino when his patience was rewarded. A barrel-like balding man with his peroxide blonde 'girlfriend' began to clamber, with difficulty, into the high-performance sports car.

Dan signalled to Gianfranco to put the bill on his tab and walked nonchalantly across the road.

Dan, in those days, was always sharply dressed in a well-cut hand-stitched suit; he had no idea where he was going to end up or who he was going to meet. His long, flowing, glossy blond hair and stubbly beard had attracted many a girlfriend – and eventually his wife.

He put on a City drawl. 'I say old man, I couldn't help noticing you have one of those Blue Badge thingies. Want one m'self – parking can be such a bugger round here.' He snorted ostentatiously. The man looked at Dan, sizing him up. Dan smiled and tapped his nose.

The man thought he was a good judge of character. Clearly here was someone with too much money and no morals. 'Do you have a spare twenty grand?'

Dan smiled his agreement.

Stanislaw Nowak gave him his card. 'Give me a call in a couple of days.'

Nowak had a deep, sonorous voice with an over-egged received pronunciation accent – the result of several voice coaching sessions. He was determined to fit in with society and had been persuaded that the English make judgments based on not only what you say, but also the way it is said. Long gone the guttural accent from his native Poland.

Dan examined the embossed card. 'Thank you, Mr Nowak. May I call you Stanislaw?'

Nowak's smile and nod of assent was sickly sweet. Dan inwardly shuddered.

'Twenty-grand shouldn't be a problem. I'm away for a few days, then I'll get back to you.' Dan held out his hand. They shook; Nowak's grip was soft and sweaty.

And so, the story had started.

Dan had interviewed the Secretary of State for Transport, Geoff 'Buff' Hoon who promised reform, but couldn't say when. He had spoken to and covertly photographed many people who had fraudulent Blue Badges – several well-known faces were going to make the front pages whether they liked it or not. What they all had in common was spare cash and no conscience.

Ten weeks later after that fateful meeting, tomorrow was a big day – the start of the publishing process. The editorial team would receive Dan's story first thing by email. Lawyers. Picture editors. Subs. Researchers. In-house PRs. Snappers ready to doorstep the unlucky parkers. All there to ensure *The Weekend News* was bombproof and itself widely reported. This was a biggie. Sometimes you just know. The legal profession was going to earn a fortune defending the indefensible.

There was a crash, interrupting Dan's reverie. Stanislaw Nowak and two heavies barged into Dan's home. Dan was stunned – his front door doing an impression of a drawbridge not being a regular event.

Normal social pleasantries were ignored. 'You've been asking too many questions, haven't you?' Clearly rhetorical. Nowak nodded at the larger of the two heavies – for some reason Dan decided to think of him as Buster. He punched Dan hard in the stomach. Dan doubled over in more pain than, up until then, he had ever known.

'You've been a naughty boy. You tried to stitch me up. I don't like that.'

Nowak nodded again. The other heavy had a go, this time at Dan's kidneys – a rabbit punch with the end of a baseball bat. Dan collapsed into the armchair. His trousers wet from where he had pissed himself. The pain ricocheted around his head.

'You are a reporter, aren't you?' demanded Nowak.

Dan remained silent – not by choice, he simply couldn't speak the pain was so intense.

Nowak wandered around Dan's room – the printer had just finished whirring. The paper still warm. Nowak picked the manuscript off the tray and started to read.

'Oh, this won't do. Won't do at all. Where's this going?' Nowak answered himself again. 'You were going to publish this in your rag, weren't you? I am a very private person. I don't like being in the news.'

Dan tried bravado. 'It's already at the paper, I emailed it twenty minutes ago.'

'You are just going to have to un-email it, aren't you?'

Dan was desperate. 'But I can't.' His dignity wasn't going to tell them he hadn't sent the story yet.

'Oh, I think you can.'

Dan then experienced pain that surpassed his last, very recent record. The sledgehammer that had just performed its duty on the front door had exactly found the boat-shaped navicular bone in the centre of his left foot.

Buster was eyeing up Dan's right foot.

'Okay, okay. I'll take your name out of it,' Dan screamed. The initial shock had been superseded by body-encompassing agony.

'That's really not good enough. I don't want to read anything – nothing at all. You have stitched up some of my best clients. I want this all gone. Gone for good.' Dan could just hear a trace of the Polish accent, but otherwise Nowak appeared calm and in control – he rarely appeared to lose his temper except for show. Many an unfortunate associate of Nowak's soon learned to be most wary of him when he was overly courteous – it was usually an overture to an outburst of anger and spite.

Nowak dipped his head in an imperceptible nod at an enthusiastically helpful Buster.

Danny screamed. 'Okay. Okay. Stop. Please stop. It's gone for good.'

Buster looked disappointed – he was proud of his reputation as London's leading psychopath. Although he wasn't sure what a psychopath was.

'What do you think, boys? Is he telling porkies?' Nowak sounded almost considerate.

'No. Yes. Yes. No.' Dan had no idea of the right answer. 'It's gone away. I'll stop it.'

Dan succumbed. Cowardice, in this case, was the better part of valour.

Stanislaw leant over Dan. A few centimetres away from his face, sotto voce. 'If ever I see or hear from you or this story anywhere, I will do your other foot and the feet of your wife and those sweet little twins as well. Now you wouldn't want to hurt your family, would you?'

Nowak's nauseating sadistic grin – and halitosis – was terrifying. 'And don't think of going to the police. A car ran over your foot didn't it?'

The three left, Nowak taking the now cold paper from Dan's printer. Dan collapsed onto the floor, pulled a pillow from the chair, then cuddled it under his head for succour. His natural defences shut him down to a state between nearly sleep and unconsciousness – but with his inner-mind still whirring. He wasn't sure how much later his private contemplation was interrupted.

'My God, what's happened?' Sarah's voice came from nowhere. Dan's brain was barely in the room. 'Car accident,' he whispered.

'What? The car ran into the front door? This is bullshit.'

The relationship between Dan and Sarah, his wife of eight years, had been deteriorating for some time. 'I'm calling an ambulance – and the police.'

'No!' Dan's desperate yell stopped Sarah in her tracks. She put the phone down. 'What's going on? Tell me now. Everything.'

Dan told her everything.

'I'm going to my mother's – I'll collect the children.' Sarah was frightened. 'I didn't marry an idiot. Lately you have been behaving like one. You've put us all in danger.'

One week later Dan's editor was incandescent. This was his first face-to-face since the 'car accident'. They had been discussing the lack of a story. Perhaps not discussing, more a one-way Anglo-Saxon harangue without repetition.

'You promised me you had the scoop to start the New Year with a bang. I gave you ten weeks and almost thirty grand in cash. Then you come up with bloody silly excuses. And now, nothing. Bloody nothing. What have you been doing? Fucking sitting there with your hand on your dick?'

'But...' started Dan.

'Don't bloody interrupt. You're a useless shit.'

Dan could see his point. But his family came first – had he been single, he might have published. Or would he? Was he simply kidding himself? He was building his career as an investigative journalist.

'Just fuck off. Get out. Now I've got to bloody well tell the publisher we don't have the big story. You're sacked. Fired. Don't even think about arguing. You're finished in newspapers. And, if I had my way, you'd owe me thirty grand.'

The editor turned to his screen and ignored Dan as he limped out of the glass-walled office overlooking the newsroom. The other hacks turned away – they knew when to desert a wounded colleague. Curiously none were available for a pint.

Word quickly spread in the cafés and mainly pubs where the newspaper journalistic community congregated; Dan had bottled it. Of course, they all 'knew' that none of them would have spiked the story – publish and be damned was their booze-fuelled consensus.

Things at home weren't much better. Sarah and the children moved permanently to his mother-in-law. Six months later Sarah filed for divorce. Dan didn't contest it. His injured foot throbbed.

Dan was damned. Danny needed a new life.

3
THURSDAY, ELSTREE STUDIOS

'ARE YOU ALL RIGHT?' DAISY WAS CONCERNED for her friend.

'Yes, fine. Must have been something I ate.' Danny was in shock – meeting the man who had changed his life, love, health, career and foot is not an easy thing to handle.

Today was always to be a curate's egg for Dan. He wondered about Martha – but she was the one who had invited him. But now the egg was well and truly scrambled. He had been looking forward to seeing Daisy again.

'Where's Nowak?' Danny didn't want to see him again. Ten years after the event he hadn't been recognised but didn't want to take chances. For now.

'I think he's trying to sort out the riggers – his way,' replied Daisy. 'Why?'

The high-volume excruciatingly condescending Anglo-Saxon-littered language ricocheted around the studio and out the doors. Those not involved made themselves scarce. No one had ever heard Nowak about to lose it.

'Just wondering,' replied Danny non-committedly.

Daisy had found a bucket of water, taking her duties beyond those of a PR further than normal.

Danny relaxed – a little.

The inconvenienced deckchair, now more or less clean, was moved into the sun to dry. Shirley came out with iced water and tea. Danny and Daisy sat. He quaffed the water – slowly he stopped shaking.

'Things don't seem to be going well?' Danny thought he wouldn't get a straight answer. There was a silence as Daisy collected her thoughts. Could she trust Dan? She sipped her tea.

'Stanislaw is investing everything he has in this – and more from anonymous backers. No one really knows who or from where. He seems to be taking everything very personally, too. Things happen in rehearsals – that's what they are for.'

Daisy inwardly acknowledged she had taken the decision and was about to go off-piste. 'Between us? Off the record.'

Danny nodded. He was beginning to feel better – his investigative journalist juices, long dormant, were beginning to reawaken.

'This is the oddest tour – the schedule just doesn't seem sensible. Okay, we are all used to a lot of criss-crossing countries but on this one we are doing a few days in Europe, then back to the UK for a few days. Then back again to Europe. We are going to African venues too – Martha isn't really known there. No one can work out why. And this is the first major tour that Stanislaw has ever promoted, he's been involved with music for some time at his own social clubs. And several events across the UK, mainly tribute and jukebox shows – you know, several acts from the seventies or eighties all on one bill.'

Danny, without realising, had seen a couple of Nowak's shows at the Roundhouse in London. 'He doesn't use his own name, does he?'

'No, he has kept a low profile. He has several promotion companies – Festival Gigs, Hypersonic Heroes and a couple more. I'm not involved.' Daisy frowned. 'It's weird that with this tour the production company is Martha's temporary management, tour promoter and producer – the ultimate three-sixty deal. And he seems to be over-riding the tour manager Jimmy Patrick's advice and decisions.' She stopped speaking, fiddled with her mug in the vague hope it would give her help – and let out a long breath. 'Oh, I don't know…'

Danny was intrigued. 'Maybe he is being very clever? The promoter is usually the one that pays for the venue and pays the artist a fee to show up, plus all the expenses to run the show. If the ticket sales are less than the expenses to put on the show, the venue still makes money and the artist still makes money, but the promoter loses money.

But in this case, he's covered – ticket sales have already gone manic.'

'But ticket sales aren't always enough.' Daisy had worked for years in the industry and had a good working knowledge of the business side. 'We do have some sponsorship.'

Danny held up his legs to demonstrate the Nike trainers. They laughed – the earlier tension subsided. Just a little.

'But we need more.' Daisy had been working on sponsorship presentations with the tour's sales manager. 'We have a major pitch early this evening with a global mobile phone operator. And two more next week. It's difficult. No business just wants their name on a tour anymore – they want active involvement, a squeaky-clean brand and lots of social media opportunities.'

'What about merchandising?' Danny knew that the artist usually keeps most of the gross sales, with the balance going to pay the people selling the stuff, the venue, and credit card processing fees. 'Who is covering the cost of design and manufacturing – and shipping?'

Daisy snorted, then sipped her tea. She came to the decision to trust Danny. 'Shipping is taken care of – we seem to have more trailers than I have ever seen before. And that's the weird one – from a transport company in Poland none of us have heard of. Normally we'd use Stagetruck, High Road, Edwin Shirley or one of the other experienced live event touring companies that Jimmy, and the industry, know well – and that are a hundred per cent reliable. But Stanislaw has insisted we use a company from

Poland, from Wrocław, Mazury Ostrodzko International. And why we need three or more mobile silent generators is a mystery, they're simply not needed – all venues have plenty of power and back-up generators too. It's all wrong.'

Danny's foot was beginning to throb – it did when he was stressed. Should he tell Daisy about his first encounter with Stanislaw? Not here maybe, he wasn't sure if he'd be overheard.

Jimmy stuck his head out of the rehearsal studio; he blinked in the bright spring sunshine. 'Oh, I thought you had Martha with you. Have you seen her?'

Both shook their heads. 'Sorry, isn't she in her trailer?'

'Not there. Runners don't know either. Never mind, I'm sure she's somewhere – probably gone walkabout having a look at some of the other shows. Some old mates are on with Graham Norton. Thanks.' Jimmy scuttled off.

There was an uncomfortable silence.

'Look, I'd better be off – the repairs are going to take longer than the crew thought. Let's reschedule for when everything is ready. The piece isn't set for transmission until just before the tour begins. But it would be good for us to meet again...' He hesitated. 'Soon?'

Daisy felt herself blushing as she inwardly hoped it would be more than business. 'How about tomorrow? It's Friday, I should be finished by six. We can organise a proper interview with Martha for transmission then.'

'See you at The Ivy Club then – how about dinner?'

They kissed, awkwardly three times as luvvies do, with a certain tension. *Oh well*, he thought, *main and spare –*

Martha or Daisy? He immediately felt ashamed of himself. Well, not that ashamed. He had got over the final row with Martha and assumed that she had too. *But it was great to see Daisy.*

Danny left the sound stage. There was a taxi outside the studio's main gate to take him back the mile or so to the train station.

THE RADIO YEARS 4

TEN YEARS AGO, DANNY NEEDED TO WORK. HE wasn't lazy. He was determined to reinvigorate his career, but the newspaper industry had closed its doors. *Slammed in my face more like*, he thought.

Through true friends he managed to get some shifts working freelance in the BBC's radio newsroom. It was monotonous work requiring the alarm clock to wake him at four o'clock in the morning during the week. Danny still believed in the morning calls – using his contacts in the emergency services to be up-to-date with the incident-strewn minutiae of life. Later in the morning, there were calls to his off-the-record contacts at the police, political parties and inevitable mavens – the anonymous 'well-informed source' close to whatever story was about to break.

At first it was all back-room research, but as he re-established his career, he began to put together packages for the various news bulletins, often presenting them himself. He had a natural warm, friendly voice for radio – neither upmarket nor obviously accented. Danny decided he enjoyed radio, it was more immediate than newspapers and he could react quickly. New technology meant it was easy to broadcast live from just about anywhere, yet it was a medium where he could remain mainly anonymous.

Soon he was out and about reporting on the bigger stories of the day. The various public relations and public affairs companies also began to court him on behalf of their clients – each convinced that their story was worthy of broadcast. Nine times out of ten the only reaction was his delete button. He turned down most of the invitations to lunch or a 'quick coffee'.

But that's how he met Martha again – the first time since school days. The occasion was the press-launch of what was to be Martha's final album, for the time being anyway. Martha hadn't had a number one for three years and this was shit-or-bust for her.

He walked up the stairs to reception, signed in, collected his badge, a drink and joined the throng of 150 or so other journalists in the David Lean room on the first floor at BAFTA.

Danny always enjoyed the British Academy of Film and Television Arts' magnificent clubhouse at 195 Piccadilly – Mitzi Cunliffe's iconic theatrical mask, now famous as the coveted BAFTA Award, was everywhere, adding to the thrill.

At ten to eleven, the media were herded upstairs into the Princess Anne Theatre, with its plush red velvet seats – not surprisingly one of the best-equipped media spaces anywhere in the UK. There was a short hiatus while camera crews set up their equipment.

The house lights dimmed, the stage lights sparkled and Roy Sheppard, in his trademark light grey frock coat, took to the stage. Roy's job as a professional facilitator was to ensure that the event went smoothly and to defuse any awkward questions.

'Good afternoon everyone. This is an exciting day – the launch of Martha's sixth studio album. First you are going to see a short video and hear some of the new tracks she recorded at Real World Studios. Then we have about forty-five minutes for Q&A with Martha – followed by a lunch. There will be Taittinger champagne.'

The audience tried not to show their excitement.

'Those of you who have booked one-to-one interviews have already received your allocated slot – if you are late, we won't be able to extend your time. In your packs there are CDs of the new work together with background and pictures. TV, you will receive download links or tapes. Okay, let's get started. Please roll VT.'

The lights dimmed. The fifteen-minute video played on the big screen – Martha in the studio, all very arty, clearly with a massive production budget. The powerful music with its tight bass line enveloped the room. The VT finished, the stage and house lights went up – he introduced Martha and her management who sat down behind the branded table. The screen was filled with a three-metre-high picture of Martha. There was no applause – journalists can be a surly lot.

The Q&A went well enough, Roy only having to cut one journalist short – the questioning focusing too much on Martha's previous life and the loss of some of her family, rather than the forthcoming new album. Old news, unlike Martha's family, doesn't die.

Danny didn't ask a question, as he was one of the journalists who had pre-arranged a one-on-one after the melee of the main press conference – fifteen minutes in The Gallery, BAFTA's adaptable private green room. He nodded at Charlie Stayt and his *BBC Breakfast Time* camera operator and sound man as they left the room.

'I saw you in the crowd,' said Martha. 'Great to see you again.'

She turned to her PR and manager. 'Please can I have the room?' Surprised, they filed out sullenly.

When they were alone, Martha leapt up and gave a surprised Danny a big hug and a sloppy kiss.

'Oh my God, I can't believe it's you. Why are you here, I didn't think you got involved in all this?'

'Work for Starshine now – you mean you don't listen!?' Danny gently mocked her. 'Breakfast show mainly, celebrity and music.'

'What happened to your high-flying investigative journalism? Thought you were going to set the world on fire?' Martha seemed genuinely disappointed.

'Long story.'

Silence.

Martha was hesitant. 'How's, what's her name, Sarah and the children?'

'We're divorced. She's married an American. They have moved to North Carolina, so I don't really see the children very often. I speak to them on the phone or Skype every so often.'

'I'm sorry.'

'Don't be. These things happen.' Changing the subject, Danny smiled. 'You've done well for yourself. Global mega-star and all that?'

'Thank you. It's hard work. Not as glamorous as you would think.'

'A long way from after-school together.'

'Nothing is mine anymore. Trust is difficult – you'd be amazed what people are prepared to do to grab a small part of me, to hang on my fame. Music, TV, entertainment – a world full of highly paid duplicitous liars, thieves and cheats.'

'That's harsh.'

'Is it? Power. Corruption. Greed – just another day in the back office of music. Okay, there are some good guys but for every angel, there is another waiting to shaft you.'

'You sound as if you've been done over?'

'It's a permanent state. Why do you think I sent my people out? Every one of them will run a mile if this album isn't a success – then they'll be fawning over their next here-today, gone-tomorrow artiste until they can no longer provide them with an overpaid livelihood. We are disposable. The bean-counters and focus groups have taken over – the considerations of the music industry, business, whatever you want to call it, have nothing to do with art or music. The talk is of neuroscaping, emotional arousal levels and competition for the gateway of the punter's mind.'

'Wow! That's just bullshit? What happened to a catchy tune?'

'You're just a dinosaur!'

Danny didn't know whether to be pleased or offended, but they both laughed. Their eyes met – enjoying the moment and each other.

Martha continued, 'Joni Mitchell said she heard someone from the music business saying they are no longer looking for talent, they want people with a certain look and a willingness to cooperate. I thought, that's interesting, because I believe a total unwillingness to cooperate is what is necessary to be an artist – not for perverse reasons, but to protect a vision. It's the way it is. Think how many pop stars from five years ago are still in the business? Ten per cent – probably fewer. I'm lucky. This is my sixth album – if you exclude the best-ofs and compilations that the record company release without my say-so. But it's my last chance – if this doesn't do well, the PR machine will talk of artistic differences or Martha wanting to do her own thing. I'm just an expendable cash cow. There's not many that get this far – and the music business is changing. TV won't pay more than expenses for an appearance and if there is a sniff of promotion even the expenses are debatable. I'm not a Madonna or an Elton who can demand payment. Okay, I might get the occasional comedy panel show – and get paid four hundred and fifty quid.'

'So, you are pleading poverty?'

'Not yet, but I am relatively young, with my whole life stretching in front of me – there's nothing worse than a poor celebrity. I have to protect my future.'

The room was warm and comforting. They continued discussing their lives, past, present and future. Their loves, past and present – the future uncertain. And the parlous state of the world of journalism, music and showbiz. The talk was effortless and relaxed, two old friends at ease with one other. Martha couldn't remember when she had last had the opportunity to just chill and chatter. All very definitely off the record.

Danny looked at his watch, surprised to see that time had flown. He tried to bring the conversation back on track. 'So this album then?'

Before Martha could answer, her PA popped her head around the door and called time, effectively ending Danny's slot. There was little either of them could do – the schedule was tight. Phillip Schofield and his team from *This Morning* were eager to get started.

Danny was frustrated but thrilled in equal measure to catch up with his old friend. But he was still here to do a job. 'We didn't get a chance to finish what we started.'

'There's a lot we started and didn't finish.' Martha's meaning was not lost on Danny. 'Let me give you a signed picture.'

Martha had the Sharpie out. Before Danny could say anything else, he saw she had written something. He stuffed the picture in his pocket, and he was firmly ushered out.

It wasn't until that evening, in the pub, that Danny

took out the picture – the inscription read 'call me' with a private cell-phone number followed by three big kisses.

No time like the present, he thought. Dialled the number. Martha answered almost immediately.

'Jenny?' began Danny.

'There's not many that use that name now,' laughed the reply. 'Really enjoyed seeing you again today. Seemed like old times. Old times without the homework.'

'Yeah. Me too.' Danny was fumbling around for the right words.

Martha saved him, 'It would be good to catch up without my people being around. Just you and me.'

'That would be nice. Really lovely.' *Don't lose this opportunity*, thought Danny. Despite his outward confidence he was surprisingly nervous when confronted by a possible date. He felt himself blushing. 'What about lunch next week sometime?'

Martha was disappointed; she hesitated, she wondered if she was being brushed off. More brightly than she felt, she responded, 'Right, good. I'll wait to hear from…'

Before she could finish, Danny interrupted. 'How about lunch, tomorrow?' There, he had said it.

Martha felt that her heart had skipped a beat – she felt seventeen and school-girlish again. 'Hang on, sounds lovely. Let me check my diary.' A pause followed by some rustling and beeps as she checked her iPhone calendar. 'Have meetings with the record company until twelve. Then I'm off to Stockholm for a TV show – must be at Heathrow at five. Flights at six – but I get whisked through the VIP lanes. How posh is that? Don't have to queue –

apparently I am a crowd hazard!' She realised she was blethering.

'Oh, the luxuries of life as a celebrity.' Danny gently teased her. Hoping.

'Lunch it is then. Can't drink too much though.' *Probably just as well,* she thought. Martha and champagne, the cause of a loss of inhibition in the past. She wanted this to work.

'Good for me – how about twelve-thirty at The Ivy Club?'

'See you then!' They disconnected. Both of them punched the air.

The following day they arrived in West Street together – more by accident than plan. As Martha and Danny air-kissed hello, a solitary paparazzi idly waiting for anyone of interest took a few opportunistic shots from across the road. He had positioned himself halfway between the front door of The Ivy and the more discreet entrance to The Ivy Club. He might make a couple of quid on the pictures – 'Martha and the new mystery man' sort of thing. As they took the glass elevator to the second floor Danny was puzzled.

'Don't you ever get fed up with that? Being photographed without a please or thank you?'

'It's my job. It's part of the deal – I need them as much as they need me. I'll worry the day I don't get photographed. I'll get my people to speak to a few of the picture agencies to ensure you are not outed as the new love of my life.' *I wish.* She smiled encouragingly at Danny. 'Can't really stop them using the picture – but at least we can control the rumours. We'll tell them you are my gay best friend!'

Although Danny was in no way homophobic, he preferred to remain reportedly heterosexual. 'It's okay. I think I can cope with a few pictures of you and me together. Do me no harm at all will it?'

They dumped their coats with Laurence and David at reception and went straight up to the Drawing Room restaurant for lunch. No one took much notice of them in celebrity-central as they tucked into the roast of the day, carved from a smoked loin of pork on the trolley, followed by Venezuelan chocolate fondant. As promised, they each had a single glass of Corton Grand Cru and lots of water.

They picked up on old times. Lots of sentences starting 'Do you remember?' Followed by even more 'Oh My God's'.

Suddenly it was half-past three.

Marie-Clare, one of the club's managers, sashayed over to them to let Martha know her car was waiting downstairs.

Danny signed the bill onto his account.

They took the lift down to the second floor and collected their coats in silence, too many people seeing Martha and the unknown man for them to risk conversation that could be overheard – but their hands surreptitiously touched and tested, seeking a reaction.

In the glass elevator to the ground floor, they were on their own.

'It's been so, oh I don't know, nice?' ventured Danny. They both laughed.

'Nice?' Martha took Danny's hand more firmly. 'It would be great to see you again.'

'Yeah, it really would.' Danny was surprised at the strength of his feelings.

'I'll call you later.' Martha's driver held open the rear door.

She was halfway inside the opulent, leather-seated long-wheelbase Mercedes when she turned, leapt out and hugged Danny firmly. Before they knew it, they were passionately kissing – making up for lost opportunities?

The driver looked away. The paparazzi snapped.

All now water under the bridge.

FRIDAY, DEMONS AT NIGHT

BACK AT HOME, AFTER THE UNWELCOME FORAY at Elstree, Danny´s brain whirled as he tried, unsuccessfully, to sleep. The demons wouldn´t leave him. After much tossing and turning, pumping and repumping of pillows he gave up just before dawn, not far off his normal Monday to Thursday waking-up time. He made a coffee and sat down in front of his laptop.

Danny had Friday mornings off. It was guest-star day on Starshine Radio – the studio full to the brim with egos, all plugging something or other, fawning over Gordon. Danny could never use the lie-in – he was too set in his ways of the early morning alarm clock. Alexa burbled in the background streaming Starshine – he wasn't really listening. It was audio wallpaper with the occasional splash of colour, when a track he liked popped up he commanded Alexa to increase the volume, which he quickly voice-attenuated when Gordon's prattle returned.

'Bloody hell, Alexa, that man is annoying,' he said out loud.

Alexa apologised. 'I'm sorry I don't know that.'

'I don't suppose you do,' he replied whimsically.

Danny turned back to his laptop. *Why was Stanislaw Nowak involved with Martha's tour? Why was he ignoring everyone's advice on his first gig? Was Daisy involved? And Martha?* Question after question.

Bollocks, he thought to himself. *Once a crook, always a crook. The real question is why this shit from organised crime is getting into big concerts? The music industry is renowned for duplicitous behaviour, lying, reneging on deals and monstrous egos. But this is different gravy.*

He told himself he was an investigative journalist at heart – today an enforced purveyor of celebrity tittle-tattle. It paid the mortgage – but was this personal? Two old friends were involved. Perhaps he hadn't seen Martha for a few years. *And Daisy...? Well Daisy...* He realised his feelings for Daisy ran deeper. *Deeper than Martha?* Probably, especially after the split – although it was fun leading a celebrity lifestyle at the time. He wasn't sure, but it was Martha that had brought Daisy and him back together, again.

One thing was certain; Stanislaw Nowak was... is... dangerous.

He opened Google and typed in 'Stanislaw Nowak'. He

was dismayed to find over half a million results – bit like hunting for John Smith in the UK. Could be anyone.

He spent another hour searching and sub-searching. Nothing but frustration. He looked at his watch, it was just gone seven – the sun had begun to fill his office at home with the first light of day. He'd been at it for over two hours.

His window on the second floor overlooked Tooting Bec Common. He watched the pre-work dog walkers picking up their pooches' shit. Danny perversely wondered what the dogs thought, especially when they were rewarded with a biscuit treat after a particularly spectacular achievement.

Parents were taking their children to school, walking mostly happily hand-in-hand along the grass opposite. There didn't seem to be the plethora of leather satchels so prevalent from his time at school. His thoughts turned back to Martha and their times together. Happy days at school.

He gave himself a talking to. *No more maudlin introspection. Shower, walk, and brekky may clear the cobwebs?*

The phone interrupted his plans. It was Daisy – she came straight to the point. 'We can't find Martha.'

'What do you mean you can't find her?'

'She's disappeared and not answering her phone. Her driver just called us – she has a key as she sometimes has to wake her and wait. But this morning, nothing.'

Danny was puzzled. 'Why are you telling me this? I don't really understand. Full rehearsals were called off yesterday because of the technical problems – it's only nine-thirty now. She may have got ready early and pottered out for some milk or something. Surely she'll be in later when dance rehearsals begin?'

'Her bed wasn't slept in.'

'Maybe she pulled – she'll soon be doing the walk of shame home?' Danny thought that was a bit unfair. 'Or stayed over with a friend?'

'Nobody has seen her since yesterday morning just before you arrived. We all thought she was in her trailer, resting. No one saw her leave.'

'Didn't her driver take her back home?'

'We only use a driver to ensure she gets to rehearsals on time – she normally gets the train home, unless it's a late finish. She does dress down, so she's not recognised.'

Danny was amazed how even major celebrities were able to get around London without being recognised. People just don't look at each other. And if a well-known face doesn't want to be seen, it isn't difficult simply with a few clothes and keeping their head down – definitely not dark glasses! Even the former Spice Girls get the Tube without a problem; one trip Danny had sat opposite Melanie C and only recognised her when they accidently made eye contact as she got off.

'I rang the police, they took the details, but didn't seem too impressed that it was Martha, or she hadn't even been gone a full day. He told me to call if we have further information or she turns up. The officer was pretty much reading from the screen.' Daisy put on an officious voice.

'"The person will be recorded as absent and their details made available to other UK police forces within forty-eight hours".'

'I'm sure there's nothing to worry about.' Danny knew Elstree reasonably well. 'Have you asked security to look at the CCTV? The guys on the desk are pretty good at logging people in and out. She'll turn up soon.'

'I called them first thing.' Daisy was exasperated. 'Martha is now teetotal and signed a contract to guarantee she doesn't take any drugs unless prescribed by an approved physician. She's not in a relationship either.'

Danny wasn't sure which pleased him more – that she wasn't in a relationship or she was teetotal and drug free, the cause of their break-up. He was confused about the strength of his feelings – *Martha or Daisy? Is it a choice to make or am I being silly?* He realised that Daisy was still speaking.

'Sorry, where does she live?' Danny hoped he had got away with not hearing what Daisy had been saying.

'Just around the corner from the Electric Ballroom in Camden Town.' Daisy knew that Camden Town and nearby Chalk Farm and Kentish Town have long been a Mecca for those working in the creative arts – and a thriving market for recreational drugs. 'I hope Martha hasn't fallen off the wagon.'

'Is that likely?'

'I really don't think so. I'd be surprised.'

'There's nothing more you can do for now, is there?'

'I suppose not.'

'She'll turn up and wonder what all the fuss is about.'

'I hope you're right. But I have a funny feeling about all this.'

'Look, I'll see you tonight.' Danny paused. 'There's a few things I need to tell you about Stanislaw Nowak. Let me know if Martha turns up.' He rang off quickly before Daisy could ask any more questions.

He stripped and ran the shower.

After a breakfast at HOB in Balham High Road of sumac fried eggs, lamb Merguez sausages, grilled halloumi, batata harra, Moroccan beans and toast with plenty of builders' tea, he returned home to research what he could about Martha, the tour, and eventually Stanislaw Nowak's involvement. Most of it was celebrity gossip and could be ignored. There were a few useful nuggets – such as the cost of promoting a major tour. No one seemed to care about where Nowak or the money had come from, all blinded by Martha's return. He'd called a few friendly journos from his days in the papers – a few hinted at Nowak's involvement in organised crime, but nothing proven.

He did get a little further with his old contacts at the police. Most knew of Stanislaw Nowak but had never been able to pin anything on him. One did agree to meet him for a drink – Bill Kelly was an old-school detective sergeant, in Serious and Organised Crime at the Metropolitan Police. Danny thought Bill had been passed over for promotion too many times and therefore was happy to talk. Bill said that Nowak was no longer the crime boss he once was, competition becoming too great with the Russian Mafia moving in on all the most profitable ventures. But he was still a 'person of interest'.

They agreed to meet for Sunday lunch at the Crown & Sceptre in Fitzrovia.

The rest of the day Danny spent doing the day job – he still had his shows next week. He sifted through several screens of incoming emails from various celebrity contacts, agents and their 'people'. He made a few calls to arrange for guests to either come into the studio, agree to take early morning phone calls or, in a very few cases, for Danny to visit and interview. Danny had three email addresses – Starshine, his freelance address, and his very private personal one. No one had used the private address.

He then spent a couple of hours updating the celebrity posts on Starshine's website, Facebook pages and all the other social media that were part and parcel of this digital world. His content was mainly rehashed press and media releases with added colour from his catalogue of background information and the inevitable social media – where it could be trusted. He was very good at sprinkling weaselly words such as 'allegedly' or 'reportedly' and, if he was really unsure, 'according to' into both his on-air and online reporting. The folklore of artistes is legendary.

Danny had long ago learned too about the black art of PR as manipulated by the pop impresarios and promoters. First step, make up a story that played against their own artiste. Then, via anonymous third parties, leak to the media. Then strenuously deny the story – with unfulfilled threats to sue anyone that published. The more they postured and denied, the more likely the stories were to be published. Keep people talking is all that matters. What did Oscar Wilde write? Danny looked it up. *There is only one thing in the world worse than being talked about, and that is not being talked about.'*

Danny shut down his laptop, changed into something suitable for his date with Daisy, carefully chosen to make it look as if he hadn't spent half an hour choosing. He decided, after several attempts, on stone-washed blue jeans with an embroidered belt, plaid check shirt with the sleeves casually rolled-up, a hand-stitched dark grey waistcoat and brown leather loafers with no socks. He added a scarf at the last moment.

He left his house about five, walked up to Balham Tube station and took the Northern Line to Leicester Square. He arrived at The Ivy Club early to find Daisy already waiting for him in a quiet corner of the Piano Bar – on her second large gin and tonic. The post-work, pre-theatre rush was just getting underway.

They embraced. Danny ordered an Innis & Gunn craft beer – Daisy accepted her third gin and tonic. She thought his clothes taste left a little to be desired.

'Any news about Martha?'

Daisy was clearly stressed. 'No. Nothing. Jimmy has spoken to her agent – he didn't seem too worried. She said she often goes silent for a few days.'

'Maybe she has simply decided to have the weekend off – she's probably walking in the Brecon Beacons right now. When we were in school together, the geography teacher arranged a field trip there. Martha loved it. She was in her element – she said she found the wild Welsh hillside invigorating. Of course, later she had to give up geography to make room for music. But we talked about that trip – and spent a few weekends there ourselves. The mobile phone signal is patchy at best.' Danny hadn't convinced himself.

They clinked glasses – they nibbled olives and salted almonds. Daisy gave up waiting for Danny. 'Give. What is it you want to tell me about Stanislaw?'

Danny told the story, leaving nothing out.

Daisy, by now ashen, interrupted Danny. 'He did what? Bloody hell Danny. Why haven't you told the police?'

'They quietly know now – told one of my contacts this morning. But at the time Nowak threatened Sarah and the children. I was scared for them. And for me. You have no idea what it was like. Terrifying. Why do you think I was so bloody shocked yesterday?'

'So, it wasn't something you ate? And it's why you limp?' She didn't know what to do or say. She was overwhelmed. *Could she remain working for Nowak and the tour? How was she going to face Nowak next time she saw him?* Strangely for Daisy, her maternal instincts kicked in.

'Do you still see Sarah or the twins?'

'Sarah remarried seven years ago. The twins are seventeen now – I see them every couple of weeks by Skype. I get the feeling it's becoming a chore for them. Let's be honest, they have a new life and a new, err, father. Never met him. Don't want to. Sarah seems happy according to the kids.'

Daisy snapped, tears running down her face.

She got up and stormed off to the lavish Ladies to wash her face and attempt to collect her thoughts. *Danny beaten up and maimed by Stanislaw? Stanislaw's background in organised crime? Martha maybe disappeared. Maybe? Who was she kidding? Martha disappearance was too much of a coincidence. What had she got herself involved in?* She wasn't one for panic – her crisis training as a PR kicking in. But this was right on the edge.

She combed her hair and tidied her make-up. She looked in the mirror, her pale reflection looked back at her – she added a little more blusher. Looked again and gave up.

A few minutes later she returned, agitated. 'So, this whole tour is funded on the proceeds of crime? And Stanislaw Nowak is a gangland boss. How the bloody hell can I work with him? How do I know that I am not going to be arrested?'

The questions tumbled out. A long list yet to be written – Daisy liked lists.

Danny tried to reassure Daisy. 'He didn't recognise me – it's been ten years and I have changed quite a bit. So, you are safe. You know nothing about all this. I made a promise not to tell anyone – and up until now I have kept that promise.'

'Thanks a bloody bunch.' Daisy's shock had turned to anger. 'How could you let me get into this situation?'

'Hang on. I didn't – you did this all by yourself. So, don't blame me. I knew nothing about Nowak and Martha. I only found out by accident you were involved with the tour. And don't act surprised – yesterday you were the one telling me something wasn't right.' Danny was becoming angry. A couple of people in the Piano Bar looked around at the raised voices.

Daisy was still. It was a fair point. In some ways nothing had changed – but everything had changed. 'I can't stay working for that man.'

'What are you going to say to Nowak? "I'm resigning because you beat up Danny"! If Nowak does find out you know, then that puts us both in danger.'

Daisy thought about it. 'I could lie and say something has cropped up. My mother is ill. Anything?'

'And what about Martha? Are you just going to ignore her?'

'But you said she was probably walking in Wales and that we should wait until Monday.'

'I said there was nothing we could do until Monday.'

'Don't play bloody games with me. She's missing, and we don't know where she is. Or with whom.'

'It's hardly likely to be Nowak is it? Think about it. Without Martha there is no tour. And she needs to rehearse.'

'Fuck, fuck, fuck!' screamed Daisy in her perfect cut-glass accent. This time everyone in the Piano Bar went silent and turned to look at them. Joe Thompson continued playing the grand piano – he segued seamlessly into Irving Berlin's 'Let's Face the Music and Dance'. With a benign beaming smile on his face he gently sang, 'There may be trouble ahead...' Everyone laughed – the happy chatter resumed.

Danny and Daisy sat there in silence. Eventually a waiter asked them if they wanted more drinks – they nodded. 'Thank you, same again.'

'I have spent all day on this. According to my initial research Stanislaw doesn't have the sort of money needed for a tour of this size – he hasn't had a lot of success lately.

I suppose his money could be hidden. I don't know if it's crime, if he won the Lottery, or if Nowak has gone legit. My best guess is he is working with someone else – a moneyman perhaps, behind the scenes. But the bigger question is why?'

More silence.

'None of the tech crew can understand what is going on.' Daisy had settled down and was now in work-mode. 'I heard them talking yesterday before you arrived – while they were waiting for the hydraulics repair team.'

'We should talk to them,' suggested Danny. 'Who is a good place to start?'

'Jimmy Patrick is the tour manager. He seems to know most of what is going on.' Daisy thought about it. 'He's been around for years – has a great reputation in the industry.'

'We need to know if Martha really has gone missing. And, if so, is this somehow connected with Nowak? In all events we need to find out what Nowak is up to – he's a bloody crooked shite.'

'You're using that word "we" again?'

'It's going to be difficult for me, if Nowak sees me – I, we, may not be so lucky the next time.'

Despite everything, they went upstairs to the club's restaurant, the Drawing Room, to eat – both were hungry. Danny and Daisy sat in the high-back fireside chairs at the same table that Danny and Martha had shared several years ago – he didn't mention this.

Most of the tables in the elegant room, with its mirrored columns, are far enough apart to be able to have an indiscreet conversation without being overheard.

Danny was recognised by a couple of celebrities who shouldn't have been there; well, not together anyway. Danny shook his head to indicate he hadn't seen them – mysteriously a bottle of champagne arrived at Danny and Daisy's table. They all silently toasted each other across the crowded room and returned to the business at hand.

Daisy and Danny agreed over Wye Valley asparagus and hot hollandaise sauce that they wouldn't discuss the current problems. They began to relax a little as they caught up on old times, picking up on old 'war' stories, industry gossip and their life histories, mainly Daisy's. The bottle of champagne emptied surprisingly easily.

Danny was amused to discover that Daisy achieved a good first while at Pembroke College, Oxford reading History and Politics – this was the first time that they had discussed their past lives. Daisy was one of three siblings and the first in the family to go to any university – her mother came from a wealthy 'old' family ingrained with the tradition of devoting life to caring for her children, rarely working, never needing to, except for occasional part-time charity volunteering during school hours. Daisy couldn't remember her father who had disappeared when she was five and was never spoken of again, despite her best efforts to find out more. 'We don't talk about him' was all she had been told. Daisy had recurring visions of her father in a crusty London club, with a bottle of whisky and a revolver delivered on a silver salver by an old retainer. 'The members thought you might like these, sir. You might find the roof terrace convenient.' One day she promised herself, she would investigate the family and her father further.

The main course arrived – for Daisy, Gigha halibut, and Danny the spiced stone bass. The icy cold Albariño matched their food perfectly. Both blissfully relaxed in a world away from the business of the tour and the missing Martha.

Their personal history investigations continued. Daisy thought she had wanted to become a political researcher and after that, she wasn't sure where it would end up. After a few months as a virtually unpaid intern working for a rabidly left-wing back-bench MP in Westminster, her mind was changed, and her opinion of some politicians reached a nadir – too many hands on her bottom and far too many clumsy propositions. After a particularly offensive suggestion involving the offer of payment of £250, she simply walked out – leaving the senior politician worried that they might be revealed for what they were. Daisy rigorously followed the aphorism 'don't get mad, get even' – one day she would call it in.

Timing is everything – on the Tube home, she saw an advertisement for a PR course. One month later after an interview with the semi-retired, pin-striped-suited course director, she started her life in PR ending up with a post-graduate diploma in media relations and public affairs from Cardiff University. The allowance from her family trust covering the rental of a waterside apartment in Cardiff Bay, her living costs and course fees. It was there she met Martin Short, the imposing MD of 'Blimey O'Reilly', a fast-growing 'yoof-focused' PR-shop, who offered her a job on the spot – after five years she decided to go freelance working for a couple of music companies and their artistes that she had met along the way.

Now late, Daisy and Danny were alone in the restaurant, the outside dark except for the orange glow of the streetlights. The room lights dimmed as they shared an Amalfi lemon pannacotta with strawberries – all thoughts of the current issues hidden behind the unexpected comfort and intimacy of the evening.

They returned downstairs to the Piano Bar for coffee and Calvados – Joe Thompson at the piano reprising Irving Berlin's works. Danny sent over a beer in mock tribute. The spell broken, they couldn't avoid Nowak and Martha any longer.

'Until Monday there is little we, you, can do about Martha. If she doesn't turn up then, there could be a problem,' began Danny. 'But with Nowak we need to find and follow the money.'

Daisy was new to all this. 'But how? I've got no idea where to start. You, more than anyone, know he can be dangerous.'

'I am seeing an old mate from the Met on Sunday – do you want to come too?' offered Danny

'Why not? We have to find Martha.' Daisy's concerns were countered by the thought of seeing Danny again.

'If she is missing,' responded Danny. Daisy's look made it abundantly clear what she thought. And that she was worried. Danny paid the bill, despite Daisy's protests – he was a bit old-fashioned. They collected their coats and took the glass lift to the ground floor. The mock flower shop smelled of hyacinths.

They went off into the night, separately, after a tentative kiss and a longer comforting hug. The closeness of their bodies stirred them. But tonight was not a night for carnal re-exploration – both impressed themselves with their grown-up resolve.

FRIDAY EVENING – LONDON AND CAIRO. WHAT'S PAST IS PROLOGUE

ACROSS TOWN, STANISLAW NOWAK WAS PANICKING. WHERE was Martha? The rehearsals were not going well – there had been too many technical hitches, he thought, despite Jimmy's protestations that this was par for the course. And now he might not have a show, without its star. And without the show…? His plans were going to shit.

Nowak had no interest whatsoever in the lily-livered wall flowers with their demands and riders and their creative juices. He didn't really give a toss about Martha either. She was just a route to market – hopefully a cash cow. He wanted – needed – to get the show on the road. Quite literally. The three shows at the massive O2 Arena in just a few weeks were looming – then the thirty-date, or more, tour criss-crossing the UK, Europe and North Africa. The PR, marketing and ticket sales campaigns had done well. But it wasn't enough; he owed money but had 'bigger' plans. He really wanted to do the business out of this show.

It had all been going so well...

The short break in Cairo nine months ago was exactly what he needed. He had been losing his rag too often with people he trusted – not a long list. He needed to calm down and expend some of his libidinous energy. He had arranged for a 'dowry' to be transferred to a marriage broker for a *nikah mut'ah* – a 'summer marriage' – a temporary marriage allowed under Shia Islam Law to circumvent Egypt's prostitution laws. Nowak had exotic tastes that only certain specialist marriages could accommodate – the marriage would end when he left for home.

He had booked into the Nibbana Boutique Hotel in Zamalek where his highly anticipated 'marriage' would begin the following day. The hotel was a testament to the seventies, but it was clean, the bed very large and comfortable, the bathroom perfect for his needs. His bedroom was a bizarre mix of contemporary and old. The heavy ormolu picture frames clashing with the cherry wood, taupe paint work and heavy black drapes. They'd obviously bought a job lot of low voltage spotlights – they were everywhere and anywhere, lighting up the out-dated design.

On the first evening, just after Nowak had arrived, he had gone for a stroll through Zamalek town – the leafy, affluent district of Cairo in the northern portion of Gezira

Island surrounded by the ambling River Nile. He had put on solid shoes; the concierge had suggested open sandals should be avoided due to foot-level organic booby traps. It was hot and humid – his shirt was, as usual, sticking to his back. Sweat trickled down his ample legs. Tour boats were slowly meandering up-river to their overnight moorings. Nowak watched with contempt the excited camera-toting, excessively large Americans dressed in shorts and trainers. The evening sky turned deep purple and orange.

He found a bar that suited his taste on Shagaret El Dor Street – the traffic rushed by outside on one of the main arteries across the island. Lane markings seemed optional. He sipped his icy cold beer and looked around – the bar was certainly shabby and whoever had designed it had forgotten about the chic bit. A couple of men in the far corner were drinking coffee, playing backgammon and smoking shishas. The traffic fumes mixed with *ma'assil*, the tarry substance burned in the shisha, reminded Nowak of home – the smell of incense in the cathedral of St John the Baptist in Wrocław.

Egyptians call Cairo the Mother of the World. It is a modern megapolis with an ancient past, a living, breathing and perspiring witness to its thousand-year role at the heart of the Arab world. Nowak thought if New York is the city that never sleeps, try Cairo sometime. Eighteen million hustling, bustling people – ear-splitting, pulse-pounding and overwhelming. An all-out assault on the senses.

As he looked out of the bar towards the mix of new and colonial-style buildings his thoughts turned to the tour and how he was going to raise the extra funds he needed. He had six weeks to finalise the optioning deal or everything was lost – he'd already put in an extra half-a-million of his own money, leaving virtually nothing in his personal coffers. Something he'd promised himself he'd never do – *but you must speculate to accumulate,* he thought, or was he simply trying to convince himself?

Nowak enjoyed people watching, guessing who they were and what they were doing. That included listening to other people's amazingly indiscreet conversations in public places, especially on mobile phones.

Across the bar, drinking hot mint tea, Ali Baka was clearly frustrated. 'That's the bloody *monassek*'s job. It's his job to take care of one bloody thing.'

Nowak couldn't hear the other end of the conversation. 'One hundred thousand is the top. Try carrot and if that doesn't work wield the bloody stick.' Ali Baka had been educated in the UK – his use of English was excellent. There was genuine malice in his suggestion to wield the stick.

Nowak worked out that one hundred thousand Egyptian pounds was nearly nine thousand in UK pounds. *This is interesting,* he thought.

Ali Baka was suddenly aware that Stanislaw Nowak was sitting up and taking notice of his conversation. Ali Baka was a short, stumpy, muscled man clearly used to street fighting. A scar ran under his stubbly chin, obtained during a knife fight in his hometown of Kuala Lumpur. His pepper and salt, short curly hair was greasy. He stood and walked over to Nowak.

'You were listening to my private conversation? I don't like that.'

Nowak wasn't in the slightest bit intimidated by the not-so-covert menace. 'Then don't bloody shout. Sit down and have a drink.' Nowak pointed at the spare chair. Baka, intrigued, lowered himself opposite and barked at the waiter, 'Mint tea. He's paying.' Nowak also nodded at the waiter.

'You haven't answered me. Why were you listening?'

'Sounds like you were having a little domestic trouble?' countered Nowak.

A beer and hot mint tea arrived. The waiter hovered. 'Fuck off,' Nowak and Baka chorused in unison.

They eyed each other up, recognising a little of each of them in the other, like stray dogs sniffing arses.

'What's a monassek?' asked Nowak eventually.

Ali Baka sipped his tea. He didn't answer for a long while. Nowak was patient – silence is the greatest inquisitor.

'Let me tell you a story.' Baka ordered another tea by pointing at his empty glass cup. 'A friend of mine is an engineer. He moved to Cairo from Damascus. He calls himself an engineer but hasn't engineered anything concrete for many years – yet he has earned over two million of your pounds in the last twelve months from... let's call it the travel trade. He provides a social service. And like all good travel companies they supply reps on the ground to look after the travellers – that's the monassek.'

'And who are these, err, tourists?' Stanislaw Nowak enjoyed a game – and the game was afoot. 'And to where would they like to travel?'

'That depends how much money they have – or could have.' Ali Baka debated whether to say more. Nowak obviously wasn't an entirely law-abiding citizen. 'And from where and to where they want to travel.'

Their conversation carried on for a further minute or two, both hinting and suggesting, circling and testing. Neither wanting to give anything up that might be incriminating. Eventually Nowak ended it.

'Let's meet here again tomorrow, same time?'

They shook hands, exchanged business cards and each went off into the streets pondering. *Opportunity or set-up?* Business cards can be very misleading. Duplicity at the front of both their calculating minds.

The following morning Nowak was fully and enthusiastically engaged in 'marriage' activities. When he was totally satisfied, he sent his 'wife' away to return the next day. The afternoon was spent finding out more about Ali Baka from Nowak's associates and contacts.

'Ali Baka. He's a bloody shit, but a successful one,' was one response.

'Moves more people into Europe and the UK than anyone else. He has a reputation for not drowning his customers,' came another. 'The word on the street is that last year Ali Baka's team smuggled over six thousand people at ten thousand US dollars or more per delivered person – and he is hoping to increase that number.'

'He is on the Met's and Interpol's radar with requests for information from several countries. No one has enough to arrest him. He is definitely a person of interest.' The call was returned from an unavailable number. Nowak could hear Big Ben chiming in the background. 'He's under pressure from the Russians.' Nowak sympathised – the Russians were muscling in everywhere. But he was equally excited, this was someone with whom he might be able to do business. He might even be able to raise the extra funding he needed. Nowak decided that Baka was exposed; he obviously needed new 'travel arrangements'.

The following evening, Nowak and Ali Baka met again – mint tea for them both. Nowak decided he needed a clear head. Baka rarely drank alcohol when in predominantly Muslim countries. After the normal social preliminaries that seem so important in this part of the world, Nowak got down to business. 'Sounds like you have a few problems in your tourist business?'

A long pause while drinks were sipped.

'Nothing in life is simple.'

Another pause.

'I'm partly in the transport business too.'

A further pause – but Ali Baka was intrigued. 'Really? What sort of transport business?'

'Touring music – have you heard of Martha?'

'Hasn't everyone?' Baka gave Nowak an ingratiating smile.

'I was thinking that I have trailers and trucks, all sign written, and highly visible touring around Europe. It wouldn't be that difficult to arrange for them to include North Africa and maybe Turkey in their travels.'

Baka thought this sounded too good to be true. 'Surely you have no space?'

'There's no problem adding extra transport.' Now it

was Nowak's turn to return the smile. 'Of course, for a suitable investment.'

Baka ignored the question of investment. 'Surely this all attracts a lot of attention.'

'Hiding in plain sight, you mean.'

Ali Baka finished his mint tea – and nodded at the waiter to replace the ornate silver pot. They both waited while the waiter brought fresh glasses.

'A couple more vehicles won't attract attention. You'd be surprised how celebrity excites even the most stoic customs and border teams.'

'How many, err, tourists could you take?'

'Maybe seventy on each crossing, maybe a few more – depending on how luxurious you want the accommodation to be. I could offer a premium service. So, you could ask a premium price. Only willing tourists though. No chance of drowning.'

Baka remained silent again – he was deep in thought. The mention of drowning was a major clue that Nowak already knew too much about his business, but could he trust him? This was only the second time they had met. Baka, too, had spent much of the day talking to his contacts about Nowak. The opinion was generally favourable, or as favourable as anyone could be in the murky underbelly of mid-level crime.

'You said investment – how much do you need for your music tour?'

'Two million – UK.'

Baka wasn't in the least bit fazed. 'At fifteen per cent – repayable in one year.'

'Five per cent flat, repayable in two years – that's one hundred grand you earn in addition to whatever you take for your punters' travel tickets.'

Baka did the maths. 'How many crossings?'

'Let's say five for now, that's three hundred, three fifty tourists, give or take.'

'Could you offer more?' Baka was excited.

'Let's see how the tour goes – these things are fluid.' Nowak, despite his enthusiasm, didn't want to over promise.

'Two million pounds is a lot of money. How do I know I'm going to get it back with interest?' Baka's menace was palpable.

'We wouldn't want to hurt each other, would we? And I might be able to help with other aspects of your business too. I am sure some of your tourists might have lost their passports?' Nowak had been involved in the supply of stolen, lost or cloned EU passports for several years, each selling at several hundreds of pounds – he had no qualms about profiting from his trade.

The passports had been used by others to bring many people into the UK. Nowak insisted to himself that none of the tourists were jihadis or criminals.

'A UK passport is the gold standard, like winning the lottery. Once inside the UK, it is very difficult to trace someone. And I might be able to help with EU passports and identity documents too. But willing tourists only?'

'People smuggling is an emotive business – Oscar Schindler and Sir Nicholas Winton were people smugglers. And what or who exactly is a migrant?' asked Baka. 'Transporting people is a business – I deliver a service that suits the depth of people's pockets.'

They spent a few more minutes haggling. Eventually Ali Baka held out his hand and they shook. 'Okay, we have a deal. Give me two weeks to sort out the details with my associates.'

Ali Baka's grip was exceptionally firm. 'You piss me about, and your death will be long and lingering.'

'A mutual agreement then.' Nowak wasn't going to back down.

That was a few months ago, but he had done it – he had raised the seed money needed to put on the tour and not at the rates the bankers and venture capitalists demanded. His return would be at least five-fold. He might not have to work again. Or he could invest in bigger and better projects.

Until Martha had gone missing.

Nowak's introspection was interrupted by his mobile phone – the ring tone being Martha's biggest hit. Even Nowak liked a bit of irony.

'Yes?' The caller ID read 'unavailable'. He looked out of his windows – he hadn't noticed it had become dark.

It was Ali Baka. 'There you are, Stan. I was hoping you would pick up – I didn't want to leave a message. Is all going well with rehearsals?'

'We had a few issues with the staging, but all is running smoothly now. We're back on schedule. It's going to be amazing. Advance ticket sales are exceeding our expectations too. Your money is safe.'

'Even without Martha?'

Nowak was silent. *How did Ali Baka know?* He bluffed, 'Given her a day or two off. Bit of a break whilst we sorted a few technical issues out.'

'Really? That's strange, because Martha is safe. With

me. As my guest.'

'What?' Nowak went cold – he was confused. 'Why would you do that?'

'Let's just say we need to renegotiate our agreement. Does Monday suit? Let's say midday – I'll text you where I am staying at eleven. You'll come alone, won't you?'

Before Nowak could answer, the phone went dead. Nowak tried to call Baka but the number he had for him was unobtainable. The burner phone already burned.

Nowak, sweating, paced around his luxurious apartment and into the kitchen – he kicked out at the unsuspecting waste bin, which distributed its contents over the floor. The cold curry from the many half-empty take-away cartons oozed across the floor forming a vibrant yellow river, mocking him.

'Fuck it!' he screamed. Grabbed his coat and stormed out to find some submissive professional female distraction. *Bollocks to safe words, I fucking pay the tart enough.*

It was going to be a long weekend – for several people. *Why has Baka kidnapped Martha?* Nowak couldn't work it out but knew that it couldn't be good news.

He didn't like nasty surprises.

He demanded to be in control.

SUNDAY AT THE CROWN & SCEPTRE, FITZROVIA, LONDON

DANNY ARRIVED PROMPTLY AT NOON BEFORE either Daisy or Bill Kelly. He ordered a Little Creatures Dog Days Session Ale and left his credit card behind the bar, starting a tab. He was about to take his first sip when Bill and Daisy arrived at his corner table at the same time. Introductions were made. Bill had the same as Danny, while Daisy had a Brockmans gin with Double Dutch Pomegranate and Basil tonic. Danny and Bill raised eyebrows, the unspoken question being *What's wrong with Gordon's and Schweppes?*

They clinked glasses and savoured their drinks. The sun shining through the coloured glazing of the pub windows on the corner of Great Titchfield Street casting patterns across the tables.

Danny and Bill were comfortable here – each enjoying the atmosphere of the traditional London pub that makes boozers and casual visitors alike feel cosy, encouraging just one more for the road, or in London, the Tube. Danny looked across the room; leaning on the bar were three men with reddened cheeks and bulbous noses on their first of their regular Sunday session. He took a long draw of his beer and licked his lips.

'How long have you known each other?' Daisy interrupted their contemplation. As she looked around, she realised she was easily the youngest there.

'Fifteen years or so. Since you were on *The Weekend News*,' said Bill, looking at Danny. 'You were a bloody good reporter. No one understood why you left – but I do now. And if it wasn't you, I'd do you for aiding and abetting, failing to report. Stealing a Tesco trolley, anything. I've calmed down a bit now.'

'I told Bill about Nowak on Friday,' said Danny. The two men looked at each other – peace had apparently just about broken out. They made small talk to prove ostentatiously that they were now friends, as men sometimes do.

Bill's wife had died five years ago of a particularly aggressive cancer – they'd never had children. He had one sister somewhere up north, but they hadn't spoken in a long while. Bill actually looked like a copper, if that was possible. Danny was convinced his flat feet were bigger than average. Bill worked out most days and, when it wasn't pissing down with rain, ran most mornings about two miles. His bald head shone. He wore rimless glasses, on his hawk nose, which made him look a bit studious.

Small talk done, Bill laid down the rules. 'Here's the deal. We're a team. We share everything.'

'Sounds like some crass TV cop drama when both sides agree and then keep secrets,' suggested Danny.

'I'll piss off now shall I?' Bill was determined that he wasn't going to be buggered around by these two amateurs. 'My way or no way.'

Danny nodded in agreement. He smiled at Bill – mouth but not eyes. Daisy was nonplussed, she'd never been involved in anything like this before. 'Yeah. Right,' she stammered.

'Between us, the National Crime Agency has been after Stanislaw Nowak for years,' started Bill, 'but he's a slippery bugger. He disappeared off our radar about three years ago. We knew about the disabled badge thing but couldn't get the evidence.' He gave Danny a hard stare. Danny looked away – his foot throbbed in acceptance of the tacit bollocking. 'We had him in for a chat on several occasions, but his bloody brief always had his side and we had to let him go. He always seems to be one step ahead of us.'

They finished their drinks and ordered a second round. To Danny's relief Daisy moved onto the house red wine – cheaper, easier to order and he didn't get looks from some of the punters at the bar.

'Right, let's eat,' said Bill. They all ordered the full Sunday lunch – sirloin of beef, Yorkshire pudding, beef dripping roast potatoes, roasted vegetables, braised red cabbage and port wine jus.

'Why do they have to call gravy a bloody jus?' Bill could

be cantankerous. Almost without a pause he continued, 'If Stanislaw Nowak is involved, it's crooked.'

'What – the tour is actually crooked?' Daisy was appalled. 'Music is a duplicitous, competitive, shitty business and I don't trust many people. Most don't even bother to stab each other in the back, they go straight for the chest while smiling and then send out a press release. But it's never, rarely, criminal.'

Bill asked Daisy about the tour and preparations. Bill ate as she spoke. To be fair, Daisy missed nothing – her jus was congealing as it cooled. Bill stopped eating occasionally to make some notes. The mention of Mazury Ostrodzko International in Poland sparked his interest. *They were hardly rock and roll? And why Poland?*

'We were about to announce some additional dates for the tour. Dublin and Belfast,' finished Daisy, 'a story a day keeps the papers happy.'

'So, what's he up to? If Bill is right, the tour must be a cover for something.' Danny managed not to spit jus all over the table as he spoke. His late mother would have been stern with him speaking with his mouth full.

'We wouldn't be sitting here if we thought it was legit,' Bill harrumphed.

'What are you going to do?' Daisy asked.

'You're going to find out more.' Bill was addressing Daisy. 'You are our inside man.' Bill wasn't a PC sort of chap.

Daisy didn't know whether to be thrilled or terrified. 'And Martha's disappearance?'

'We don't know she has disappeared yet. Let's wait

until tomorrow's rehearsals and see if she turns up.' Danny wasn't convinced, but there was little they could do until then.

Bill handed Daisy and Danny his personal email and mobile phone number. He used the last of his Yorkshire pudding to mop up 'his' gravy. He promptly stood up. 'Right, thanks for lunch. I'm off to do a bit of digging. The office will be quieter on a Sunday.'

Which it wasn't.

NEW SCOTLAND YARD. THAMES, NORTH EMBANKMENT, LONDON

New Scotland Yard should have been named Even Newer Scotland Yard, thought Bill. The first Scotland Yard was in Whitehall Place, but the public entrance at the rear was through Great Scotland Yard – over time the street and the Metropolitan Police became synonymous. In 1890 London's Metropolitan Police moved to Victoria Embankment overlooking the River Thames – and the building was named New Scotland Yard. In 2016, after several more changes of location, the Met moved back to the north bank of the Thames overlooking the London Eye to yet another New Scotland Yard.

Bill ignored the tourists taking selfies by the eponymous revolving sign and ran up the steps into the oval glass reception with its discreet high-security features. He swiped his pass and took the lift to the lower ground floor, removed his glasses and pressed his face into the retinal scanner. The door clicked, and he walked along the brightly lit corridor to another building. The whole Whitehall Government Estate is criss-crossed with not-so-secret underground tunnels – some even connecting directly into London Underground stations.

'Detective Sergeant' Bill Kelly entered the sub-basement meeting room to be greeted by five colleagues, summoned earlier from their homes. It was illuminated with colour corrected lighting matching the time of day, apparently to provide a better working environment.

'Afternoon sir', they chorused. Three men and two women, all in jeans and various casual wear.

'It's Sunday, let's not stand on ceremony.' Bill wasn't a Detective Sergeant but it suited him sometimes to play dumb outside the office. Detective Chief Superintendent Bill Kelly led a covert serious organised crime investigation team at the National Crime Agency. He was qualified in covert surveillance, source handling and hostage negotiation, and was responsible for numerous national and international investigations into serious and organised crime, from international financial fraud through to human trafficking, arms dealing and drug trafficking.

Some of what he said to Daisy and Danny was true – he'd been investigating Stanislaw Nowak for several years. He didn't normally get out and about too much mixing business with pleasure but he'd known Danny for a while from various investigations when he was persona grata in the newspaper industry. And Danny had called him, personally – the name Stanislaw Nowak an instant trigger. Sunday lunch wasn't too much of a hardship – *despite the bloody jus.*

Bill poured himself a coffee from the side table – strong, black, no sugar. He took a gulp to attempt to overcome some of the effects of the two pints of Little Creatures Dog Days Session Ale and stave off the post-prandial Sunday somnambulance.

'Right then, I have just had lunch with two contacts. Very nice too.' The rest of those around the table traded insults. Sandwiches from the canteen was the best they could do on a Sunday without straying outside onto the tourist-infested pavements.

'For the two of you new to this, Danny Owen is a freelancer working with Starshine Radio and before that, an investigative hack for *The Weekend News* – he was the reporter that partly fucked our fraudulent disabled badge enquiries. The Home Office wasn't very pleased that we didn't get anywhere but the new digital Blue Badges have more or less stopped organised crime's involvement. He thinks we've kissed and made up. Daisy DeVilliers is the public relations consultant working on this Martha tour being promoted and produced by Nowak.'

'Do we know anything about her?' asked fresh-faced Detective Sergeant Rob Andrews.

'Not yet. But thanks for volunteering to find out,' countered Bill.

'We know that Martha may have disappeared – real name Jenny Jones. Wait for the MisPer alert when Martha hasn't turned up for work. I've alerted comms to put a flag on her name to trigger us when the call comes in, then I want you to go up to Elstree Studios and find out what the hell is going on. You can say you are part of the Missing Persons Squad. Ms DeVilliers is your new best friend and you are there to support her at this difficult time.' The rest of the team laughed.

'In the meantime, I want full surveillance on Nowak. From where does he get his money? What's he up to – no way he has suddenly gone legit. And, we need to know about Mazury Ostrodzko International in Poland. Daisy DeVilliers said there was something odd going on, using them for transport and not a regular music event tour company. Some of the tour locations and the schedule seems off too – and they have just announced Dublin and Belfast. I'll apply to the Home Secretary's office for permission to bug Nowak's phone and flat.'

There was excitement around the table – at last the opportunity to nail Nowak. The possibility of a list of offences with solid evidence cheered them all. Nowak would be going down.

MONDAY

At four-thirty in the morning Danny's iPhone sang 'Another Day of Sunshine' from the film *La La Land* – he thought that being awake at both four-thirties in any day should be made illegal.

Yesterday, after Bill Kelly had left the pub, he and Daisy had stayed on for 'a few more' – several more in truth. They continued talking about Nowak, Martha and the tour – but, after a while, the conversation turned yet again to more personal matters.

Danny had studied Journalism, Communications and Politics as an undergraduate at Cardiff University, a few years before Daisy's post-graduate course. His Honours degree won him a direct entry into the Thomson trainee journalism scheme at the *Western Mail* – Wales' paper of record. Danny and Daisy compared notes about student life at the various pubs, nightclubs and events in Cardiff. They quickly discovered many shared experiences – good, bad and ugly, with much hilarity. Before long both had moved away to pursue their own careers leaving Cardiff forever, never to return. Danny had worked his way around the UK from the regionals to the nationals; his eye and ear for a story, accompanied by a bulging contacts book, garnered him an increasing reputation eventually leading to *The Weekend News*, followed by his ignoble departure.

Right now, he wasn't feeling as perky as usual – Daisy and he had gone back separately to their own homes, but it was a close-run thing. The argument of Friday night largely forgotten and forgiven, but Daisy was still very worried.

Danny realised his feelings for Daisy were getting stronger. At some point he would have to tell her about the tryst and subsequent break-up with Martha if Daisy didn't already know from the tabloids – preferably before *or if* Martha and he were reacquainted. He didn't want there to be any misunderstandings. *Women could be so fickle.* His thought was best left unsaid.

He had agreed to meet Daisy at ten-thirty to watch rehearsals, which were scheduled to continue at eleven. She had assured Danny that Nowak never turned up at the studios before mid-afternoon – and if he did turn up earlier, the jungle drums would let everyone know. No one wanted to be caught unawares by the arrival of *The Producer*.

Any weekday morning when he was on-air, staying in

bed was not a luxury he could allow himself – bed to shower in less than twenty seconds was the only way, no matter how much his brain and body begged him otherwise. The shower kick-started him. He slurped his usual Nespresso Rosabaya – chosen simply because of the metallic pink colour – and knocked back a bowl of granola. The dirties went into the dishwasher – no need to press the button yet as he hadn't been there much. He was out of his home by five. A brisk walk to Balham Underground station followed, to catch the first Northern Line Tube of the day. He was in Starshine's Leicester Square studios by ten to six.

More coffee with the morning papers, gossip columns and emails started the working morning – spotting fake news was an art form. He had been alerted to a few stories by email from his contacts over the weekend, he printed them out and wandered down to the studio well before the six-thirty on-air time, hoping that DJ Gordon wasn't in one of 'his moods'.

He bumped into Alan coming out of the news studio having just read 'the six' – the heavy double doors silently closing against their magnetic soundproof seals. Studio was a little optimistic, more a tiny cubbyhole off the newsroom lined with sound-deadening panels.

Alan's own news was not good. 'He's in a filthy mood. All-weekend bender with one of Friday's guests.'

Danny inwardly groaned, put on his game face and walked into the breakfast show's control cubicle. Gordon was already his side of the glass in the studio – where Danny could not be heard.

The breakfast team confirmed Alan's assessment.

'Good luck,' wished the sound engineer and producer.

Until exactly 06h30:00 the sustaining feed of music, idents and commercials was entirely pre-programmed and automated, except for the news. Just one engineer oversaw the five Starshine networks. The high energy, pompous news jingle roared out and Alan offered his second news-read of the day. Two minutes, thirty seconds later Gordon was on-air with the usual jangly jingle – no sign of his foul mood, just early morning enthusiastic bonhomie. Six million listeners not exactly hanging on his every word but using Gordon and the music to kick-start their morning routines, commutes, or whatever they were doing. Danny had a perverse daydream of a million Londoners seated on their collective toilets all performing in unison. It kept him amused.

The three hours continued with the normal array of banal content demanded by 'Zoo Radio' – music, news, sport, traffic, travel, showbiz, and tittle-tattle. This week's listener phone-in competition offered a 'holiday-of-a-lifetime' to Orlando – for which JetAway holidays had paid £25,000 for the privilege of giving away the prize.

There was little talk in the studio between links while the music was playing, but all of them came alive when it was their turn. After all, they were professionals. At nine-thirty they fell off air, handing over to the next show with the now famous carefully rehearsed ad libs.

Danny rushed out of the Starshine studio without saying goodbye and made his way north to Elstree Studios.

Danny checked in at security, he was expected. As he

walked up the central drive, he couldn't help being aware of the studio's history – Hitchcock went into the record books by directing *Blackmail* there, the first British talking film. Empty studios are simply versatile spaces with blank walls, dowdy lighting, big doors and soundproofing – yet when in production they come alive, sparkling with energy and pizzazz. *Strictly Come Dancing* was rigging for a 'special' in another studio – three long articulated trailers were being emptied by a fleet of gas-powered forklifts. The freelance crew from Gallowglass sweated as they manoeuvred the large wheeled flight cases full of cables, lights, and power distribution hired in from Media Powerhouse. It was, to all intents and purposes, another normal day in the fantasy factory.

'Martha Movin' Out' had booked the George Lucas Stage 2 – one of the seven film and TV stages at Elstree. James 'Jimmy' Patrick, the production manager, had insisted that they use this stage with its fifteen-metre headroom, so they could ensure that the massive stadium tour could be fully rehearsed and ready, following the likes of Take That, Madonna, Robbie Williams, Kylie, and the Spice Girls.

Jimmy had known Elstree's MD, Roger Morris, for several years, from when Roger had produced the very first show on Channel Four – they had done a deal to slot in Martha's rehearsals when the George Lucas studio was 'dark'. The industry thrived on relationships and 'the deal'. Timing was ideal for them both.

Danny contemplated if Stanislaw Nowak was sullying Elstree's magnificent history? He probably would not be the first or the last to besmirch the industry. Showbiz can be a two-faced affair. Danny did not wonder why some production offices and many prostitutes of all persuasions shared the same streets – both offered temporal pleasure in exchange for money. No such offering within the security cordon of Elstree though.

When Danny arrived at just after ten-fifteen the rigging team had finished the repairs, the hydraulically operated thrust stage was able to glide silently in and out, up and down, round and round on command, its motion carefully synchronised with the music. There was silent concentration as the tech team continued to programme the sequences that they lost on Thursday and Friday. Hundreds of moving lights each had to be told what to do, when and where. The moving beams of light highlighted by the 'foggers' – environmentally friendly 'smoke' machines used for creating special effects, to make lighting and lighting effects visible. No show without smoke.

Every element was pre-programmed ensuring the live performances were the only thing left to chance.

On this tour the keyboard player was triggering the computers, with back-up from the front-of-house sound mixing position. Everything synchronised to a twenty-fifth of a second. Once started SMPTE timecode, click tracks, MIDI, backing tracks, motion control, motors, light control, video, graphics all distributed and run until the next stop, when the artists might talk to the audience often using the same ad lib every performance. 'Hello – you are our favourite city', 'Are you having a great time?', 'You are a great audience'.

On long tours, some artists often had no idea which

city they were in – a reminder prompt card with the name of the city was often gaffer-taped to the stage monitors. The whole industry sympathised when Axl Rose, Slash and Duff McKagan of Guns N' Roses greeted their fans with a rock 'n' roll, 'Hello Sydney' after taking to the stage at the Melbourne Cricket Ground – leaving the 70,000 strong crowd booing or bemused in response.

Daisy arrived two minutes after Danny. 'Have you seen Martha yet?' No hellos. No acknowledgement of yesterday. No kisses. Just panic.

'What time is she due in?'

'Ten-thirty.' Daisy looked at her watch for the umpteenth time.

'Well then, hurry up and wait.'

Daisy and Danny waited in the studio watching the crew continue to set, focus and fine programme the array of Vari-Lites, line-up, check forty radio mic channels and in-ear monitors. The front-of-house sound is the easy bit – what the audience don't realise is that there are another twenty mixes for the singers, musicians and, of course, Martha. All a massive undertaking rarely understood by the audience or those outside the business.

Ten-thirty came and went. At eleven, still no Martha.

The show-caller and stage manager kept the rehearsals going – each segment of songs took hours to set and rehearse. They had reached about the halfway point of the show last Thursday, when the moving stage had failed in an explosion of sticky amber fluid.

Eleven-thirty came and went. Still no Martha.

Jimmy had been on the phone to everyone and anyone.

No one had seen Martha since last Thursday morning. He walked across the alleyway between the studios for privacy and called Nowak on his private number. 'We have to call the police Stan.'

Stanislaw hated being called Stan, but that wasn't an argument for now. He disagreed.

'No, not yet.'

'But Stan—'

'I said no. She'll turn up soon enough.' Nowak's mind really wasn't on this conversation.

'But what about rehearsals?'

'You can carry on without her. I want to see a full tech run with everyone Wednesday at three.'

Jimmy had no choice. Nowak was the boss. He didn't like it.

'We may not have everything set. We lost two days with the rigging failure.'

'Wednesday at three.' Nowak ended the call.

Jimmy returned to the studio to give the team the news.

In his Docklands penthouse flat, with views over London City Airport, Nowak sweated – he was a big man and sweating came easily despite the air-conditioning. He changed his shirt for the second time – the Paul & Shark striped shirt now discoloured with large patches of damp. Inside he was panicking. The phone call he had received on Friday was disturbing and ruined his weekend's carnal exploits.

His phone buzzed. A text from an unknown number – but Nowak knew who it was. He called his driver to be ready and gave him Ali Baka's hotel address in Soho.

He left his apartment, took the lift to the ground floor.

Ray, his driver, held open the back door of the Lexus LS with its rear reclining seats and seven shiatsu massage programmes.

Nowak was unaware of the watchers and the technical team that had then entered his apartment. BT Open Reach engineers get everywhere.

As do London black cabs – the ubiquitous vehicles largely ignored, making for a perfect cover. There was almost no chance of it being spotted as it followed Nowak's Lexus.

10
SOHO, LONDON

ALI BAKA, WHEN IN LONDON, LIVED LUXURY TO the full – unlike many in his line of business he wasn't overtly ostentatious with his demands. He eschewed the massive global brands along Park Lane favoured by many of the rich, famous and infamous. He preferred the smaller luxurious boutique hotels where he could enjoy anonymity away from the concierges and doormen whose hands had been greased by the media and paparazzi.

He aspired to be a part of history – it suited his massively inflated ego. He revered the greatest of all English essayists and critics, William Hazlitt, who lived in Frith Street in the heart of London's Soho, now Hazlitt's Hotel where Baka had an ornate room. Hazlitt knew all the literary figures of his day, including Wordsworth, Coleridge, Shelley and Keats. Hazlitt's great friend, the celebrated author Charles Lamb, was with Hazlitt when he died. At the time, number six Frith Street was a boarding house. The landlady, anxious to re-let the room, had his corpse laid out under the bed until it could be collected for burial in nearby St Anne's churchyard – today still the only green space serving the dense urban area of lower Soho. Ali Baka kidded himself he was part of the glitterati of London. If things didn't go well, he fantasised how he could get away with hiding another corpse under the bed.

At ten minutes before noon, Stanislaw Nowak pressed the intercom beside Hazlitt's discreet panelled-glass, Georgian front door. The gentle buzz indicated that the door had been released. Nowak did not notice the wood panelling, the oil paintings or the ochre and mulberry painted walls as he approached the reception desk.

'Ali Baka,' he barked. 'Nowak, he's expecting me.'

The receptionist was unfazed. 'Of course, sir, please take a seat.' He pointed to the George III mahogany settee with walnut legs, the pink damask immaculately embroidered with yellow silken threads. Nowak lowered his portly frame; the settee creaked ominously.

In Ali Baka's glorious two-storey Duke of Monmouth suite, the phone rang beside the vast marble bath, filled with water from the beak of a life-sized eagle. He levered himself up. 'Yes?'

'There's a Mr Nowak to see you sir.'

'Send him up in twenty minutes.' Nothing like a bit of waiting to help the meeting skip along, thought Baka.

Ali Baka towelled himself dry and considered what to wear. He chose the hotel's monogrammed thick, towelling dressing gown. He wanted to give the impression of an informal and unimportant meeting. His suite included an intimate sitting room and a small outdoor garden with a sliding glass roof. Today closed. Baka took a bottle of champagne and one chilled glass from his full-size refrigerator, popped the cork, drank one glass and immediately refilled it.

A few minutes later there was a buzz followed by a heavy knocking. Ali Baka waited thirty seconds before opening the door, champagne glass in hand.

'Stan, how lovely to see you, do come in. I won't offer you a glass as I am sure you won't be staying that long.'

'You fucking shit. What have you done with Martha?'

'Come in and sit down, Stan.' Baka pointed to one of the leather club chairs. 'She is very safe and well cared for.'

'I don't want to bloody sit down. Where's Martha?'

'We agreed we would use your tour to transport my goods. And that's why I agreed to loan you two million pounds. Just a couple of small adjustments, that's all.'

'Where's Martha?' Nowak lunged at Ali Baka, who nonchalantly side-stepped, spilling a little champagne.

'Now look what you've made me do – I don't like waste.' Baka put his glass on a side table.

Nowak was shaking with rage. Baka spun around and grabbed Nowak by the throat, forcing him against the wall. 'I asked you to sit down, so we can have a chat, man to man.'

Nowak tried to break free without success. He wasn't as fit as he once was.

'Why have you kidnapped Martha?'

'Kidnap is a little harsh. I am just protecting my investment.'

'Bollocks, you've kidnapped her.'

'Sit down.' Baka was insistent.

Nowak sat.

'There, that's better – we can discuss this like civilised businesspeople. My associates and I have re-run your transport arrangements against our business plan, and the numbers don't work for us. We have to double the numbers you transport.'

'What?! That's not possible. You and I had an agreement.' Nowak paused and thought for a moment. 'And who is "we"?'

Baka ignored the question. 'Why not? One or two extra trailers, that's all. We continue to use the stripped-out generators for our premium service. But like the airlines who have two classes, I want to do the same. We transport additional guests in economy class.'

'Who are these additional guests?'

'Let's just say they are less fortunate and will be working for their passage.'

'No. Absolutely not,' countered Nowak. 'We agreed we would safely move a few well-off people. Mainly Syrian and other migrants who want to apply for asylum once here in the UK. You're talking about people trafficking – that is something else.'

'They're all people. Come on Stan, you are a people person?'

'I'm not getting involved in trafficking. And I want Martha back now. Where is she?'

In hindsight, the irony of the tour's name 'Martha Movin' Out' was not lost on Nowak.

'She is at a very private facility without phones or internet. She thinks you have given her a few days off in isolation for complete rest and recuperation. Obviously, I have security there – we wouldn't want anything to happen to Martha, would we? She is being very well taken care of.'

'Without her there is no tour.'

'Then you would owe me four million pounds. Interest can be very burdensome.'

'We agreed five per cent – one hundred thousand.'

'Ah yes, that was assuming you could transport my goods. If there is no tour, then my associates and I don't get the return we anticipated. And we would want all our investment back plus compensation for loss of earnings – as per the contract you signed.'

'Fuck you.' Nowak stormed out. He didn't close the door. He rued the day he ever met Baka – that bloody café in Cairo and his inquisitive nosiness.

Ali Bakar smiled, picked up his champagne, finished it, and poured another – he embraced alcohol in Christian countries after he left Malaysia, determining never to return. He picked up a phone, one of several burners, dialled a number. When the other end answered he simply said, 'Looks like we are in business. First batch in about four months.' He had business associates in the massage, escort, farming, nail bar and hospitality industries who were always looking for willing hired hands – and Baka didn't disappoint. He took the battery and SIM out of the phone, ready for the trash cart.

Nowak stormed out of the hotel and into Frith Street. A few minutes later a relaxed couple exited their taxi without paying the fare and hand-in-hand entered the hotel. At reception they let go of each other's hands and showed the receptionist their warrant cards.

11
MONDAY AFTERNOON

At Elstree studios they had broken for lunch. They had rehearsed all morning to recorded backing tracks that included Martha's vocals. During the tour, Martha's pre-recorded vocals were always available at the touch of a channel button on the massively powerful Solid State Logic L550 Plus sound desk – just in case. Very few people would spot that she would be lip-synching. A foot switch by Martha's mic stand could also trigger the pre-recorded vocals and back to live when she needed.

The crew had been indifferent to Jimmy's news that everything had to be ready for a full run on Wednesday afternoon – they were all working flat out. They would either be ready, or not. All were used to the false deadlines set by some producers who thought they were being tough. They still had twelve days booked in the George Lucas studio to finish the show, so why rush it?

The dancers, rehearsal band and backing singers had caught up the lost time. The technical problems that had beset the earlier rehearsals were now solved. All they needed was Martha, the star of the eponymous show.

Shirley and her team from Starring-Meals-on-Wheels were serving their usual array of freshly cooked food. It seemed everyone was hungry and, with Martha not on set, they had a rare opportunity to enjoy lunch. The salmon and prawn pasta with garlic bread was particularly popular.

A few had escaped to Elstree Studios' Star Bar and Bistro by the main gates, normally quiet at lunchtimes. The bar fills up in the evening for the pre-home 'quick one' or for an informal 'after-show' – a water cooler with booze. The bar was simply designed, a few archive production stills from Elstree's past, garish yellow and green bar stools and some comfy-looking chairs. The run of windows looking out onto the central drive allowed anyone and everyone to see who was arriving and departing. It was a working environment in a world where alcohol is not always considered to be the devil in disguise. The bar was a meeting point for the thirty or so independent businesses based at the Elstree Production Village – production companies, equipment hire, action vehicles, set construction, animation and the freelancers working there, all engaged in the business of show.

Most, particularly those working on TV programmes, were in show blacks – black trousers or shorts, black shirts and soft-soled black trainers. Others in jeans and tee-shirts, none particularly smart or glamorous. A couple of 'suits' sat on the sofas in the corner munching sandwiches and drinking water, iPhones, laptops and designer briefcases all ready to go.

Despite every member of the Martha team having signed supposedly watertight non-disclosure agreements, word travels fast within the industry, especially after a couple of lunchtime pints. The talk in the bar inevitably was of the missing Martha. Nearby, a make-up artist working on a celebrity reality TV show had been keenly listening to the unguarded chatter – men can be such fools when they start showing off. An envelope with a thousand pounds in cash would be delivered later from the red-top newspaper after her phoned-in tip off. Nothing remains a secret for long.

Thirty minutes later Daisy's phone rang. The caller display showed it was Kelvin Edwards from *The Daily Tribune* – allegedly the UK's leading celebrity daily newspaper and online blog spot. Daisy prepared herself.

'Kelvin, how are you?'

'I'm fine. But I hear you've lost Martha?'

'What? Really? No!' Daisy thought quickly. How the hell did he know? 'We gave her a few days off that's all. We have the backing tracks, rehearsals are on schedule. No point in wearing her out when we don't need her here. It's a big tour, we want to save her energy.' Daisy didn't realise how close to the truth she was.

Danny was the only journalist let anywhere near the rehearsals. And Daisy knew he wouldn't spoil his exclusive or let her down. Someone had been talking.

'So why were the rehearsals cancelled on Thursday and Friday?'

Daisy's PR experience kicked in – give Kelvin something that he would think was a story. 'Between you and I, off the record, you can say it's from a source close to the tour?'

'Okay.' Kelvin wasn't convinced but let's hear what had to be said.

'We've had a few technical issues. We are using a brand-new type of hydraulic stage and it failed on Thursday morning – you should have seen the mess. We're really excited about it, no tour has used this system before and it's going to be spectacular. But you know with anything new, there are teething problems. Everything is working perfectly this morning but we decided to carry on testing to backing tracks. Everyone else is here, working and absolutely thrilled. It's a game-changer.'

She amazed herself with her ability to sound so enthusiastic and genuine. Base anything on some truth. But had she done enough?

'So, you know where Martha is?'

'Yes, of course.'

'Where?'

'Kelvin, I love you dearly,' which Daisy didn't, 'but I'm not going to tell you. We're trying to give her a little time off before the tour. She'll need it – it's her biggest tour ever.'

Kelvin wasn't convinced – it did sound plausible enough. But his source was normally one hundred per cent reliable. Before he had a chance to say more, Daisy continued.

'I remember you said your wife loves Martha, doesn't she – I'll send you two tickets to the golden circle for the opening night and an invitation to the private after-show party where she can meet Martha and get a couple of selfies.'

They disconnected after the normal insincere pleasantries. Kelvin decided he needed another source – although the 'the exciting new staging' would make a paragraph or two in tomorrow's paper, and an excuse to publish a couple of pictures of Martha. Always good for circulation.

Daisy, ever the professional, immediately emailed to Kelvin a couple of candid photographs of Martha rehearsing on stage a couple of days ago – control and own the story was her mantra. She had turned a bloody disaster into an opportunity for one-and-a-half million people to read about Martha plus the audience of lazy reporters, *you couldn't call them journalists*, she thought, who would simply rehash Kelvin's story in their media.

But Daisy was still worried. *Where was Martha? What would happen if this all got out? And what of Martha's health and well-being?*

TUESDAY

Stanislaw Nowak had not slept well. Yesterday's meeting with Ali Baka had seen to that. He was royally fucked – between the devil and the deep blue sea. The deep blue sea had some appeal. He couldn't remember which of them suggested the idea of using a concert tour to smuggle migrants. Maybe he'd been showing off a bit?

He considered the past and how he had arrived in the shit he was now in.

Nowak had met Martha via Piers de Petrelli, Martha's sanguine manager, at an artistes' showcase two years before. Petrelli was on the verge of being sacked for not doing enough, so was trying a little harder – not that Martha had generated much income for him recently, so he hadn't extended himself.

A couple of days later, Roka was noisy and full-on, mostly with junior investment bankers braying at each other. It was the go-to Japanese fusion restaurant of choice on Canary Wharf near Nowak's apartment. The entertainment business revolves around 'having a chat over lunch', where Petrelli had slowly reeled in Nowak – hook, line and sashimi.

'You have a great reputation for promoting live music.' Petrelli was in full obsequious mode. *How some crumble under the assault of flattery*, Petrelli thought as he sipped his perfectly chilled Condrieu from the Viognier vines on the right bank of the northern Rhône – he was a wine snob, par excellence.

'At the clubs the tribute acts really work. The pissed singing along to their golden oldies from when they were courting.' Nowak understood the whims of his audience – the acts were just a way of enticing people into his social clubs where he made his money from the bar selling illegal imports of wine and cigarettes, relabelled spirits and bulk beer, alongside anything-but 'home-cooked real pub grub'.

'Martha won't pull in audiences at your clubs. Wrong age group – you attract the greying pound, the sixty-plus. Get up to date. You want Generation X – they're the ones with the money. Think nothing of blowing a hundred, two hundred, three hundred quid or more on a night out.' Petrelli could be magnificently patronising.

'Yeah, all right. I've done well promoting seventies and eighties acts on one bill too.' This was also true; he had filled several of the smaller music venues around the UK such as King Tut's Wah Wah Hut in Glasgow, and even had some success at the 02 Academies in Newcastle and Birmingham. But he always dreamed of filling the large arenas in Manchester, Liverpool and the domed 02 in the loop of the Thames. This didn't seem that much of a leap from the UK concerts he had been promoting. Nowak didn't have the *cojones* for massive stadia yet – maybe one day. Maybe.

'Pop Revival is massively commercial, Stanislaw. Acts from five, ten, fifteen years ago are popular because the generation that loved them when they were younger, now have the money to spend on gigs. Look at Erasure, the Spice Girls tours, Melanie C solo, Take That, Pink, even Elton John and Paul McCartney. And then we have Martha – someone with flare and entrepreneurial spirit could make a killing. She is perfectly ready for a revival tour.'

There was a little more background that Nowak largely ignored – but he was convinced.

'What are we talking about?'

'I'm suggesting I give you a one-year option to put together a tour.'

'How much?'

'Fifty thousand.'

'Oh, do piss off. Twenty-five and eighteen months.'

The to-and-fro continued for a couple of minutes – neither wanting to show weakness.

'Forty and twelve months. Final offer.'

'Maybe.'

'We'll keep it simple – a three-sixty deal. If you do get it together,' which Petrelli doubted, 'Martha personally gets sixty grand a show, minimum thirty shows – you supply and keep everything else, except back catalogue and sales of music from the tour. Fifty per cent up front once you confirm.'

'Fifty a show, final offer – and first show is free, my option money back. I get twenty-five per cent of sales of music from the tour.'

Petrelli did the maths. Twenty per cent plus costs on a minimum of one point five million, that'll do for his pocket with an artiste that had done nothing for quite a few years. Plus, his share of the music sales. It was a good day's lunch.

Nowak did the maths too – no brainer.

'Done.' They shook hands.

'Email me the contract and I'll have a look.'

They clinked glasses, looking into each other's eyes. Neither blinked. Both smiled. Neither genuine. But this was show business.

And that was it. The lawyers took a month to finalise the deal. Nowak and Petrelli signed, and £40,000 arrived in Petrelli's client account from one of Nowak's 'production' companies. Two months later Martha received £9,000 from Petrelli – what was left after 'costs'. But Martha was back on the road again, hopefully. And Petrelli wasn't sacked.

Nowak's issue was bankrolling the tour. He now had a year to fix it.

Nowak's maxim was always OPM – 'other people's money'. Risk and reward. They took the risk and he took the reward. He was prepared to put in a million personally but needed another two or so to get the show on the road.

Few conventional banks would listen to him; he didn't have a track record. And those specialist banks that did make an offer discussed punitive interest rates and personal guarantees. Nowak had been burnt by personal guarantees in the past and vowed never to sign one again.

But Nowak was a showman. His hero Phineas Taylor Barnum's credo was, 'To put the money in my own coffers.' Barnum is also credited with, 'There's a sucker born every minute.' Nowak couldn't disagree, but this time he was to be the sucker, if only he had realised.

He formed a new company, 'Martha Movin' Out Limited', and quickly recruited the trusted from his teams in his existing businesses. They were all used to working for a different company depending what day of the week it was, but Nowak always paid them on time and with a small premium. Staff loyalty was vital both to do the job, sometimes putting in long hours, and to keep their mouths shut.

The first eight venues in the UK had been pencil booked and publicised, to test the market. His sales, promotion, online and marketing teams were fully occupied organising sponsorship, cross-promotions and advertising. Even Nowak was surprised how well ticket sales were going – the small print 'subject to contract', 'subject to license' and twenty-five per cent non-refundable booking fee ignored by the enthusiastic fans. Nowak was always amazed at how often the small print was ignored.

There are some people that cannot keep it straight no matter what, there were always 'extras' to be had – Nowak was one of them. The increase in mass cyber-communication, on which many a scam has its foundations, has had massive lucrative impact on the criminal classes. Before the tour planning had really got underway, he was already thinking of profitable sidelines. He'd made a few extra thousands of pounds from illegally selling the valuable emailing lists of those who had signed up – he'd salted the list with a few false names to track anyone reselling the list without his permission. If anyone failed to pay his 'fee' for stealing the list, he had another strong-arm team ready to go in and persuade them otherwise. GDPR compliance optional.

His recent recruit was media and public relations consultant, Daisy DeVilliers – as pure as the driven snow and about as far away from criminal activity as it is possible for a PR to get. Daisy the independent freelancer with a fabulous contacts book; she had the home and mobile phone number, and personal email addresses of anyone and everyone in, reporting or influencing showbiz. Nowak had given Daisy strict instructions to keep his name out of it.

'It's all about Martha, the tour and reliving their youth. Talk about the sizzle, not the sausage.' And that was pretty much the end of the brief. Daisy quickly became a member of the trusted team; she could be left alone to get on with her job, which was just as well. Nowak thought she understood what he was trying to achieve.

But Nowak's thoughts returned to his current issue – he never said he had a problem, too negative, it was always an 'issue'. But this one was a very big issue. Bloody Ali

Baka, blackmailing him into turning the whole tour into his people trafficking operation.

Despite Nowak's colourful and criminal past, he didn't shit on friends – rule one. Rule two, see rule one.

A few months ago, with Ali Baka's loan beginning to be drawn down, Nowak had returned to his hometown of Wrocław in Poland to meet with a long-time friend who had a transport company – Mazury Ostrodzko International.

Nowak had left Wrocław aged eighteen and had returned only a few times to see his family and a select group of trusted mates. Trust was important, even in Nowak's shady basement life.

Nowak was one of four children who had shared with his mother the cramped two-bedroomed apartment at the top of a six-storey tenement. He didn't know his father. His childhood night-time memories were the sounds of trains shunting, clanking and whistling from the nearby nineteenth-century Wrocław Główny, the largest railway station and sidings in the Lower Silesian Voivodeship – the red-brick castellated building and archaic platforms the centre of many of the main Polish railway routes. He used to sit for hours watching the apparently morose activity as steam shunters chuffed back and forth, stopping for what seemed like ages, the driver doing nothing except quaffing rough potato vodka and occasionally being visited by 'ladies without a drink'. The shunter returned an hour or two later maybe with a few wagons and a happy driver. Nothing worked at any speed or with apparent logic – but everything arrived where, not necessarily when, it was meant to.

He missed the old town with its ornate medieval and Eastern Bloc architecture, traditional cobbled main square surrounded by outdoor cafés and bars, with the clock tower keeping watch. He fondly remembered the permanent smell of cooked cabbage and paprika floating through the air.

Unless you were in university, there was little to keep anyone in Wrocław. The UK beckoned – getting in was easy enough as an EU citizen. Five years later he obtained a legitimate UK passport with dual citizenship of both the UK and Poland. Whenever he travelled back to his home country, he used his Polish passport, giving him the same citizens' rights and duties as Polish people who live in Poland as permanent residents.

Pietr Ostrodzko and Nowak had been in school together for the whole of their childhoods. Both had worked reasonably hard and achieved respectable enough results, but neither good enough to get them into the university. Both were grafters, not shy of a hard day's physical labour where they earned a few złoty to go drinking and chatting up girls.

Now, years later, they had met at the European HQ of Pietr Ostrodzko's transport and trucking company – the modern warehouses and wharfs lining the banks of the River Oder and Wrocław's canals. Forklift trucks scuttled around apparently haphazardly but everything seemed to work. More than seventy trailers and a couple of barges were being loaded and unloaded, preparing to criss-cross Europe with anything that needed transporting, a further two hundred trucks already on the road in their now familiar grey and orange livery. Pietr Ostrodzko was the grand master of all he surveyed.

They hugged. After the normal small talk Pietr got down to business in their native language.

'So, what have you got going Stanislaw?'

'You've heard of Martha?'

'The singer?'

Nowak nodded.

'Of course, I have. Permanently in the charts here a few years ago. Great songs and big tits?'

'That's the one. I've signed her for a European, UK and North African concert tour.'

'Wow. Bloody hell. That's massive. Your empires grows!'

Pietr, successful himself, was seriously impressed.

'You're not doing bad yourself.' Nowak looked around. Pietr's operation was exactly what he needed.

'What do you need me to do?'

'Tour transport.'

'That's a new one for us.'

'Never too old to learn. The big one is timing – cannot afford to be late. Non-delivery is not an option. We have some very tight schedules and some complex journeys.'

Pietr exhaled a massive sigh. He wanted to help his old friend.

'It'd have to be at proper rates but I'd do you the best deal I can.' Sounded a good booking – he might even drive one of the trucks himself. He'd always fancied Martha.

They continued for a while talking about logistics, costs, dates, venues and timescales – and back-up. One spare tractor unit, with a tyres and recovery vehicle at all times. On some legs, with long distances to travel, doubling up on drivers.

Nowak continued, 'And I need you to buy three one-hundred-and-fifty kilowatt silent generator units, mounted on trucks. I'll give you five hundred thousand złoty and you get to keep the generators.'

Pietr was puzzled. 'What? Why?'

'Well, that's the point. Might have a little side-line.'

'Go on.' Pietr was now hesitant, his fast and loose days behind him.

'These silent generators are lead-lined to kill the noise. X-ray and scanners at ports can't totally see through the insulation, just vague shapes. And if the vague shape looked like the gubbins of a generator, everyone would be happy.'

Pietr wasn't stupid. 'I won't have anything to do with drugs or people trafficking.'

Nowak agreed. 'But the odd migrant stowaway who wants to move to the UK is different – especially if you and I don't know about them. That's the drivers' problem.'

There was a long pause while Pietr considered his old friend's request.

'I might need to reconsider the costs.'

'Of course, but we are old mates?!'

After a little hesitation Pietr Ostrodzko and Stanislaw Nowak shook hands and hugged. The deal was done.

And so, the 'generator' trucks and other trailer units painted and sign-written in the Martha Movin' Out branding were on their way. Another piece of the jigsaw in place.

In his apartment, with the tour just six weeks away, Nowak was sweating. Was he about to break a promise to his oldest friend – and get involved with something that was way beyond what he considered to be decent, even by his misguided standards?

He really had no choice, he had to agree to Ali Baka's new demands. Without Martha he didn't have a show. Without a show he'd have to return ticket money and sponsorship. He couldn't return Baka's £4 million, never mind the £2 million he had 'borrowed' – why he had agreed to such punitive arrangements he had no idea. He hadn't read all the small print.

But he simply didn't want to get involved in people trafficking, a huge jump from helping a few people seek asylum in the UK. If they were caught it was pretty certain that jail was on the cards for him and his best friend Pietr Ostrodzko.

Nowak never thought there would be a time when he had a moral dilemma.

He spent the rest of the day in silent contemplation – he had turned his phone off and refused to look at email. The sun was shining. He sat on his balcony and watched the planes land and take off from London City Airport. Below him, on Gallions Point Marina, a RIB was loading tourists ready to give them a thrill ride. Further over he could just see the Woolwich Ferry plying its trade. And, to his right, was the great dome of the 02 Arena mocking him.

Eventually, as the sky was turning deep orange, he picked up the phone and called Ali Baka on a burner number he had given him.

Baka answered simply, 'Hello.'

'Okay, you have a deal. I'll transport your goods. But I only return one million of your loan and that's it.'

'One and a half, no interest repayments and it's a deal.' Baka was thrilled – he was in business, but he wasn't going to make it easy.

'What don't you understand about one million? Take it or leave it.'

'You are in no position to negotiate.'

'Neither are you.'

Baka thought about it. He disconnected, leaving Nowak hanging. He took the battery out of the pay-as-you-go phone and later that day dropped it in the Westminster waste.

WEDNESDAY

STILL NO MARTHA. IT WAS TEN-THIRTY. AND NO one could get hold of Nowak – he'd been impossible to get hold of all day yesterday and Daisy had been trying to speak to him this morning.

'What are we going to do?' she asked Jimmy. After all, he was the tour manager.

Jimmy was in a quandary. 'I don't think we have any choice. We must call the police again – Nowak doesn't know we called them on Friday. Our secret for now.'

Daisy agreed. 'I suppose I could ask them if there has been any progress?'

'Okay, do it. My decision. I'll straighten it with Stan and take the shit storm. What's the worst he can do, sack me?'

Daisy kept her counsel – just. She called the police, who were surprisingly receptive. None of the officious palming-off from last time. Someone would be on their way.

Daisy then called Danny, who picked up on the tenth ring. 'Make it quick, I'm with George Ezra about to pre-record for next week. He's got a new album out.' A signal to Daisy he wasn't alone – he was surrounded by George's 'people'.

'Martha still hasn't turned up. Jimmy and I have called the police. They said they'd be here soon. Please come and be with me – I'm out of my depth. Could use a friend.'

'Okay. What about Nowak?'

'He said he wants to stay away from the police, so he shouldn't be here. But I haven't been able to speak to him yet today.'

'What!? You called the police without speaking to him?'

George Ezra's people looked shocked at Danny's outburst.

'Jimmy and I agreed.'

Danny wasn't sure it was the right decision – but not his call. 'See you in a couple of hours, but I'll have to go before the scheduled rehearsals. Nowak'll be there for those – and I don't want to bump into him.'

Less than an hour later Detective Sergeant Rob Andrews from the 'Missing Persons Bureau' arrived at the front gate. He spent ten minutes talking with the security team – one who was ex-job – before being shown up to the George Lucas studio.

Daisy greeted him; they shook hands. DS Andrews briefly showed his warrant card, not long enough for Daisy to register he wasn't from Missing Persons.

'You were quick, on Friday no one seemed to care.'

'Martha is a high-profile person.'

'Let's go somewhere quieter,' insisted Daisy.

Daisy wanted to avoid the Martha Movin' Out production offices. She didn't want the busy back-office team to hear what was being said. They walked past the BBC's temporary technical facilities, through a maze of stairs and corridors, past several dressing rooms – on the doors, the names of stars appearing in today's TV shows. They eventually found Elstree's small, soundproof, unoccupied twenty-four seat preview theatre with the screen at one end and projection portals at the other. They chose to sit at the front of the four rows of plush red velvet seats, near the screen and low stage where they could stretch out their legs.

DS Andrews flipped out the concealed table from the arm of his chair and opened his pocketbook. 'I am known as the initial investigating officer. It's my job to learn all we can and to help assess the next steps. You reported Martha missing on Friday. She hadn't been gone long – seemed a bit quick? Are you sure she is missing and not simply taken a few days off that you didn't know about?'

'She didn't turn up for rehearsals. Which is unlike her – she is never late without calling in.'

'I see.' DS Andrews was having fun playing the part of a Missing Persons policeman rather than National Crime Agency. 'When did you last see her?'

'Thursday morning. She went back to her dressing room while the riggers tried to fix a fault with the stage.'

'Did anyone else see her?'

'We assumed she stayed there. Although I did think it a bit odd when Jimmy...'

'Jimmy?' DS Andrews interrupted.

'Sorry, Jimmy Patrick, the tour's production manager. I thought it a bit odd when Jimmy asked Danny and I if we had seen Martha.'

'And who is Danny?' Rob Andrews kept a straight face. *This would be interesting.*

'Danny Owen is a reporter from Starshine Radio who had come to Elstree to interview Martha. He's an old friend of both Martha and me.'

'So, what is your relationship with Martha?'

'I run the PR and marketing for the Martha Movin' Out tour – I've known Martha on-and-off since her first successes.'

'You know her pretty well then?'

'Professionally, as well as more or less anyone else in this business. Not personally really, I wouldn't say she is a close friend. My job will be to look after her public face as the tour ramps up. Protect her. I am also running her assistants team – dealing with requests for photos, autographs, appearances, radio and TV. Plus, all the proactive stuff.'

'Where does she live?'

Daisy passed over a sheet of paper with the details, including phone numbers and email.

'Have you been there?'

'I haven't, but her driver has. No answer Friday morning. That's why we began to worry about her. Her regular driver has a front door key – she occasionally has to wait. Martha gave her the key, so she could have coffee or something while Martha was getting ready. She went in. Her bed hadn't been slept in.'

Much of this had been reported the first time. Rob Andrews had this in his slim file. 'It would help if we could have that key please, so we can have a good look around her home.'

'I'll see what I can do.'

'What about family?' Rob Andrew knew the answer, but what is often key in any investigation is the variance in the perception of truth.

'There's only her sister left – Vikki. Martha was one of six, her other two sisters and two brothers were killed together with both her parents in a late-night accident coming home from a gig on the M1. Twelve or fifteen years ago. It was all over the news.'

Rob Andrews vaguely remembered. He wasn't really one for the celebrity papers, although it had made a couple of the broadsheets and even sixty seconds, one hundred and sixty words on BBC Radio Four news. The story was more about the multiple motorway pile-up than the death of an up-and-coming family band of whom few had heard – long forgotten.

'Her sister, Vikki, is the only one left? Almost the whole family killed at the same time must have been devastating.' Rob Andrews was trying to pretend he gave a toss. Once you can fake sincerity and all that.

119

'The minibus driver was stoned. According to the first responders, before he died, he was ranting about the demons hiding in the fog.' Daisy was reluctant to go into the finer details of the night of the accident or where Martha and Vikki had been partying.

'The M1 can have that effect on you.' Daisy wasn't impressed with the policeman's black humour. 'What about, err, Vikki? Their relationship now?'

'Their relationship now?' Daisy thought carefully before answering. 'Off and on. On and off. I think both sisters had counselling after the accident. Vikki has always been jealous of Martha's success and celebrity status. For a while neither Vikki nor Martha spoke to each other, I don't really know for certain how their relationship stands now. When I spoke to her about it, Martha suggested they are back on reasonable speaking terms. I needed to know in case it came up – the press can be inquisitive. I think Vikki sometimes gets off on being mistaken for Martha which leads to occasional trouble when Vikki is off her head – the paparazzi do get confused.'

'Where does Vikki live?' Rob Andrew wondered if Vikki was involved in Martha's disappearance or could help find her – she was certainly a person of interest.

'I don't have the full details. Acton, I think?' Daisy scrolled through her iPhone but couldn't find a contact for Vikki.

'I'm sure we can find it.' The questioning went on for another ten minutes, going over old ground. Daisy realised how little she really knew about Martha. They were professional friends, but she had never been to her flat in Camden.

'I now would like to talk with Jimmy please.'

Daisy called his mobile and then they waited in silence. Five minutes later Jimmy arrived. Daisy was making the introductions when her mobile rang.

'Sorry, have to take this.'

She walked up the shallow stairs to the back of the preview theatre.

'It's me,' said Danny. 'I'm at main gate security.'

'You were quick,' she whispered. 'The police are here talking to me and Jimmy. We're in the preview theatre.'

'Come and get me – don't know where it is.'

'I'll be down now.'

Daisy was pleased to get away. Jimmy could cope with the questioning, thought Daisy. After all he was as keen to find Martha as anyone. No Martha meant no tour and no pay for his crew – many long-time friends. He was ultimately responsible for ensuring Martha's safety and security; it wouldn't take long for the blame game to catch up with Jimmy and ruin, maybe unfairly, his reputation.

THE WYE VALLEY – MONMOUTHSHIRE

MARTHA WAS HAVING A WONDERFUL TIME – THE promise of a whole week of privacy and pampering. Her whole life was an emotional roller-coaster.

On Thursday she had been sent a text telling her she was going on a special luxury break to help her relax. It apparently came from Nowak, with instructions to be ready at one-thirty, to be picked up by car from Maxwell Road, the side entrance to Elstree Studios, usually used for audiences excitedly attending one of the many shows recorded or broadcast live from the studios. The excess glitter from too many enthusiastic audience members' outfits was still on the floor from last night's celebrity ice-skating show. As Martha left, the entrance was deserted. No one saw her leave, the CCTV ignored.

The subterfuge reminded her of her time as a major celebrity. In those days, she became too familiar with the kitchens, goods entrances and side streets of most up-market restaurants, hotels and venues – avoiding the reporters, photographers and crowds that grew larger and larger outside the main entrances of wherever she went. Unless, of course, she wanted to be seen; this then ensured the front cover and several pages inside virtually every celebrity gossip magazine and red-top newspaper in the world, and a complicated nightmare for her personal protection team.

She had been told by today's driver, who she had never met before, she wouldn't need to pick up her own clothes or cosmetics as absolutely everything was provided. Back in the day she relied on John, her regular driver – he provided her bonkers world with stability and normality, someone she trusted. That luxury was long gone.

Stanislaw? Trust? she asked herself. Long ago Martha had learned to trust no one. *Something is definitely off on this tour. Danny will help – maybe. Maybe not? Or am I being paranoid? But I'm back in the game.* She laughed out loud. *Just like the old days again*, she thought as she stretched out in comfort.

The old days? Really? Nostalgia isn't all it's cracked up to be. Her thoughts turned back to that night. Guilt racked her. She should have been on the bus. She shouldn't have survived – the guilt of the living. Just her and her sister all that was left of her large family. That awful night when

Danny and she had argued. A nasty, vitriolic, spiteful battle – both had said things that once said, couldn't be retracted. She was stoned and Danny was right.

Martha sobbed out loud. A massive, racking sob.

'Everything all right ma'am?' Martha's maudlin introspection was interrupted by her driver.

'Yes fine. Sorry. Something in my throat.'

A letter signed by 'Stanislaw' had waited beside her on the back seat of the long-wheelbase S-Class Mercedes with the darkened rear windows.

The letter told her she would be away for a week or so at a private luxury spa where she would be known by her proper name of Jenny Jones. She was not to tell absolutely anyone she was going to be away, as word always spreads and the paparazzi would find her. The letter also insisted that she hand her phone to the driver for safe-keeping and total privacy, which she did. But too late for secrecy – she had already sent an excited text to her sister, Vikki:

'See you in a week sis. #secret #excited #pampered. #spa. xxx'

Vikki had quickly replied:

'When you back? Wanna see rehearse. Good 2CU. xxx'

Martha and Vikki had made an effort to restore their sisterly relationship – neither had spoken openly about or planned the reunion. It sort of happened. *Maybe maturity has its plus points*, Martha mused.

She was exhausted from rehearsals – the timing was perfect. She attempted conversation with her driver.

'Hello I'm Jenny.' Martha was doing as she was told.

'Good afternoon ma'am.'

Further attempts at conversation were either ignored or all she received were monosyllabic replies.

There were a few bottles of water beside her and a selection of magazines in the pockets of the seats in front of her. She picked one at random – *Horse and bloody Hound. Who the hell did they think she was?*

Once they hit the M4 westbound, her eyes inexorably closed. She gently drifted off as the tyres hummed, barely audible in the air-conditioned leather luxury of the limousine.

She dreamed of her past and her *journey* to today. The tears continued to roll down her cheeks as she remembered her late family. Memories of happy days as a child playing on the double swing in their small lawned garden. Music college. Those first gigs with her brothers and sisters. The accident. The guilt of not being there. The loss. The pain. Round and around it went.

In her somnambulant state she drifted randomly through her life. Adoring fans. The crowds. The high life. The low points – being dropped by her record company and then her management. Long periods of her life were inaccessible, her memory deleted by drug- and alcohol-fuelled demons. And then, inevitably, to Danny. School. Homework. Those few weeks of bliss – the first and only true love of her life. The meal at The Ivy Club, their first 'proper' date after seeing Danny again at the press conference. She remembered it as if it were yesterday – vivid, in full colour, the smells, the sounds of happy diners.

Every word of that conversation…

'Okay, here's what I suggest. I need someone to put together promotional radio packages for me – you're freelance. You do it.' Martha remembered the stunned look on Danny's face.

'Warts and all?' Danny's reply.

'Nothing off the table, but I do get final veto. A girl must have some secrets.'

They laughed. The squeeze of Danny's hand. The frisson as they touched.

'Just you and me? No PR, no management?'

They hugged – they kissed goodbye. Properly.

Then the next time they met. Martha remembered the skip of her heart as she saw Danny in reception of The Sound Company in Gosfield Street, the old Victorian building, once the All Souls Girls' Poor School, close to the theatrical and media heart of London, just around the corner from the BBC's Broadcasting House. They drank water whilst waiting for their booked studio time – the sign above the coffee machine recommended that voice artists and interviewees do not drink tea, coffee and especially milk before a session, as they affect their voices.

The unmistakable voice of Brian Blessed barrelling around the art deco corridors as he took his far from subtle leave from Studio One. He greeted Martha at considerable volume, who introduced him to Danny. 'Marvellous, marvellous. Good to see you darlings.' And with that he went off into the street.

They had talked about the music industry and how it was changing.

'Motown started it all in the late sixties.' Martha remembered telling the story. 'They owned their artists' likenesses, touring, publishing, record royalties, told them what to wear, how to walk. The three-sixty deal is the big one. The business relationship between the artist and the music industry company – often through a manager or agent. Everyone gets a slice of the pie. The music company agrees to provide financial and other support for the artist, including cash advances, marketing, promotion, touring and so on. In turn, the artist agrees to give the company a larger percentage of their revenue streams.'

'Seems a bit heavy handed?' Danny was appalled.

'Everything has changed. Profit margins from recorded music have plummeted. The three-sixty deal reflects the fact that much of a musician's income now comes from sources other than recorded music, such as live performance and merchandise. It does have some advantages – with Motown it made for great entertainment but if you look at every one of those artists, what happened? Sooner or later they said, "I'm not going to go on the road for hundreds of shows because you tell me so. I'm an artist! I'm a creative person!" Eventually all their artists left.'

'Seems a bit like the old Hollywood film studio system?'

'Not far off – but we don't have to sleep with the producers to get a gig. The thing to remember is that there are two things about creativity, you can't force it and you can't really control it.'

The sound engineer arrived spot on time, she shook hands with Martha and Danny and showed them up to

Studio Five. Danny had booked two hours to record the interview. He said he would personally edit it on his laptop later for syndication around the world.

Danny and Martha entered the studio, with its carefully controlled acoustic and burgundy baize-topped studio table – everything was ready for them. They chatted for a couple of minutes until the engineer through the glass was happy with the levels, the red light went on to indicate that no one should enter, followed by the green cue light. They were off.

Danny started. 'Martha, your sixth album. You've come a long way since Solihull Soultrain. Tell me about your journey...?'

Ninety-five minutes later they were both exhausted. The engineer tidied up the recording and handed Danny the memory stick. 'I'll email you a copy too. We keep the archive here for six years.'

Danny told Martha he was thrilled with the interview. Her life story had come alive with several anecdotes no one had heard before.

To be fair Martha made no amendments to the final edited interviews. Danny had prepared several versions at various lengths for sale, distribution and syndication, including commercial one-hour and half-hour documentaries illustrated with Martha's music old and new.

Take-up exceeded his expectations – it seemed that the world was still interested in Martha. Radio news bulletins and 'arts programmes' used the interviews as the foundation for longer pieces, with Danny taking part in several of the studio discussions. Some radio stations around the world transmitted the full-length versions trailing them to be exclusives, and selling the advertising spots within for a premium.

Danny had told Martha in bed one night that it was the one-hour documentary version that attracted the attention of Starshine Radio, although they never transmitted it. A few days later, after a couple of phone calls and a formal recruitment interview with the station manager, he was offered a full-time job as the music and celebrity radio reporter on Starshine's breakfast and other shows. Apparently, the paparazzi's shots of Martha and Danny in *Hello* was a clincher.

Martha woke briefly somewhere near Swindon. She sipped some water, unwrapped a blanket and settled back down. Dreams and nightmares soon returned.

She remembered 'that' meeting. Some faceless record company suit – and a grey one at that – telling her that they could no longer support her. Martha was dropped by her label as often happens in the rotten world of music; sales simply were not good enough. She had been told that she went on a record-breaking bender around the pubs, clubs and seedy bars of London's Soho – eventually passing out in a pool of vomit outside Groucho's. A friend, she had no idea who, found her. All Martha could remember was waking up in bed with a pile of stinking clothes in the corner – and a distant voice persuading her to drink water. A dark memory. After that nothing for weeks and months. No memories. Nothing. She later read – and saw – in back-issues online of the red tops that she took refuge hiding in a world of booze and drugs. Personal tragedies are easy fodder for the tabloids exploiting the stories for their own profits; these stories sell newspapers. More headlines for the wrong reasons until, like the record companies, the press had become fed up with her fall from grace and inability to generate advertising income.

The relationship with Danny broke down – she loved him deeply and he, in return, had tried to save her from herself. But she didn't want saving, all she cared about was her next fix and next bottle. The arguments became worse and worse. Then one day Danny had simply walked out never to return. *Love doesn't conquer all*, Martha remembered him screaming at her.

Martha's memory clicked. Danny leaving was the final straw. Something deep inside, maybe the body's basic survival instinct, persuaded her to seek help. An hour later she was in a very private rehab clinic.

Martha and Danny hadn't seen or spoken to each other since. The text Martha sent to Danny inviting him to rehearsals was the first contact in years.

She woke up with a start, when the car turned off the M4 at Chepstow – no more stopping at the tolls of the Severn Bridge. She had friends in the business living on the Welsh side who had told her house prices had rocketed since the tolls were abandoned – mainly commuters moving in who worked around Bristol. Martha looked out the window at the wide expanse of the River Severn and across to the green hills beyond.

They passed the racecourse, the remains of Tintern Abbey and continued up the beautiful Wye Valley. Twenty minutes later the car turned onto a gravel drive. The signs read 'Strictly Private. Beware of the dogs'.

As the car glided to a stop outside the portico of the eighteenth-century neoclassical house, she was greeted by a man in striped trousers, black coat without tails, plain waistcoat, grey tie and a white shirt with turned-down collar.

'Ms Jones, welcome to Piercefield Park. I'm Williams.'

Martha had spent many years staying in hotels under assumed names – her favourite was always Delia Clementine. For a moment Martha was confused, then smiled – her outstretched hand was ignored.

'Let me show you to your room ma'am.'

The views through the first-floor massive sash windows were spectacular, across the valley the trees verdant in the afternoon spring sunshine. Below her, a security guard patrolled with a muzzled Alsatian on a short lead.

Williams showed Martha the long, silken pull cord. 'This will summon your maid. She will be here in a few minutes.' Without saying anything further, he left.

Martha opened the wardrobe. A variety of monogrammed sports clothes and silk pyjamas greeted her. In the chest of drawers, a selection of expensive underwear in her size, together with a one-piece swimsuit. The dressing table was laid out with cleansers and skin care products by Oscar de la Renta, Farragamo and Bvlgari. The bathroom was well stocked with toiletries, luxurious fluffy towels and a dressing gown. There was nothing for which she could have wanted.

By the bed, a remote control that endlessly varied

the air conditioning and the lighting from bright, sunny daylight to moody deep blue and everywhere in between. A library of books and magazines was displayed in the bookcase. A media server provided an almost limitless source of films on the massive screen and music via the studio-quality Genelec loudspeakers.

No rehearsals. No pressure. No interruptions. No internet. No mobile phones. No television or radio. This was going to be heaven – the knock on the door interrupted her reverie. Without waiting to be let in, her personal maid entered.

'Good afternoon ma'am. My name is Natalia.' Her Polish accent was light.

'Please call me Mar…, Jenny.'

'Ma'am, I am your maid. Mr Williams has asked me to show you around and to take care of your every personal need. Anything. I am exclusively at your service day and night.'

Martha smiled. Her outstretched hand yet again ignored.

'May I suggest you change into the lightweight sports clothes? I'll take your street clothes away to be cleaned.'

Natalia left. Martha undressed scattering her clothes on the floor and luxuriated in a hot bath with some of the very expensive bath foam, chosen at random. She read the label and laughed – 'Bvlgari's Goldea is a tribute to the golden goddess of beauty and sun. This pearlescent bath and body gel wraps skin in intoxicating notes of the eau de parfum – transforming every cleansing ritual into a moment of casual luxury.'

'Cleansing ritual? And there I was thinking I was having a fucking bath,' she said out loud.

After twenty minutes, before her skin became prune-like, she got out, wrapped her bobbed blonde hair in a towel and tried some of the creamy matching body lotion – 'a refined bath line combining mysterious *Eau Parfumée au Thé Noir* fragrance notes with cleansing and softening ingredients.'

'*Will that be milk and sugar with your Thé Noir, ma'am?*' She giggled.

She was about to put on her new underwear when Natalia re-entered the room without knocking – she didn't seem to notice Martha's naked body with the intricate tattoo on her lower back and buttocks. She picked up Martha's 'street' clothes and left again without a word.

A few minutes later Natalia returned with something in her hand. 'For security we ask all our guests to wear these ankle bands – they are completely heat and waterproof, also the key to your room. Please do not try to remove it.'

Before Martha had time to ask questions, Natalia had attached the reinforced neoprene ankle strap with the built-in long-range RFID tag.

'There is a breakfast card by your bed – please let me know what you wish to eat, I'll bring it to you in your room every morning at ten o'clock. You can ring me for tea, coffee, refreshments, anything you wish at any time. Your personal refrigerator is stocked with a selection of fresh juices and mineral waters. I'll restock the fruit bowl every day – is there anything you particularly enjoy? We have no alcohol here. You are here to detox, cleanse and for your personal well-being.'

Martha wasn't disappointed, she had promised she would remain off the booze as part of the deal – she had been reasonably good for several years. Alcohol wasn't an addiction but an occasional weekend party celebration and a glass or two of wine with a meal. She was proud that she had never taken an illegal substance since her fall from grace. She knew of ex-friends who had resorted to prostitution to fuel their habit.

She also knew she had to improve her fitness for the gruelling tour to come, and maybe this was one of the reasons that Stanislaw had sent her here? She had been puffing a bit after nine or ten songs with their energetic dance routines. Her personal trainer had done his best and she was improving but it was going to take a while to bring her back up to full fitness after too many binge sessions with her Camden mates. But that was all behind her.

Natalia led the way following the ornate corridor, down the massive oak staircase to the treatment room.

'We have an indoor and outdoor pool, both with hot tubs nearby. There is also silent sensory relaxation area.'

Martha was seriously impressed as she looked at the outdoor infinity pools with a perfect vista. It felt like a wealthy owner's home.

They walked a little further where Martha was shown the heated tepidarium with its tiled bed. Then the thermal experience sequence of herbal steam room, laconium and ice cave. Finally, the gym with weights, rowing and running machines and several contraptions she did not recognise, but was sure she would learn about.

Apart from a couple of staff, they had seen no one else. Martha had only had a sandwich from Shirley for brunch – she realised she was hungry. The sun was just setting.

'Where do I eat?'

'In your room – I'll bring it up to you.' Natalia showed Martha a simple menu card.

Martha was about to protest, but then thought it wasn't such a bad idea. She needed the rest away from other people. She chose the local Wye salmon, Jersey Royals and a mixed salad, followed by some berries washed down with some icy still water.

By nine-thirty she was ready for bed.

Each day followed a similar routine. Breakfast at ten in her room. Gym, with a personal trainer who refused to engage in any sort of conversation except to berate her to work harder, followed by pampering spa sessions and massage, a light lunch on the terrace or in the conservatory, an afternoon swim followed by a couple of hours with a book. Then dinner in her room – she was surprised how easily she fell asleep.

But by Wednesday morning she was bored senseless; there is only so much relaxation and pampering one can take. There seemed to be no other people staying. The staff, whilst polite, remained generally distant. Undoubtedly, she felt fitter, mentally and physically, and ready for the gruelling tour.

That afternoon she decided to go for a long walk around the forests of the Wye Valley. She followed the high fencing around the gardens for what must have been at least half a mile, looking for a gate – there wasn't one. The only way in and out was the long gravel drive down which she had been driven what seemed like ages ago, but in reality only six days.

She was surprised by the burly gardener working alongside the closed main gates. 'Can I help you ma'am?'

'Oh hello. I was going for a walk and looking for the way out.'

Martha appraised the man – late thirties, not tall, but clearly muscled and toned. His blond hair and sparkling blue eyes instantly attractive. He was wearing blue jeans and a black polo shirt embroidered with Piercefield logo, his black Hanwag LX boots perfectly lightly polished.

'I'm sorry ma'am, guests are not allowed to leave the grounds – for security reasons.'

'What? This isn't a prison?'

The man smiled – which ratcheted a few more points up in Martha's bloke-scale.

'I'm Jenny.'

'Oliver Mellors.'

The first member of staff to shake hands. They were rough and calloused. The name seemed familiar to Martha.

'What do you do here?'

'General handyman, gardener, look after the horses – bit of security.'

No rings on his fingers, Martha noted.

'How long have you been here?'

'Not long.'

'Where were you before?'

'Army.'

Clearly not a conversationalist, thought Martha.

'Right. I'd better be off.' Martha made for the gates.

'That way please ma'am.' Mellors' grip on her arm was firm.

'That bloody hurt.'

'As I said ma'am, guests are not allowed to leave the grounds – for security reasons.'

To Martha's surprise Natalia, her maid, arrived and firmly took her other arm. Martha tried to shake off the surprisingly powerful grip. Together they marched her, struggling, back to her room.

'Let me fucking go!' Martha screamed. 'That hurts.'

Her pleading fell on deaf ears. Martha's elation crumbled as she realised this was not a luxurious indulgence – she was a prisoner.

What the fuck is going on? Her stress levels returned.

WEDNESDAY

Two hours or so east, Jimmy hadn't been able to add anything much about Martha.

'Tell me about Stanislaw Nowak.' Detective Sergeant Rob Andrews surprised Jimmy.

'What about him?'

'He's promoting and producing the tour?'

'Yeah, but he pretty much leaves me to get on with it. I sign the cheques and authorise online bank payments. Everyone gets paid on time, which is rare in this business.' Jimmy thought about what else he could, should say. 'He has a short fuse occasionally. He said he would be in later. We are meant to be rehearsing with Martha at three.'

'But that's not going to happen is it? What has he said

about Martha going missing – I thought he'd be up here by now.'

'We haven't been able to contact him.'

Rob Andrews frowned. He made a note. 'Isn't that strange?'

'I suppose so, yes. But, as I say, he does leave me to get on with it.'

'How long have you known him?'

'It was Martha actually. She suggested me to Stanislaw. I managed her last tour – what, five or six years ago? We got on.'

'And Nowak?'

Jimmy puffed his cheeks. 'I suppose five or six months. I put the budgets together for him and suggested some venues. A few things he insists on doing his way, but generally it's my gig.'

Daisy, with Danny, arrived in the preview theatre. Daisy introduced Danny to Rob Andrews, not that it was needed. The look between them clearly telegraphing that there was to be no acknowledgement of previous meetings.

'Thank you, Mr Patrick, you've been most helpful. If I may, I'll watch the rehearsals later – you said three o'clock?'

'Yes. But please be discreet. We're trying not to make a fuss about Martha being missing.'

Daisy interrupted.

'We've already had the press asking questions. The story at the moment is that we have given her a few days off whilst the stage rigging was fixed and programming completed.'

'Indeed.' Rob Andrews removed that morning's *Daily Tribune* from his bag and held up the inside celebrity page. There were the pictures of Martha that Daisy had sent accompanied by an innocuous headline in 196pt bold, 'MARTHA RETURNS!' Daisy wondered why the exclamation mark was needed but was thrilled, every little helps to sell tickets.

'Thank you all, I'll see you later.' Rob Andrews didn't give a damn about headlines. The three of them got up to leave.

'Perhaps you would stay here, Mr Owen. I have a few questions for you.'

Jimmy left, Daisy more reluctantly. When DS Andrews had checked that the soundproof, heavy door of the preview theatre was shut, he turned to Danny.

'Bill Kelly asked me to send his regards.'

Danny was taken by surprise. 'How do you know Bill?'

'Detective Chief Superintendent Bill Kelly is my boss – we work together.'

Danny paused. 'So, you're not in Missing Mersons and Bill isn't a sergeant?'

'No shit Sherlock. Detective Chief Superintendent Bill Kelly leads the covert serious organised crime investigation team at the National Crime Agency. After your lunch on Sunday, Bill decided you could be trusted – I don't know you, so the jury's out. For now, Daisy and everyone else is kept out of the loop about who I am. It's our little secret. *Capiche*?'

Danny nodded, but thought he'd think about that one later. 'So why are you here?'

'Let's just say Mr Nowak is a person of significant interest.'

'What about Martha?'

'We're more interested in Nowak. But don't worry we're on the lookout for Martha too. Bill tells me you and Nowak have history?'

'We've only met a few times – ten years ago and again last week, very briefly.' Danny remembered the incident very clearly. His stomach churned.

'Didn't he recognise you?'

'Didn't get the chance. I, err, left quite quickly – and Daisy hadn't introduced us.'

'So, what are you going to do when you do meet?'

'I'm hoping to avoid that. It's been a long time. He might not recognise me, I've changed a bit.'

'Tell me more about Martha. Bill said you knew the family from back in the day.'

'Not a lot to tell really. Most of her family killed in a tragic accident. Both her parents and four of her siblings. Her twin sister, Vikki is still alive – lives somewhere in Acton.'

'Does she have a partner?'

'Not as far as I know, but Daisy would know more about that.'

'Okay for now. I'm sure Bill will be in contact.' DS Andrews stood up. 'Right then, let's get over to the rehearsals.'

Danny led the way. After a few wrong turns they were led by Martha's voice coming from the studio, the soulful words of 'Missing You, Loving You' belted out of the 20,000 watts rehearsal system. On stage, Martha's stand-in was making most of the right moves to playback. The deep blue Vari-Lites gently tilted down to encircle her in backlight – as the music finished, the stage plunged into dead blackout.

Jimmy's voice boomed over the PA and foldback. 'Looks great everyone. Well done. Thank you. Let's reset to rehearse from the top. Ready to go at three please.'

As the team scurried around to grab a cuppa and make last-minute adjustments, the house lights came up to reveal Nowak sitting on a large chair where the front row of the audience would be during the tour. He levered himself out of the chair and headed towards the catering truck.

Daisy, shocked, grabbed Danny and ushered him backstage into Martha's enclosed quick-change area where no one could see him.

'Oh my God, he's here. Did he see us?'

Danny shook his head. 'Don't think so – if he did, he didn't recognise me. Remember you have to act normally.'

'How can I, knowing what he did to you?'

'You must. You are safe as long as you don't know a thing.'

'But I do.'

'If we are going to find Martha, and get to the bottom of this you have to.'

Daisy wasn't sure – she shook her head and grimaced.

'This is a chance for me to get even... and for us to find out what he is up to.'

DS Andrews was surprised as anyone to see Nowak. He knew exactly who he was. He approached Nowak, badge extended with his thumb partially obscuring the details. 'I'd like a word about Martha please, Mr Nowak. As you know she's been reported missing—'

'Missing? What? Of course,' Nowak was temporarily lost for words. 'Who called you?'

'Ms DeVilliers and Mr Patrick – must be a big thing, your star missing? You must be very worried?' DS Andrews elongated the word 'very' for emphasis.

Nowak didn't know that the police had been called. The last thing he had said to Jimmy was 'no police'. But he had survived police questioning before – he could also think on his feet.

'There must be a mistake. I simply gave her a few days off – we're rehearsing without her as you can see.'

'That's not what Ms DeVilliers and Mr Patrick said. They seemed concerned for Martha's welfare.'

'Communication breakdown. That's all.' Nowak smiled. He could be charming when needed. 'Cup of tea? Something stronger – or are you on duty?'

Nowak tried to usher DS Andrews towards catering, but he stood firm. Jimmy Patrick saw the two of them and rushed over.

'We've been trying to get hold of you Stanislaw. Martha is still missing, no one can find her. We've looked for her at all her regular haunts. No one has seen her since Thursday.'

Nowak was ever the smooth operator. 'Didn't you get my email? I gave her a few days off.'

'What, in the middle of rehearsals? You didn't say anything when I called you on Monday.' Jimmy was furious – and confused. He tried to hide it.

'With all the technical and stage issues, it seemed a good time.' Nowak was trying to be at his avuncular best. He was beginning to bead up.

'You called for the full rehearsal for three today.' Jimmy spat the words.

DS Andrews chipped in, 'So where is Martha, Mr Nowak? You gave her the time off. You must know where she is? I hope police time isn't being wasted? What's it to be? Is Martha missing or not?'

Jimmy looked at Nowak.

Nowak was in a quandary – he started sweating even more profusely. If he said Martha was missing, the police would be all over them. If he said she was safe, it would be expected that Martha would turn up. But to get Martha back, he would have to agree to Ali Baka's demands.

Nowak was about to say something, anything, when his phone rang. No caller ID. He was tempted to ignore it but changed his mind. Saved by the bell?

'Sorry everyone, I have to take this.' He gesticulated at the group, pointing at the phone in his pudgy hand. 'Hang on, let me go somewhere quieter,' he said to the phone not knowing who it was.

Nowak waddled across the studio, to behind the stage. He stood just outside Martha's quick-change area.

'Yes?' Danny could hear every word Nowak spoke. He prayed Nowak would not walk in on him. Danny quietly locked the door – a hand tested the knob and quickly gave up. Danny heaved a silent sigh of relief.

'Have you thought about it?' Ali Baka on the other end of the phone didn't bother with pleasantries.

'Oh yes, I've thought about it.' Danny wondered what Nowak had thought about.

'Well?' Baka was aggressive.

'The police are here – Martha has been reported missing.'

'That's not my problem.'

'I told you – one million, final offer.'

'From where I am standing, you don't have a lot of choice. There's only so long you can keep the police from demanding to see Martha. Then you'll have some very difficult questions to answer.' Baka knew he held all the cards, and was doubling down.

'Listen, Baka. You're the one who changed the deal.'

'Well then, Martha will be staying where she is.' Baka rang off – as usual he removed the battery from the phone together with the SIM. He threw the phone into the back of a passing pick-up and dropped the SIM down a drain.

Danny had heard one side of the conversation. Who is the backer? What deal? Why was Nowak offering one million and for what?

Nowak waddled off. Now he had two problems. The police demanding to see Martha. And no tour. Was he just being stubborn not agreeing to Baka's one and a half million deal? Reward versus risk?

Nowak texted Daisy. *See you Friday with Martha.* Which of course was a lie but might give him some time.

He called his driver to meet him outside the studio. Within a few minutes he was on his way to Baka's hotel.

The journey took over an hour in the London traffic. Roadworks and temporary traffic lights seemed to thwart his driver's every turn. Nowak was not in a good mood as he kept his finger on the doorbell at Hazlitt's. The receptionist seemed to be completely unfazed by the campanological attack and the big man's threatening bluster.

'Ali Baka,' Nowak barked.

'Mr Baka checked out earlier, sir.'

'Did he leave a forwarding address?'

'No sir. But may I please ask your name, sir – and see some ID please, sir?'

'Why?'

'He has left a note addressed to one person, sir. Mr Baka said that person may call by. I was to give the note to that person and that person only, sir.'

Nowak took his driving licence from his wallet and handed it to the casually dressed receptionist.

'Thank you, sir.' The driving licence was handed back. 'Please wait one moment, sir.'

Nowak did not notice or did not care about the serial sycophantic, sarcastic 'sir's.

The receptionist disappeared into the back office. A few moments later he returned with a stiff white envelope with the Hazlitt's crest embossed in gold, the address in raised hand-engraved black ink. Nowak's name was scrawled in biro.

'I believe this is for you, sir?'

Nowak grabbed the envelope and turned to leave without saying a further word.

'Thank you, sir,' said the receptionist to Nowak's disappearing sweat-stained back, which he didn't hear. Neither did Nowak hear the receptionist's sotto voce, carefully considered character assessment: 'Fucking twat.'

Inside the envelope was a phone number with a message. 'Call me when you are ready to deal.'

16
THURSDAY MORNING

DANNY'S PHONE VIBRATED IN HIS POCKET halfway through the breakfast show – Danny was trailing his interview with George Ezra in a jovial, all-studio chat. He was familiar with having to process multiple sources of information while speaking, so he was not fazed. Gordon segued straight into the new single and muted all the microphones. 'I told you to switch your phone off before coming into the studio.'

Danny ignored Gordon – he was a trumped-up DJ, not his boss. The word was that there was going to be a DJ-reshuffle that didn't include Gordon – one of the big names from BBC Radio Two had apparently been seduced into joining Starshine. Whether the rest of the breakfast team were included in the reshuffle was a matter of open conjecture. If Gordon was aware of all this, he didn't let it show – unless his extra grumpiness this morning was a sign?

Danny looked at the email on his private email address: 'Meet me. My office. Ten this morning. Bill.'

Danny simply typed 'OK', pressed 'send' and smiled at his colleagues.

Danny couldn't believe, as he left the studios a few minutes after nine-thirty, that it was exactly a week since he had become embroiled with Daisy, the missing Martha, and Stanislaw Nowak – and here he was voluntarily agreeing to meet again Detective Chief Superintendent Bill Kelly of the covert serious organised crime investigation team at the National Crime Agency.

His stomach rumbled. The five-thirty breakfast needed replenishing – slightly out of his way, but worth it for a good coffee, he crossed Leicester Square and walked across to Francisco's. He was greeted with open arms and an over-the-top hug from Francisco himself.

'Hey, Danny. Where have you been? I miss you!'

'Morning, Francisco. You miss my money, not me.'

'Okay, okay. Maybe a bit of both.'

Danny ordered a large cappuccino, with an extra shot, together with a fist-sized cannoli Siciliani.

'Ah, you like my mother's recipe from Piana degli Albanesi.' Francisco ostentatiously crossed himself in memory of his late Sicilian mother.

Danny sat outside and waited for his second breakfast to arrive. He checked his emails and Facebook page, just a few odds and sods, but nothing that needed immediate attention. No news from Elstree yet after yesterday's shenanigans – he expected that to change. Francisco arrived with his coffee and a large plate covered with this morning's calorific treat. Danny cut up the tube-shaped shells of fried pastry dough filled with the sweet, creamy filling of figs, honey and ricotta and popped a bit in his mouth. He didn't have to wait long for the sugar-buzz. The coffee was strong and smooth.

At ten-to-ten he handed Francisco a tenner, took a couple of pounds change, and made his way down to New Scotland Yard, a ten-minute walk past the National Gallery and the Prince of Wales' monstrous carbuncle, across tourist-strewn Trafalgar Square and into Northumberland Avenue. He decided a few minutes on the Thames embankment would clear his head ready for whatever lay ahead – he never failed to be thrilled by London's skyline, particularly along the river. The trains rattled across Hungerford Bridge as they delivered the last of the daily commuters and the first of the shoppers into Charing Cross station. He walked through Whitehall Gardens with its beautifully tended flower beds and sub-tropical trees – couples were sitting together on the benches taking al fresco breaks. As Westminster Bridge and the Houses of Parliament loomed into view ahead, he limped up the steps of New Scotland Yard.

Bill Kelly was waiting for him in reception.

'You're a dark horse, aren't you? Detective Chief Superintendent – when did all that happen?'

'You're just out of touch – you didn't ask, and I didn't tell.' They shook hands.

'You'll have to sign in.'

Danny signed on the touch screen. The civilian welcome team then took his photograph, scanned his Starshine ID and printed a pass which they attached to a branded dark-blue lanyard embroidered with the Metropolitan Police's logo intertwined with the words: 'Professionalism, Integrity, Courage and Compassion'.

'The brand gurus get everywhere,' said Danny to no one in particular, 'they'll be selling souvenirs next.' He looked across the reception desk to a display of postcards, a Bobby Teddy Bear and sets of cufflinks adorned with the Metropolitan Police crest. His dreams realised.

'Come on through,' said Bill, indicating one of the sophisticated airport-type security scanners. 'You'll have to leave your phones in one of the security lockers – you pick it back up when you leave.'

The guest lift took them directly to the fourth-floor meeting suites – no chance of visitors getting into New Scotland Yard proper.

Bill made the introductions to the eight people seated in the room. Danny instantly forgot almost all their names.

'Of course, you have met Detective Sergeant Rob Andrews.'

'Missing Persons?'

There was gentle laughter.

'Right, I have asked Danny to be here today because he is our route to Nowak and Ali Baka – and may have information that will help us with our enquiries.'

Danny looked up when Bill said the name Ali Baka. Suddenly it made some sense of what he overheard

Nowak saying on the phone. Danny was about to speak. Bill stopped him. 'Let's get some chronology into this. We might begin to fit this jigsaw together. So, what do we know – stick to the facts, then we can discuss?'

The screen burst into life. *Not bloody PowerPoint*, thought Danny. But he opened the notebook that had been left in front of him.

Bill stopped Danny. 'By all means make notes, Danny, but they cannot leave here. This meeting must remain confidential – I don't want to see or hear anything in the media. No one, and I mean no one must know who this team is, who I am, or that we are talking to each other – and that includes your mate Daisy DeVilliers. Not Martha either – if ever we see her again.'

Danny nodded his agreement and put the Metropolitan Police branded pen back on the table.

'I'll make a start.'

A picture of Stanislaw Nowak was displayed on the screen.

'Danny here called me last Friday. He was enquiring about Stanislaw Nowak and his involvement in the Martha Movin' Out concert tour. He was concerned that...' Bill consulted his notes '...and I quote, that "this piece of crooked shit" was promoting and producing what appears to be a legitimate tour. Danny couldn't understand why Nowak was involved with Martha. Neither could I.'

The screen changed to a picture of Martha.

'For those of you who live in a cave, Martha was a massive UK and European pop star ten or so years ago. Her career ground to a halt about six years ago when what was to be her final album bombed. She pretty much fell apart too – alcohol and drugs.'

Danny said nothing about his and Martha's past intimate relationship.

'I have them all,' interjected one of the women at the table.

'All what?' asked Bill.

'Martha's albums. Great to iron by.' Two others nodded that they had the same enthusiasm for Martha.

'Shagged my first girlfriend to Martha.' The room turned to the young constable and let out a collective 'Eeeugh – too much information.'

The grumpy older man wearing a smart sports jacket was never seen without his ex-military striped tie. His name badge declared him to be Detective Sergeant Michael Maguire. He harrumphed a meaningful, 'Jesus Christ, give me the Stones and a bit of Morrissey any day.'

Bill ignored them all.

'Obviously I asked Danny how he knew about Nowak.' Danny's foot did its traditional throb. 'He told me, in strictest confidence, about a story he was writing ten years ago for the now defunct *Weekend News*. Danny here stumbled across organised crime's involvement in disabled Blue Badge fraud involving our friend Nowak. We discussed why he didn't report all this to the police – and we have, let's say, reached an understanding.'

The screen switched back to a different picture of Nowak, struggling out of a low-slung sports car – a couple of the men took more interest in the peroxide blonde woman's legs, her skirt riding up as she got out from the passenger side – they exchanged glances of non-PC admiration. Bill distributed bundles of A4 paper to everyone. Danny realised that this was a copy of his, until now, unseen story.

'How did you get hold of this? Even I don't have a copy – I thought I'd destroyed them all and wiped the file?'

'The law works in mysterious ways,' offered Detective Sergeant Michael Maguire. His grin was challenging.

'So why didn't we charge Nowak, Guv?' asked Rob Andrews.

'Oh, we had a couple of chats under caution, but his brief extracted him before we could press charges. Then a message came down from on very high via my guv'nor, subsequently retired, that it was not in the public interest to take this any further.'

Knowing looks all around. Most smelled a cover-up. DS Michael Maguire stirred his coffee.

'What about the transcripts and tapes of the interviews?'

'All disappeared in the move to here. The only thing of any certainty, well as certain as we can trust any bloody journo, is this story – I have copies, with photographs, in several secure places.'

'Cock up or conspiracy?' asked Rob.

'Not for today,' replied Bill, looking meaningfully at Danny.

Bill waved the A4 printout about – reminiscent of Neville Chamberlain at Heston aerodrome returning from seeing Herr Hitler. 'Danny, perhaps you'd like to give us the highlights of your unpublished magnum opus.'

The room turned to Danny.

'Ten years ago, Blue Badges – disabled parking badges – were easy to forge, not any longer by the way. They were effectively bits of cardboard or printed plastic with a rotary clock. Stolen badges were easy to sell too – no photographs, no holographic watermarks, names were handwritten in what was meant to be permanent marker pen, easily wiped off. It seemed that almost every high value car and Chelsea tractor had one on its dashboard, it was virtually impossible to tell which were genuine and which were false. Back then wardens didn't have mobile phones or access to internet records. The admin was simply too much. Fraudulent badges meant disabled parking spaces were often full – leaving no space for those who genuinely needed them. With parking in Central London even then costing forty pounds a day or more, no wonder organised crime had muscled in. The Government estimated it was a fifty million pound-a-year business.'

'Bloody hell,' said Detective Sergeant Michael Maguire, back to being grumpy as ever, scanning the article. His gentle Northern Irish accent became more pronounced. 'There are some very big names here – some still active. Very big. Bloody hell, that's—'

Bill interrupted. 'Local councils and uniform, often tipped off by residents and gallant citizens, came down hard on drivers caught using the bollocks badges. We were much more interested in organised crime who were leading the sale and distribution – which is how we came across Nowak.'

Danny picked up the story. 'As I researched, I discovered a huge list of high-profile names using them – businesspeople, bankers, celebrities, public servants, sports stars and even several of your police, err, colleagues.'

Maguire looked uncomfortable.

'This would have been a major exposé for *The Weekend News*. We confidently expected resignations and prosecutions – and increased circulation of course. I photographed several caught in the act and subsequently tried to interview a few. Most tried to fob me off saying that illegal use of a Blue Badge was a victimless crime. Several threatened me with their lawyers.' He read from the first paragraph of his unpublished feature. 'For disabled people, Blue Badges are a vital lifeline that helps them get out and about to visit shops or family and friends. Callous thieves and unscrupulous fraudsters using them illegally are robbing disabled people of this independence.'

'All jolly interesting,' Maguire grumpily leant back, 'but how does all this fit in with bloody Nowak?'

'The evening before I was going to submit the story, Nowak and a couple of his chums visited me at my home – it wasn't a social call. Nowak was pretty pissed off. Nowak then ran the biggest Blue Badge syndicate in the UK and it seems he has or had friends in high places. I have no idea how he cottoned on to me in advance. He said that if I published, or spoke to you lot, he would hurt me and my family. One of his thugs took a sledgehammer to my foot as further persuasion.'

'That's why you limp?' asked the Martha-loving sergeant.

Danny nodded. 'I wasn't prepared to risk my family for the sake of a newspaper story, so I canned it. My editor and several colleagues didn't quite see it that way – and I sort of resigned. Nowak made it very clear he never wanted to see or hear from me again. Which he hasn't until last week.'

'I suppose you have a disabled badge now?' Detective Sergeant Michael Maguire could be a cantankerous shit when he wanted to be. Even so, nobody understood why he had taken against Danny – this was the first time they had met. Maguire fiddled with his pen.

'I would, but I don't own a car.' *Fifteen all*, thought Danny, he wasn't going to let Maguire take the piss. 'And it only hurts when I'm tired or stressed.'

'The reason that this doesn't leave the room is because of some of the names in Danny's story. We don't know who may still be involved with Nowak. Professional Standards have been investigating for some time. As I said that's not for now,' said Bill, looking again at Danny. Eyes communicating a message.

'We know that Nowak isn't clean. He has several nightclubs and a couple of production companies. Apparently legit – all aimed at the more mature clientele.'

'Suits you sir.' Bill glared at the interrupter.

'We think he deals in stolen passports too – not personally but has a well-developed network. We need to know more about that. He pretty much disappeared off our radar three years ago as the Russians moved in and we were diverted to other interests.'

Bill directly addressed Danny. 'What we are about to discuss now is privileged information – you shouldn't be here. Do I have your word you will keep this absolutely secret?'

Danny agreed. Bill continued, 'Is there anyone here unhappy with Danny remaining in the room for the next discussions?'

Sergeant Martha-lover spoke for them all. 'If you say Danny is okay, good enough for you, we'll back you, boss.' Everyone nodded. Little did Danny know that this was a carefully rehearsed scenario.

'Thank you, really appreciate that. I think if Danny hears this, he may be able to help us put two and two together?'

Bill walked over to the oversized white board and started scribbling bullet points.

'So, what have we learned, what do we know? We put Nowak under twenty-four-hour surveillance as from Monday – three days ago. We persuaded the Home Secretary's office to issue a warrant to allow us to bug his flat too. He uses several burner phones, so those are impossible to track, and WhatsApp, which we still cannot break. No one has seen Martha since Thursday. Daisy deVilliers, Nowak's PR, called it in on Friday morning – Missing Persons didn't take too much notice as it was difficult to say if she was missing or not. Not even a day had gone by, so didn't trigger their protocols.'

Danny defended Daisy. 'She's not Nowak's PR, she is the PR for the Martha Movin' Out tour.'

'Same thing in my book. As some of you know Danny, Daisy and I met on Sunday.'

'Yes, yes for a very nice Sunday lunch whilst we were waiting back here for you – eating Friday's leftover sandwiches and drinking stale coffee.' They were a good team and Rob Andrews knew he could take the piss.

'The big question is how Nowak is funding all this. A tour of this size takes millions of pounds. But I'll come back to that in a moment. Against the advice of his tour manager, Jimmy Patrick, Nowak is using a trucking company from his old hometown of Wrocław. Don't expect me to pronounce it properly – Mazury Ostrodzko International. What do we know about them?'

Detective Sergeant Michael Maguire picked up the story. 'Seem straight enough. Big operation run by an old school chum of Nowak's – Pietr Ostrodzko. They have a few hundred trucks and commercial barges, work directly for quite a few of the large companies and also provide wholesale services as well. According to their website, European logistics and just-in-time solutions – whatever that means. Nothing criminal showed up from Interpol or the local *Policja*. They have been struggling for the past couple of years as the big boys such as FedEx, DHL, UPS and TNT are increasingly working at national levels. They don't seem set up for the kind of Amazon and eBay direct-to-door business.'

'The tour schedule isn't right, according to Ms DeVilliers. We need to follow up on that. Did you get anything from Jimmy Patrick?' Bill looked at Rob Andrews.

'Not yet. Now, I am just a plod from Missing Persons helping to try and find Martha. We'll have to decide how we handle that.'

'According to Daisy they are about to announce Dublin and Belfast, straight off the back of several European and African dates.'

Detective Sergeant Michael Maguire picked up again. His job was desk research. 'The port of Dublin is expanding rapidly. They have just announced several new super ferries

– twice as large as anything before. Up to six hundred lorries to and from European ports, completely avoiding the UK land bridge. As we know, once in the Republic of Ireland it's pretty easy to get into Northern Ireland and across to the mainland.'

'Smuggling maybe? But what? Drugs?' Martha-lover number two suggested.

'You may be right,' continued Bill, scribbling a note on the white board. 'Monday morning Nowak met with our new person-of-interest, Ali Baka, at Hazlitt's Hotel in Soho. We don't know what they discussed – and Baka checked out soon after. So, no point bugging his room. We didn't have the team on the ground to follow Baka, we stuck with Nowak. After an enormous lunch in Wardour Street on his own he seemed to spend the rest of his day visiting various people in and around Soho and Westminster. Surveillance are compiling a list of residents at those addresses. He returned to his flat about five. Also, on Monday, our tech team posing as BT Open Reach engineers entered Nowak's flat in Docklands and it is now well covered for sound. Tuesday, Nowak stayed at his flat all day – he didn't see anyone or speak with anyone until early evening when he made a phone call on one of his burners. It doesn't give us a lot as we could only hear Nowak's end.' Bill clicked the link on his laptop:

'Okay, you have a deal. I'll transport your goods. But I only return one million of your loan and that's it.'

Silence. Apart from Nowak's laboured breathing.

'What don't you understand about one million? Take it or leave it.'

Silence.

'Neither are you.'

Sound of a crash.

'Bollocks.'

'We tried to enhance the audio to hear the other end, but there was too much background noise. So, all we know is that Nowak has taken out some sort of loan for over a million. Quid, I assume. And he is trying to renegotiate payments. More importantly what goods has he agreed to transport? Is this a separate deal or part of the Martha tour? Wednesday, Daisy deVilliers called Missing Persons again as Martha still hadn't turned up. This time we were ready. Rob was up at Elstree within the hour. Rob?'

Rob took his cue. 'As I said, I was posing as a plod from Missing Persons – I didn't want to raise suspicions, although I think Nowak might have clocked me, don't know how. Strange. Not sure. Daisy said that Martha hadn't been seen since Thursday. I checked with security on the front gate – one of them I vaguely knew, ex-job. He seemed to know what he was doing. So, we don't know how Martha left without being seen. I spoke with the production tour manager, Jimmy Patrick, he didn't have a lot to add – he did seem a bit surprised when I asked him about Nowak. Hopefully I got away with it. Jimmy seems straight enough. He said that Nowak left him to it. I asked why Nowak hadn't visited the studios when he learned that Martha was missing, he just repeated that Nowak left him to get on with it. Interestingly he said that Nowak had been uncontactable. Then I spoke with Danny here – alone.'

'I was a little taken aback when Rob said you sent your regards.' Danny stared at Bill. 'And I learned you weren't a sergeant.'

The room laughed.

'Danny told me about how he met Nowak last Thursday – a week ago today. Messy by all accounts. But Danny wasn't recognised,' Rob continued. 'He filled me in with some of Martha's background. We were both surprised to see Nowak had arrived yesterday in the studio to watch the rehearsals. Nowak clearly didn't know we had been called, he said it was all a communications mix-up. He had given Martha a few days off. Jimmy Patrick was annoyed – delete that, bloody furious. Nowak couldn't tell me where Martha was, he was blustering when his phone rang. He said he had to take the call and I didn't see him again that day.'

'Daisy said she received a text from Nowak saying that Martha would be back on Friday,' offered Danny.

'So, he does know where she is?'

'Or he is playing for time?'

They all silently reflected. Not everything was making that much sense.

'Where were you during all this?' Bill asked Danny.

'Obviously I didn't want to be seen by Nowak. When he arrived, Daisy hid me around the back of the stage in the quick-change area. But I did hear Nowak on the phone as he took the call right outside. I was shitting myself he might walk in on me. I locked the door – Nowak didn't try very hard to get in.'

'What did you hear?'

'Nowak said he had thought about something. Martha was missing, and the police had been called. He did say one million was his final offer. I didn't understand the next bit, but I do now – he said Baka, you're the one who changed the deal. I thought he said backer – as in financial backer, not a person's name.'

'Well maybe they are one and the same? But we do know that Nowak and Baka are talking to each other and doing some sort of deal. According to surveillance Nowak went back to Baka's hotel yesterday – we must assume to meet with him. We know that Baka had already checked out. But he did collect an envelope from reception. The receptionist wasn't that enamoured with Nowak or Baka for that matter. Only Nowak could collect the envelope after proving his ID. We have no idea what was in it. Our priority for now is to find out much more about Ali Baka.'

DS Michael Maguire nodded – his list of things to do and research grew. He hated this part of the job. More laughter from the room at his discomfort. But at least it kept him at the centre of things.

'That must have been straight after he saw me,' said Rob.

'What is the relationship between Baka and Nowak? What is this million Nowak keeps going on about? Where is Martha? What is Nowak doing involved in a massive concert tour? Why the abnormal tour schedule? Why are they using Mazury Ostrodzko International instead of a regular touring transport company? What else…?'

'More coffee,' said DS Maguire, now really grumpy, 'and I want a piss.'

'Far, far too much information,' countered Sergeant Martha-lover.

While the others did whatever they needed to do, Bill escorted Danny back to reception, where he collected his phone.

'Take care, Danny. Nowak is a nasty piece of work. Leave this to us now – nothing you can do.'

They shook hands. Danny crossed the road and looked across to the London Eye whilst he wondered what to do next. The wheel had temporarily stopped turning he assumed while someone with walking difficulties was helped on. An MBNA Thames Clipper lazily stayed in synch with the flow of the mighty river, waiting for its pier to be clear to offload and take on board passengers wanting to go upriver to Millbank and eventually Putney. In a few weeks' time he hoped excited Martha fans would be taking the River Bus Express down river to the O2 – but he was concerned there would be tens of thousands of disappointments.

He took out his phone and switched it on. He zipped up his leather bomber jacket as a cold un-spring-like wind whipped up the Thames. There was a delay while the phone did whatever it did to wake up, then spent the next thirty seconds vibrating, pinging and other annoying noises.

He scrolled through his public email accounts. Mostly publicists trying to court him with their latest 'star of the future' – deleted. Various newsletters, newspaper synopses and alerts he scanned – deleted. A couple of emails he popped into his follow-up folder for later. Facebook was the normal selection of friendship requests from people he had never met, trolls, fans' comments and know-alls commenting on what he had said about George Ezra – he wasn't sure who wound him up the most. He was surprised by the WhatsApp from Gordon apologising for being *'snappy and a bit off-form this morning'* – deleted.

The private email from Daisy simply read, *'Any news? xxx'*

He felt a little guilty as he replied, *'No. I'm going home for a kip. Will contact you later. How are rehearsals going? Any news of Martha?'*

A few seconds later Daisy replied, *'No Martha news. Nowak said tomorrow. Rehearsal plodding through. Ticket sales spiked after Kelvin's piece in The Daily Tribune. I'm pitching for more sponsorship this afternoon. Jimmy trying to keep everyone's enthusiasm up. Laters. Xxx'*

Danny turned and walked towards Westminster Underground station. The Jubilee Line train pulled into the station just as he walked onto the platform. He changed to the Northern Line at Waterloo – half an hour later he flopped onto his bed and fell, exhausted, into a dreamless sleep.

17
THURSDAY AFTERNOON

DANNY WOKE, AT FIRST CONFUSED. HE RARELY had a sleep during the day. Outside it was light – he looked at his clock. Three o'clock. He'd been asleep for two hours. He washed his face with cold water and pottered into the kitchen to make a cup of tea to have with a piece of Sainsbury's carrot cake, possibly past its sell-by date. He wasn't a big cake eater, he tried to kid himself, but one always appeared in his fortnightly shop, somehow.

He took his mug of tea, and the now half-eaten cake into his office – once the spare bedroom, but he rarely had visitors that stayed. And if an occasional female visitor did stay, she shared his super-king bed – normally only for one night, sometimes two. His last regular girlfriend had departed a few months ago, being awoken most mornings at four-thirty was the final straw in an already rocky relationship. It suited him. He didn't particularly want a long-term relationship, but that could change for the right person.

So, who is Ali Baka, he asked himself? He flipped open his laptop, opened Google and typed the name into Advanced Search. He thought of Google as his cyber-mind. In a recent pub quiz he learned that Google's original name in 1996 was BackRub. He was a collector of trivia – always useful to fill on the show.

He thought he could ignore the Facebook search results, he didn't believe that the Ali Baka he was looking for would be bold enough to prominently display himself. Nothing anyway. He tried Bing, Yahoo, Yandex, DuckDuckGo, Blippex, Wolfram Alpha, Blekko, Naver, Pipl, Baidu, Yacy – there were a few possible mentions, but nothing that immediately sparked his interest. He was simply overwhelmed – too much or too little. He had to narrow it down.

Outside it was beginning to get dark, thick black clouds scurried across the late afternoon sky – he pulled the curtains and made another cup of tea. He looked at the diminishing carrot cake and pinched a bit off with his fingers by way of a compromise.

He wasn't prepared to leave it to Bill Kelly and his team despite his promises – he was too personally involved. One side of him contemplated a return to investigative journalism as he was bored senseless with the world of celebrity and show business and its duplicity, posturing, petty in-fighting and egos. Not for today though.

Something to think about when, if, this – whatever this was – was over.

He had lost count of the times someone had said to him that they were 'very excited'. 'Very excited' until it all came crashing down to reveal the next 'very exciting' prospect. Getting up at four-thirty for the foreseeable future didn't appeal either. He rather hoped that the rumoured change in the breakfast show team would make his mind up for him, force his hand. He was lucky to have a job on Starshine, a major London radio station – he had heard that some of the small digital-only stations paid their morning presenters seventy-five quid a show. He certainly wouldn't get out of bed for that.

He realised he had become lazily comfortable on a salary that most would say was excessive, plus what he earned from appearances, awards ceremonies, corporate gigs, talks and a bit of freelance work. He wasn't an A-lister able to demand forty grand for a night's work, but he was able occasionally to get three, which he happily accepted for a night in the spotlight wearing a self-tied dicky-bow – his late mother always insisted on standards. Like the Duke of Edinburgh, she could spot and criticise a pre-tied dicky at a hundred paces.

As he returned to his office, passing the door to his bedroom, he was reminded of a very pleasant few days and nights in the company of Yuliet Spooner. Yuliet worked part time at the Centre for Covert Media Studies – together they had been researching a story about the increase in surveillance cameras in the UK and their potentially inappropriate use. One thing led to another, both agreed it was very pleasant, but they each had their own lives so parted without any acrimony and the promise to maybe pick it up again. But it did give him an idea.

He found the Centre for Covert Media Studies' website, clicked on 'Our People' and there she was – a headshot in glorious black and white. He clicked the envelope suggesting an email link and Outlook opened. He was about to start typing when the thought of hacking crossed his mind. The Centre for Covert Media Studies had ruffled many feathers in the past, especially when working with whistle-blowers wishing to remain anonymous. He didn't trust Bill Kelly and his team not to have put a surveillance team on him. He closed down Outlook.

If they had got into his computer or phone, he may already be too late. *Christ, I am becoming paranoid*, he thought and re-opened Outlook.

Then closed it again.

He looked up the Centre for Covert Media Studies' postal address and found it was just off Gray's Inn Road, not far from Kings Cross.

He took a blank sheet of A4 out of his printer, thought for a moment and then with his Parker ball point, a gift from some record company or other, wrote:

'*Dear Yuliet, long time. Might be onto something. I haven't changed my number. Please call ASAP to arrange to meet. Keep it simple. Regards, Dan.*'

Good journalists never delete anyone's contact details from their little black book – or whatever the e-equivalent is. Danny still had his original leather-bound A5 desk address book. A few years ago he laboriously transferred all the contacts into Outlook, but couldn't bear the thought of getting rid of the beautiful, rich, brown-leather hand-tooled tome with his name, Dan Owen, embossed in gold leaf on the front.

He used the first name he was known as when they worked together. Would she remember him – after all it was, what, twelve years ago? He added a PS for good measure:

'It's not about surveillance cameras.'

He folded the paper and put it in an envelope, simply addressed to 'Yuliet Spooner'.

He looked at his watch – five o'clock. If he left now, he could be there in thirty to forty-five minutes. He threw on his leather jacket again, grabbed his wallet and phone, and made his way back to the Northern Line. Due to an incident at Elephant & Castle he didn't arrive until six-fifteen. He walked down from Kings Cross St Pancras, found the offices closed, so put the envelope through the letter box just as the clouds burst – pixies dancing on the pavement. *What now?* he thought, sheltering in a nearby doorway. He WhatsApp'd Daisy. *'Drink?'* Almost immediately there was a ping. *'Yes. Where?'* asked Daisy. Danny was delighted. *'Club. I'll be there in fifteen.'*

Someone was on his side as a taxi deposited two passengers right beside him, the yellow light came on and he darted into the back. He didn't normally take black cabs, preferring the London Underground. He refused to use Uber. Sometimes the weather won.

Daisy beat Danny to the Piano Bar – in addition to Daisy's gin and tonic, there was a cold Innis & Gunn beer waiting for him. They kissed on the lips, for some reason they were much more comfortable with each other. Maybe the last few days did have a silver lining? They were both thinking the same thing. At least tomorrow was Friday, so he didn't have to get up early.

All seemed well with the world.

18
FRIDAY MORNING

Danny's phone was ringing.

His head throbbed, caused in all probability by an unquantifiable number of late-night Long Island Iced Teas – allegedly created by Charles Bishop, a 1930s moonshiner in the then dry Tennessee during the prohibition. The mix of tequila, vodka, rum, triple sec, gin, orange juice and a splash of Coke seemed very quaffable last night.

To add to his woes, sometime overnight, the Bird of Paradise had obviously taken a very satisfying shit in his mouth.

The naked body lying beside him stirred.

He found his phone just before it went to voicemail.

'Yes,' he croaked.

'It's Yuliet.'

He took a drink of water from the glass beside his bed. It partially persuaded his vocal cords to restore and his tongue to become unstuck. 'What time is it?

'Seven-thirty, you did say ASAP.'

Daisy left the bed and padded across to the bathroom – naked. For a moment Danny lost his train of thought.

'You start work early?'

'Catches the worm and all that. You said you wanted to meet? How about nine-thirty.'

'Okay. Francisco's?'

'See you there.' Yuliet rang off, brevity always her forte. Francisco's was an old favourite of theirs back in the day.

'Who was that?' asked a naked Daisy from the en-suite bathroom door.

Danny explained. Leaving out the bit about sharing the same bed that Daisy had just left – and no mention of Ali Baka.

'We're meeting her at nine-thirty just off Leicester Square.'

'Why?'

'I'll explain when we get there. We don't have to leave for an hour. Come back to bed.'

'Not until you've cleaned your teeth.'

Two hours later, after further careful bed antics, coffee and a shared shower, Danny and Daisy arrived at Francisco's.

Neither noticed their watchers.

Yuliet arrived a couple of minutes later. They managed to find a cramped table by the partially steamed-up front window. Introductions were made. Danny had explained to Daisy what Yuliet did on the Tube on the way up from Balham – Yuliet and Daisy silently acknowledged, without animosity, their shared intimate knowledge of Danny. Danny thought what with Martha, Yuliet and Daisy, he might as well reinvent Friends Reunited – this could get complicated.

Danny was distracted by an ebullient Francisco. 'Twice in two days. You do miss me?'

They shook hands. Danny avoided the Italian bear hug. 'Francisco's mother's cannoli Siciliani is amazing with a cappuccino.'

Yuliet and Daisy enthusiastically nodded their assent.

There was a brief silence before Yuliet asked, 'So why am I here after, what is it, ten, twelve years? What's so important that it's suddenly an ASAP?'

Yuliet never did beat about the bush.

'I'm trying to trace someone called Ali Baka. Connected with a crook called Stanislaw Nowak. Nowak is promoting and producing Martha's forthcoming concert tour. Daisy is running the PR for the tour.'

Yuliet smiled at Daisy.

'I saw that she was touring again – Martha was pretty good. Had a couple of her CDs back then but did wonder why she was being revived on such a grand scale. I've bought tickets for me and a couple of mates for the O2, second or third night.'

'Why are you suddenly interested in this bloke, what did you say his name was, Ali Baka?' Daisy was puzzled, this was the first time she had heard Baka's name.

'I heard Nowak talking on the phone to him when you hid me backstage. Nowak said he had thought about something. Martha was missing, and the police had been called. He did say one million was his final offer and Baka had changed the deal.'

'Martha's missing?' Yuliet was intrigued. 'Does this mean the concerts are off?'

'Does Bill know about this?' Daisy's turn.

'Who is Bill?'

Danny could see he was about to be drowned with questions. He was saved by Francisco arriving with the coffee and cannoli.

'My mother's finest – *prego, si goda donne adorabili.*' He winked at Danny.

'Detective Chief Superintendent Bill Kelly – Daisy and I met him last Sunday when it was realised Martha was maybe missing. And I wanted to find out more about Stanislaw Nowak, Daisy's boss – and his involvement in everything. Nowak and I have history from the *Weekend News* days.'

Daisy interrupted, 'I though you said he was a Detective Sergeant?'

'Long story.'

Yuliet's turn, she had knowledge. 'Detective Chief Superintendent Bill Kelly is a big cheese – he doesn't do Missing Persons. He leads the covert serious organised crime investigation team at the National Crime Agency. Financial fraud, human trafficking, arms dealing and drugs. His name has come up several times in investigations we've been running at the Centre for Covert Media Studies. We've sometimes helped each other – by mutual consent we always kept his name out of it. Wouldn't do for us to be seen collaborating with the police. We occasionally exchange tip-offs and information when, let's say, it would be difficult for police involvement to be seen. We are not subject to the Police and Criminal Evidence Act. Sometimes our investigations are on the edge of legality – but sources are sources.'

Daisy raised her eyebrows at the admission. She discarded her two packets of sugar onto the table. Yuliet picked them up and added them with hers into her coffee. Daisy looked askance.

'I've got a sweet tooth.'

'Ali Baka – do you know anything about him?' Danny was determined to bring the conversation back on track.

'Doesn't ring a bell. But I'll ask around the Centre, I'll put a quiet enquiry out to a few of our freelancers. We are the mavens of journalism – seek and thou shall find. Hopefully anyway.'

'This is wonderful,' said Daisy, speaking with her mouth full of cannoli Siciliani.

Danny gave Yuliet his private email address.

'That's no good – emails can be traced and hacked, even if you set up a new account using a fake name. We use PGP, a system for encrypting emails. But still if you send emails using PGP, the sender and recipient addresses remain visible, but the content of the message is encrypted. WhatsApp is probably the best – but suggest we always use it to arrange to meet somewhere face-to-face. But not here again.'

'Why not here?' asked Daisy.

'You've rattled a few cages. I expect Bill told you to leave it to them? If he is involved, this is much more serious than you can imagine. And it also maybe explains why you are being followed.'

Daisy was horrified – she looked out the window and couldn't see anyone. 'How do you know?'

'That couple over there on the bench outside have been studiously pretending to ignore us. They don't talk to each other. They did photograph us as we arrived. I'd be careful what you say in your flat too, Danny.'

Daisy blushed – she had been quite vocal that morning.

'Can they hear what we are saying now?'

'No, they wouldn't have had time to set up a laser microphone onto this window – and we are not suspects. But by now, Bill will know we have talked. He'll want to know why. I know someone who can sweep your flat if that would help.'

Danny nodded at Yuliet. It was just like the old days.

'If I do this, I want first night tickets – golden circle, after show and a greet-and-grab selfie with Martha too.'

Daisy liked Yuliet. 'It's a deal.'

'What are we going to do about the watchers?'

Yuliet was more experienced in the ways of surveillance. 'I suggest one of us, probably you Danny, out the back door – and Daisy and I leave by the front having a noisy row. Then storm off in different directions. I can't believe they will have put any more than two of them on us. They might not notice Danny has disappeared for a while.'

'That won't achieve anything apart from telling Bill we know we are being watched.'

'That's not the point – it will send a message. And stick one up at them!'

All would have worked fine, except Bill Kelly sat down at their table. 'Room for a big one?'

'Hello Bill, we were just talking about you.'

'I know!' He nodded at Daisy and Yuliet by way of a greeting. 'But what I really want to know is why you three are here – together?'

'Old mates. Time for a catch up. The cannoli Siciliani are wonderful.'

'Bollocks. Don't take the piss Danny. I wasn't born yesterday.'

Francisco took advantage of the extra custom. 'Four more cappuccinos – and my mother's cannoli Siciliani for you sir?' Even he couldn't sell-in a second cannoli to the others.

'Mug of best builders' please,' said Bill. The other three agreed to the cappuccinos. No cannoli.

'Who is Ali Baka, Bill?' asked Yuliet. 'And what's he got to do with Stanislaw Nowak and Martha?'

Bill gave Danny a hard stare. 'That's what we are investigating. And let me reiterate, be quite clear. We do not need any help. This is strictly a police matter.'

There was an uncomfortable silence. The stale mate interrupted by the arrival of the tea and coffees and Bill's mobile ringing. Four yesses and several pauses didn't give a lot away. 'I'll be there in twenty minutes – just having a cuppa.'

'What happened to "we're a team, we share everything"?' asked Danny.

'What happened to you giving me your word you will keep this absolutely secret?' countered Bill.

'This is not a pissing competition you two. We're trying to find Martha.' Yuliet tried to keep the peace.

'No, but I am mightily pissed off.' Bill Kelly attempted to keep his anger in check for the sake of the other customers. Not that he really cared.

'Why are your people following us?' Danny demanded.

'For your safety, that's all.' Bill smiled.

'Yeah. Right? If it's for our safety, why have they gone?' Yuliet had noticed the watchers had gone when Bill had arrived.

'They haven't.' Bill imperceptibly nodded at two men, dressed in golf casual, at the table by the door.

'Then who were the couple outside?' asked Yuliet.

Bill finished his mug of tea and, without a further word, got up and left.

'We need to get up to Elstree,' said Daisy.

'And I need to start finding out about Ali Baka,' said Yuliet.

'And we all need to watch our backs,' said Danny.

The golf duo, cover now blown, smiled at Danny and Daisy and followed them at a distance out of the café. It didn't take long for them to pick up their additional watchers, being careful not to let them know they had been blown.

FRIDAY – NEW SCOTLAND YARD

'WE MAY HAVE A COUPLE OF PROBLEMS.' BILL WAS standing at the white board addressing his hastily assembled team.

'Firstly, Danny and Ms DeVilliers met with our old friend Yuliet Spooner this morning.'

'Oh, for fuck's sake.' Detective Sergeant Michael Maguire's face looked really, really grumpy. 'What has she got to do with it? She is a pain in the arse – their brief is still after us for allegedly keeping their information on our Domestic Extremism database. I don't like her and don't trust her not to stick her nose in where she shouldn't.'

Bill was surprised at Maguire's outburst, but ignored him.

'Danny, as we expected, hoped, broke his promise and started investigating Baka and his connection to Nowak and the missing Martha. But that's not the problem. They were being watched.'

'We know that. You asked us to set it up – I got onto SCD10 straight away.'

'Had a call. SCD10 told me that Danny and Daisy were meeting Yuliet in the café – I was nearby, so I thought I'd have a word. But Yuliet had spotted another team of watchers outside, who disappeared when I turned up. We need to know who they are.'

The team's interest was piqued.

'No one outside our tight little team knows about all this. Suddenly we are holding coffee mornings.'

'The only way we'll find out who they are is to set up followers on the followers. Has SCD10 been warned to keep an eye out?'

'Not yet. And I don't want to, before long we'll be doing the bloody conga – our information is leaking. Have a think and get back ASAP.' Bill didn't mention that his watchers were already on the trail of the unknown other two.

Notes made.

'We will know later today if Martha turns up with Nowak.' Rob Andrews consulted his pocketbook. 'I'm going up to Elstree this afternoon to follow up on the Missing Persons investigation. Hopefully I'll find Nowak there and have another chance to speak with him. I might have to break cover.'

'Not yet, Rob. Stay Missing Persons for a few days more – or until Martha turns up, if she does. But you should speak with Danny and Daisy again, they seem to know what is going on.' Bill was thoughtful. 'Michael, you called me, you said you had some new gen.'

'I looked into Ali Baka. He is a person of interest on the GLAA database.'

'GLAA, yet another bloody TLA?' More room laughter.

Grumpy Michael harrumphed. 'The Gangmasters and Labour Abuse Authority. They have been investigating serious and organised crime's involvement in human trafficking. It gave me a starting point. It seems that Baka may have been illegally moving people into the UK for a couple of years, but so far no one has been able to get any evidence that will stand up to CPS scrutiny.'

'So, Nowak and Baka?' asked Bill. 'More importantly, do we think that Nowak is being protected? Every time we get close to him evidence disappears or we are told to leave it alone.'

'I'll speak to my contact in the MSHTU.' Bill was enjoying winding up Michael. 'An FLA for you! The Modern Slavery Human Trafficking Unit – they work closely with the GLAA, UK Border Force, Immigration and several other international agencies. See who else knows about Ali Baka.'

'You said a couple of problems? What's the second?' asked Rob Andrews.

'Nowak's flat was already being bugged.' Bill dropped the bombshell.

'What?'

'By who?'

'How?'

'Why?'

The questions came thick and fast.

'I don't know. Our team might have been overheard doing their job – so we might have been compromised.' Bill was phlegmatic. 'I suppose the question is whose team do they play for? Our lot left the rogue surveillance in place. It was sophisticated long range, powered by the lighting ring.'

'So, that might explain the extra followers?' asked Rob Andrews. 'I suppose we need to establish who they are following? And is there a team on Nowak? And why and who are they following – Danny, Daisy or Yuliet or all three? That may help us to understand who they are reporting to? Or do we simply ask them?'

'Not yet. This whole thing stinks. Something isn't right.'

The meeting broke up.

20
ELSTREE–
FRIDAY LUNCHTIME

DAISY AND DANNY ARRIVED AT ELSTREE AT quarter to one. They hadn't spotted anyone else other than the golfing duo following them on the Tube, train and walking up from the station, but by their own admission, they didn't really know what to look out for, especially if their followers were professionals. It was unlikely that anyone without a police warrant card would be able to get into the studio complex itself – security is always tight on the main gate and perimeter fences.

As they approached the studio, the familiar high-energy music was pouring out of the open doors. Martha sounded superb. Danny was surprised that they hadn't had complaints from the media companies in the offices surrounding the studio, but he supposed noise was normal in this 24/7 environment. The working sound stages and TV studios kept their massive soundproof doors shut during critical periods – 'the red light and bell' system that had been used for years in the film industry indicating no entry and silence on the set. Underpaid interns, runners, otherwise known as third or fourth assistant directors were stationed outside the doors to ensure no one ignored the no entry signs – and to prevent unauthorised people getting in. Daisy told anyone wanting to get into 'the media' that it isn't a glamorous life, especially when it's cold and raining.

'She's back,' said Daisy with an enormous smile on her face. It quickly changed to disappointment as they entered the massive studio and watched the stand-in going through the motions – she looked nothing like Martha but was roughly the same height and build. For each part of the show she wore similar clothes to those Martha would be wearing 'on the night'. She was a resting musical theatre actress recruited on the basis she would hit her marks, be available and understand the humdrum repetition demanded of the business. Convention meant everyone called her Martha while she was working – a hangover from TV and film where everyone uses the character's name while on set.

Martha's band were giving it their all. Up until now they had been relying on keyboards and samplers for rehearsals to save the budget during rehearsals. Now with the full percussion section, backline, brass and the strings of the full twenty-two-piece orchestra the sound was rich and multi-layered. Martha back in her hey-day

had a full-time foundation band that solely worked for her
– occasionally augmented by session musicians on bigger
gigs and some TV. On this tour Jimmy and the musical
director had recruited freelance session musicians who
could 'read the dots' and who could be relied upon to give
the same excellent performance night-after-night, session-
after-session, all on Musicians' Union recommended gig
rates or more.

Lights, staging, scenery all moved in perfect
synchronicity. The massive screens and multiple Barco
Mitrix displays were awe-inspiring.

'This should be a fabulous show that will thrill the
crowds of eager fans,' she said to no one. Daisy's emotions
were on a roller-coaster. 'If only. If only…'

Jimmy came bounding up. 'Any news of Martha?'

Daisy sprang into semi-cheerful PR mode. 'We'd hope
you know. Is Nowak here?'

'Haven't heard from him. The show is pretty much
ready to go – all we need is the star. We've had a week.
Can't really fine tune it more until we have Martha.'

'What are you going to do?'

'Nothing we can do. I'll send everyone home at three
– they'll enjoy an early finish and save a bit of money. Give
them the weekend off. Next week should be our final week
of rehearsals here, then get all the kit back into flight cases
ready for the road.'

Danny realised he was hungry – he had eaten nothing
apart from Francisco's mother's cannoli. 'Is Shirley still
open for some food?'

'All the time the artistes and crew are here, she never

shuts,' replied Jimmy. 'I haven't stopped so I'll come over with you.'

Daisy spotted their official followers and made the universal sign for a drink and some food. They beamed with delight and came over.

'No point in hiding as we know who you are. Have a brew and lunch on us,' Daisy offered.

As they sat down Daisy thought everyone should be introduced.

'I'm Daisy, this is Danny and Jimmy.'

'We're Dick and Dom.'

Jimmy was confused.

'Who is Dick and who is Dom?' asked Daisy. They all laughed – as good as any other names.

Shirley had performed her usual miracles, they all had lamb hotpot with Jersey Royals and green beans followed by an overly boozy trifle. 'It is Friday,' chirruped Shirley with a grin, 'and I have some white wine chilling, or a beer if you'd prefer?'

Everyone stuck to water, soft drinks or a 'nice cup of tea'.

During lunch they talked about Martha, her fame and showbiz gossip. Jimmy was about to ask who Dick and Dom were, when he was called back to the stage to sort out some sort of issue, nothing serious. 'No peace for the wicked,' he sighed, taking a slurp of tea. 'Keep an eye on that for me. I'll be back!'

'We were all followed,' Dick, or was it Dom, said when Jimmy was out of earshot. 'Same two who were outside Francisco's. Didn't recognise them, but they were good.

Wouldn't have known they were there unless we knew they were there. Assume professionals. We made sure they didn't know we had seen them.'

'Waiting for us in McDonalds opposite the main entrance,' said Dom, or was it Dick?

'That's useful, we know it was one of us they are interested in, not Yuliet,' suggested Danny.

'Unless Yuliet has her own watchers we don't know about?' said Dick, or was it Dom?

'Don't leave here until we get back – I reckon I fancy a Millionaire's Iced Frappe.' Dick and Dom ambled off through the stage and up the main street of Elstree Studios away from the main gate.

A large picture of Colin Firth and Geoffrey Rush beamed down on them – a reminder that *The King's Speech* was made in the same studio in which Martha's show was rehearsing. The pair turned right just before the site of the former Big Brother house and exited the studio complex via the private load-in gate.

Jimmy returned to the catering area, tried again. 'Who were those two?'

'Police, helping to find Martha,' replied Danny quickly.

Jimmy's phone rang yet again. He exhaled with a combined string of profanities. 'Can't even stop for a cuppa.' He answered it, grunted a couple of times and rang off.

'Vikki, Martha's sister, has turned up unexpectedly at the main gate.' He looked at Daisy. 'Would you mind?'

Daisy finished her tea and set off for the gatehouse. Jimmy disappeared into the darkness of backstage to sort out one of the many things on his list of things to do. Danny sipped his post-lunch cup of tea and worked through the latest cyber-arrivals on his smart phone.

Ten minutes later Daisy arrived back with Vikki, both chattering away. Although Danny hadn't seen her for over ten years, he was amazed to see how alike the twin sisters still were – different clothes sense and make-up but otherwise identical. 'Wow! Great to see you again. It's been a long time.'

They didn't know whether to shake hands, hug or kiss. In the end all three in an embarrassing concoction of mistimed dance steps and head moves. They both laughed in that way that people do when trying to hide behind difficult situations.

'How much you look like Martha!' Danny exclaimed, defusing the stand-off.

'Or she me,' smiled Vikki. 'A few years ago I did some of her appearance work to give her a rest – no one knew as long as I wasn't asked to sing. I practised her autograph. It was a bit of fun. Her musical ability passed me by – we haven't always been close. Pain in the arse sometimes, but a bloody breeze if I wanted to get in somewhere without paying.'

Laughter, but Daisy and Danny couldn't stop staring. There was some stilted small talk as they fulfilled the need to settle down.

'Came to see my sis – see the rehearsals. Then I thought I'd suggest we could go out to eat and have a couple of drinks this evening.' Vikki eventually got down to business.

'She's not here.'

'Blimey, how much time has she been given off? She said a week.'

Danny and Daisy were intrigued.

'So, you know where she is?' asked Danny. 'We've been worried about her.'

'Had a message from her last week. I don't know where she is. Surely you know?'

Danny and Daisy both shook their heads. Vikki was surprised, fiddled with her iPhone and passed it to Daisy, who passed it on to Danny. There was the message time-stamped last Thursday at 12h45:

'See you in a week sis. #secret #excited #pampered. #spa. xxx'

'So, Nowak wasn't lying.' Danny was surprised.

'Who is Nowak?' asked Vikki.

'Lying about what?' asked Jimmy, who had just returned to his now cold cup of tea. As he sat down, he saw Vikki for the first time. 'Martha, you're here? You look different.'

'This is Vikki, her sister – I almost made the same mistake!' said Danny.

'Vikki knew that Martha was going away.' Danny passed Jimmy the phone, to read the message.

'So, do we assume that Nowak does know where she is? The message isn't clear.'

'He said she'd be back today,' Daisy reminded everyone. 'I guess they should be here sometime soon. Especially as Vikki is here.'

'Well that's the end of our early finish – we'd better stay until official knocking-off time,' sighed Jimmy. 'I'll go and give the crew and band the news they are staying until six.'

'Martha,' cried Shirley. 'Where have you been? Would you like some lunch – I've made your favourite?'

As one they turned to Shirley. 'This is Vikki, Martha's twin sister.'

'No! Really? Has anyone told you that you are the spitting image? Like two peas in a pod.' They all laughed. Shirley went back to her catering truck shaking her head in amazement muttering, 'Never seen such a thing. Whatever next?'

Jimmy stood. 'As you are here, Vikki, while we are waiting, would you like me to show you around?'

'Hang on a sec,' interrupted Danny. 'Was Martha expecting you?'

'No. I just turned up on the off-chance – hadn't seen her in a while. She said I could come around when I fancied.'

'So, this wasn't planned?' Daisy took up the questioning.

'No,' Vikki felt she was being interrogated, 'as I said just decided to see her. Friday. POETS day.'

They all laughed. Pissing Off Early was not now on the cards.

Jimmy, with Vikki in tow, walked off to the stage area. Several of the crew thought they were seeing Martha, especially as she was expected back. Jimmy had to explain 'twin sisters' several times.

Vikki was amazed at the size of the set, staging and tour. 'Bloody hell. This is bigger than she has ever done before.'

'It's all moved on over the last six years. The technology has developed enormously – and competition between acts is massive. Lots of LED screens and lighting – not around when Martha was touring last time. We must live with the times but also play homage to your sister's past. She was a huge star. My job is to recreate that – and relaunch her career.'

Vikki and Jimmy walked to the centre of the enormous empty stage and looked out. The keyboard player and sound department chose that moment to play back one of the songs that had been giving the dynamic EQ a challenge – there had been distortion within the massive sub-woofers, caused by the pitch-shifting octave effect box on the synthesised bass. It had to be fixed – the sound team knew the bottom end choreographed the audience's emotional response, so it had to be perfect. And they wanted to win a ProSound and a few other awards.

For a laugh Vikki stood behind Martha's vocal mic and started to mime – the effect on everyone was the same. Martha looked like she was back. The stand-in looked concerned that she might be out of a job.

Nowak was shocked. *Martha had returned at last?* But then his head took back control – he knew it couldn't be Martha but was still impressed by the likeness. His devious mind considered his options as he waddled across the studio floor. He had more important fish to fry.

Nowak stood over Danny's and Daisy's table. 'Nice to see you again Danny, or is that Dan?'

Danny didn't throw up this time, but it was a close call. His stomach did a couple of somersaults. Daisy wasn't too thrilled either.

The music stopped. There was an almost eerie silence.

'You and I need a word.' Nowak stabbed his podgy finger into Danny's chest. 'In private.'

'I'm happy here, thank you.'

'I said, you and I need a word – in private.'

'Whatever you say to me I will tell Daisy. And I'm not going anywhere with you alone.'

Stand-off. Neither blinked. Daisy looked uncomfortable.

'What are you up to?' Nowak was not as aggressive as Danny thought he could have been, but there was still an underlying menace.

Daisy stepped in. 'As I told you last time Danny is the celebrity and music reporter for Starshine Radio, he is putting together a piece about Martha and the tour. He knows Martha from school – and I've worked with him for many years. Martha asked him to watch the rehearsals.'

Nowak looked enquiringly at Daisy who was upfront. 'Yes, I also know about the disabled badges and what you did to Danny. I'm not sure how long I can work for you.'

'It was a long time ago. Different times?'

'Bollocks. You're still a fucking crook Nowak,' Danny was trying to keep his bile in check. 'What are you up to? What have you done with Martha?'

Nowak sat in one of the chairs and shouted across to Shirley, 'Best builders please love – strong, four sugars.'

'You can't prove a thing now – too long ago. And anyway, I have friends who will look after me.' Nowak was in full poseur mode. 'I suppose you are here to write one of your nasty little investigative pieces?'

No one knew what to say next. Nowak's tea arrived with a Nestlé big assorted mixed biscuit box for the table. Shirley scuttled off – she sensed the tension. Not a time for idle chatter, she thought. Nowak stirred his mug of tea, put the spoon on the table and carefully picked out a Toffee Crisp, unwrapped it and shoved the whole thing in his mouth in one piece. He took a large, disgusting slurp of tea and smacked his lips. Daisy and Danny both chose a KitKat – eaten slowly, with more decorum.

'Until last week I had no idea you were involved with Martha. I was here for the tour story and to interview Martha.' Danny wasn't going to let it go. 'Now I know you're involved it's bound to be crooked.'

'But you're not going to hurt your old school mate are you – I am giving her a second chance to live the high life. Do we have an issue with that?' asked Nowak.

'What do you think? You crippled me for life and then waltz in hoping I'm going to be your best friend. Do bugger off.'

'You really don't want to be my enemy.'

'Fuck you. I don't give a toss about you.' Danny was in danger of going off on one. 'I'll report this fair and square, but don't expect any favours. Anything I do will be solely about Martha and her music. I hear or see one fucking thing out of line and I will out you for what you are. I repeat, where's Martha?'

There was a long, thoughtful pause. Nowak slowly replied, 'I really don't know.'

Both Danny and Daisy were surprised by Nowak's admission. He suddenly sagged, bluster dissolved, the weight of the last few days overwhelming his bravado. Daisy noticed his complexion was sallow and there were bags under his eyes – obviously he hadn't been sleeping.

But Danny was still outraged. 'What do you mean you don't know where she is?'

'I mean I don't know where she is. What part of that don't you understand?' *All true.* He thought he daren't explain Ali Baka or his other plans. 'And without her I am screwed. I really have no idea where she is.'

Nowak realised, in a glorious irony, that the whole tour looked like it was going to be a massive success – his money team reckoned a profit of over ten million even after he had returned all Baka's money. But could he extract himself from the people smuggling? For possibly the first time in his life he had a successful legitimate business.

'Daisy and Jimmy were right to involve Missing Persons then?' Danny demanded.

Nowak didn't know how to respond. He needed Martha back. But he had to keep Ali Baka out of it – his life would be in danger.

And with that, DS Rob Andrews arrived, and Danny's phone pinged.

21
MEANWHILE FRIDAY

As soon as Yuliet got back to her office, she had sent out a secure enquiry message about Ali Baka and Stanislaw Nowak via the Centre for Covert Media Studies' heavily encrypted systems. She then did a bit of digging herself in the research folders.

There were a few search returns on Ali Baka's name in deep background from a couple of years ago when one of her team had been doing some preliminary investigations into working conditions and employment in nail bars and massage parlours. Nothing concrete, but enough to give some clues that Baka could be involved in trafficking and slavery. She discovered that the Gangmasters and Labour Abuse Authority had been investigating serious and organised crime's involvement in human trafficking – Baka's name cropped up a few times.

Stanislaw Nowak was a different matter – he showed up in any number of research notes. Mid-level organised crime with fingers in lots of pies.

There was nothing on file connecting Baka and Nowak.

Yuliet decided to wait for responses to her messages before carrying on. She had several other investigations on the go that were taking her time – including a long-running fight with the European Court of Human Rights to force governments to review how they intercepted the media's communications.

The Centre was also investigating Frontex, in theory the EU's external border agency – but having little power as it battled to operate within the bureaucracy created by the collective failure of EU member states to fully commit and cooperate with it. The result of these EU-wide fiascos had been thousands of people drowning at sea – and organised crime making its fortunes. Yuliet was appalled to discover data protection issues had meant the personal details of suspected people-smugglers could not be shared between Frontex, Europol and National Crime Agencies. Yuliet was incensed by the red tape – particularly self-imposed.

At twelve-forty-five Yuliet left her office, wandered up to Gray's Inn Road and along to her favourite bakery, 'Aux Pains de Papy', her regular routine when working at the office. The smell of fresh baking tantalised anyone within fifty metres, reminding Yuliet of her days at the Sorbonne in Paris – she felt like she was back there. She was greeted by the French staff, who had over the years got to know her reasonably well. She ordered, in fluent French, a camembert, tomato and honey baguette together with a challengingly strong, milky coffee.

Despite, maybe because of everything she did, Yuliet liked routine. As usual she wandered across the road to sit in St George's Gardens, an oasis of calm. Yuliet had done some research into the gardens and, as a result, had joined the Friends' scheme – it was her private me-space. The Gardens were once the burial ground for two nearby churches – the Nicholas Hawksmoor church, St George's Bloomsbury, and the church of St George the Martyr in Queen's Square, now known as St George's Holborn. Back in the day, London was growing fast, and churchyards were overflowing, so burials moved to what was then open country and a high protective wall, subsequently demolished, was built around the gardens to keep out body-snatchers who supplied the nearby anatomy school – now the School of Pharmacy. Many students, unaware of their murky past, had taken most of the benches. Yuliet managed to grab a seat as one group left, no doubt to return for afternoon lectures.

'Hello, Yuliet. I hear you are interested in Ali Baka?' She hadn't noticed the arrival of the woman on the bench beside her. She was simply dressed in black jeans, pink Planet drop-shoulder hoodie and Converse trainers. Her face was smooth, a few laughter lines around the eyes and just a touch of make-up – nothing on the lips, her eyebrows black. Her hair was jet black in a short bob – obviously a wig, thought Yuliet. The woman blended into the surroundings, just someone else talking a break.

'Do I know you?'

'I've no idea. Do you?' She spoke with an educated London accent.

'Well, no.'

'That's a good start. We do have mutual friends.' Yuliet turned to look at the woman.

'Ignore me.' She snapped before putting that day's *Evening Standard* on the bench between them. 'When I've gone pick up this newspaper, look at the front page then put it in your bag, open it later. Wait at least ten minutes before leaving. Don't try to follow me.'

'Who are you?'

'Let's just say that I am a big fan of Martha. You might be able to do more with this than my friends. But I am told we are now even.'

'Who's we…? asked Yuliet. But the woman was already gone, drinking her takeaway tea down Handel Street, merging into the ordinary day.

Yuliet picked up the paper as instructed, glanced at the front page – more Mayoral and self-serving political shenanigans – and shoved it in her blue tote bag. As instructed, exactly ten minutes later Yuliet stood up, brushed the crumbs off her clothes, and left the opposite way to the mysterious woman, along Heathcote Street to her office. She took off her coat, sat at her desk and carefully opened the newspaper.

A plain brown padded envelope was hidden inside the folded paper. Yuliet carefully examined it. What was in there? The woman seemed to know what was going on – but Yuliet had no proof, this could be a set-up? There had been stories circulating about Anthrax and explosives – and, of course, Novichok.

She felt like a child at Christmas sneaking under the tree, trying to work out what their present was by feeling with their fingers and shaking to hear what noise it made. Yuliet thought today's present felt like sheets of paper, some A4 with a few smaller, stiffer pieces on what felt like thin card. Centre for Covert Media Studies protocol demanded without question all packages should be swabbed and X-rayed – they had an airport-type machine downstairs in the post room.

'Bollocks,' she said out loud to nobody. 'Let's do it.' Never one for the rules. She took her hallmarked silver letter opener – a present from a former boyfriend who didn't understand her – and was about to carefully slit open the flap when she stopped. Further muttered profanity followed as she picked up the phone to the post room.

'Hi Kenny, I have a package to check out. Please can I bring it down right now?' Kenny was not a jobsworth and had a great can-do attitude that endeared him to everyone at the Centre. 'See you in five.'

Yuliet finished her now cold coffee and put the reusable mug to one side to wash later. She then took the stairs down to the post room.

'What have we got?' asked Kenny with an eager smile.

Yuliet handed Kenny the padded bag. 'Some bombs can be initiated by X-rays.'

Before Yuliet could stop him, he inserted the package into the scanner. 'No explosives or curious packages inside. Look, you can see.'

Kenny showed Yuliet. 'Nothing orange or dense. Looks like paper to me. But let me do a trace detection test. If it was infected, probably too late as there will most likely be residue on the outside.' Kenny swabbed the package and inserted the test paper into the Ion-Mobility Spectrometer. 'Nope, nothing obvious. I can send it out for more tests if you like?'

Yuliet thought for a moment. 'Think I'll risk it – doesn't look like anything obviously suspicious?'

'You'll be fine. I'll pop up in half an hour if you like to check you are still alive?' Kenny laughed. Yuliet laughed too. *Hangman's humour*, she thought. She thanked Kenny and went back upstairs to her office.

Once again picking up the hallmarked silver letter-opener she slit open the flap and tipped the contents onto her desk, then remembered to breathe. Nothing went bang and there was no peculiar powder. The package contained photocopies of a confidential file with several sections redacted with thick black lines. She held the paper up to her strong desk light – whoever had redacted the contents did so before photocopying, so no hope of analysing what might have been underneath.

There were several candid colour photographs labelled with the name Ali Baka, appended with a file number. All good quality, but obviously taken from a very long way away judging by the depth of focus. Difficult to tell where the pictures had been taken – a few were obviously from somewhere hot and dusty, others looked like a city which could have been London, one had the deep azure sea behind.

Yuliet began to read. Within a few minutes she understood that this was gold dust – an hour later Yuliet realised this was a story that could run and run. *Who was the woman?* She had an idea but couldn't work out why the files had been sent over.

In all events Danny, and Daisy too, could be in considerable danger. Nowak wasn't safe either. Where did this leave the missing Martha? She took out her phone and sent a message. Up at Elstree, Danny's phone pinged with a WhatsApp message.

'Need to meet ASAP. Yx'

22
FRIDAY AFTERNOON

'MARTHA STILL MISSING?' DS ROB ANDREWS looked directly at Nowak.

Nowak shifted uncomfortably. He looked at Danny and Daisy for support.

Nowak was about to lie, when the full orchestra burst into life making further conversation almost impossible, drowned by the heart-stopping ultra-bass. The brass kicked in with a tower-of-power rock fanfare. A single guitarist spot lit upstage-right joined in with an E-minor-nine funky vamp. The risers either side of the stage, with the rest of the musicians on-board, smoothly lifted and rotated into position. The ultra-bass was joined by an ostentatious tympani player upstage-left, building the tension. Fog and dry ice poured on and around the stage. The Vari-Lites circled.

The ten banks of 5x5 Par30 light matrixes illuminated the would-be audience at full brightness, 'blinding' them so they wouldn't be able make out what was happening on the stage. Suddenly dead black out – synchronised with a massive snare roll. In perfect synchronicity the massive Mitrix screens displayed a glorious cascade of gold discs that resolved into the words 'Martha Returns', as Alan Dedicoat's pre-recorded voice-over boomed out in a rising cadence – 'It's time. It's time. It's time for the return of… Martha.' The production team knew this would be a 'cause-for-applause' once the show went live – every show had pre-determined points when the audience thought they had spontaneously decided to cheer or applaud. But they had been conned. The magic of show business?

Stage centre, there she was wearing a long, gold evening dress – Vikki had been quickly hydraulically lifted from below the stage while the 'audience' would not be able to see what was going on. Thin straps, demur décolletage and the high heels gave the sophisticated look the costume designers and art direction team had carefully selected to appeal to her new, more mature, audience. The gold discs sewn into the fabric sparkled like personal mirror balls from the six follow spots illuminating her from back, front and sides. The whole studio – the set, walls, ceiling, floor and where the audience would be on the night danced to the reflected sparkling gold. The ten-metre ultra-high-resolution video screens showed Vikki's laughing face in massive close-up – a first for any tour, it was using the new 16K video system. The music kicked into the opening of one of Martha's most high-energy songs, the perfect show-starter.

The effect was mesmerising. The audio-visual experiential effect spectacular. No one, not even the critics, could fail to be totally enraptured.

The production stills photographer clicked away.

Before Vikki began to 'sing' Jimmy's amplified voice brought everything to a halt. 'Thanks everyone. Let's reset from the top. Heads of department conference please. Everyone else tech-check and set-up to go again in fifteen.'

Rob Andrews, Daisy and Danny and even Nowak were almost speechless. This was the first time any of them had seen the show in full action – and it was going to be fabulous if the first few minutes was anything to go by.

Nowak turned to Rob Andrews. 'Martha returns.'

'That's not Martha.' Daisy confused DS Rob Andrews; he was convinced Martha was back.

'What?' he replied. 'Then who is it?'

'It's her twin sister, Vikki.' Even Daisy acknowledged Vikki standing in was simply awe-inspiring.

'Bloody hell, that's amazing. So where is Martha then?' Rob Andrews was interrupted by massive tom-tom beats – sixteenths with the kick drum on the up-beat – making further conversation almost impossible. The front-of-house sound mixer's voice could be heard asking the drummer to include the snare and a hi-hat ride.

'Shall we go outside?' shouted Rob Andrews.

The four of them left the area to find somewhere quieter.

Danny interrupted. 'Look, you don't need me – and I have some urgent business to sort out. Gotta dash.'

Daisy joined in. 'Me too. Sponsorship meeting.'

Danny and Daisy left. Rob Andrews turned to Nowak. 'Well?'.

'As I said, Martha isn't missing – she is resting, back soon. It was remiss of me not to let everyone know. But rehearsals must continue if we are going to have a perfect show. Vikki turning up was just luck. So sorry for wasting your time.' Nowak was twitchy, but back on full ebullient form. 'I'll have a word with the team to ensure it doesn't happen again. Communications cock-up. Left hand. Right hand.'

DS Rob Andrew inwardly laughed – he was certain he knew what the right hand was doing.

They shook hands. Nowak slapped Rob Andrews on the arm in a man-on-man show of solidarity. Nowak turned back into the darkness of the studio to give a couple of production notes to Jimmy.

Rob Andrews stood there, mouth open. *The whole bloody thing is getting out of hand. What the fuck is going on?*

He decided to pretend to accept – softly, softly catchee monkey. He did not believe Nowak's attempts to assure him that Martha was away on a rest-break. But it didn't make sense, not unless Nowak was perpetrating one of the biggest cons in music history and having Martha's sister stand in for real on the tour?

He decided not to conduct any further interviews, they were in the middle of rehearsals and he wanted an excuse to be able to return once he had reported back. Nowak, not Martha, was the focus of his attention. But he did want a word with Danny and Daisy.

'Wait for me,' Rob shouted at the backs of the disappearing Danny and Daisy.

They stopped just before the main gates.

'I'll give you a lift back into town?' offered Rob as he caught them up.

Daisy's phone rang. 'Hang on a sec, have to take this.'

Danny silently acknowledged, pointing at Elstree Studios' Star Bar and Bistro on the right – a pint would be welcome.

Daisy walked away from the other two. Bloody Kelvin Edwards from *The Daily Tribune* again.

'I hear Martha's still missing?' He didn't even have the manners to say hello or make any sort of small talk. 'My source tells me you have been rehearsing without her.'

'Hello Kelvin, how nice to hear from you.' Daisy was determined to be a professional.

Kelvin didn't appear to notice the sycophancy; neither was he going to be put off from his exclusive front-page story. 'Well?'

'I've just watched an amazingly spectacular full-dress rehearsal.'

Kelvin was silent. He had been assured an hour earlier that Martha was still missing.

'I'll send a couple of pictures – exclusively yours. I'll give you the weekend as a head start as we are such good friends. Don't say I don't do anything for you. They'll be great for the *Sunday Celebrity* pull-out. You can quote a source as saying tickets for the first two days are sold out – and we may well be adding a fourth day at the O2 due to overwhelming demand. It'll be your exclusive until Monday.' *Damn, I'm good,* thought Daisy.

'How do I know the pictures are recent?'

'I'll send you some with the full orchestra in shot – I am sure your unreliable source will confirm that today is the first day they have been on stage?'

Kelvin knew that this was true. Condescendingly he thanked Daisy and rang off.

Daisy immediately called their stills photographer and asked for half a dozen shots to be sent to her from the rehearsals, a couple with the orchestra in shot. 'Don't worry about grading or cropping them – I want them to look very recent and rushed.'

She joined the other two in the far corner of the bar. Two pints of lager, with the top third missing, sat in front of them. Rob had a frothy moustache.

'Do you want one?' offered Danny.

Daisy nodded. 'G&T. Low calorie please.'

As Danny returned with a house gin and Fever Tree Naturally Light tonic he looked around – apart from the two bored bar staff they were alone and far enough away not to be overheard.

'So where is Martha?' Rob Andrews was pretty pissed off. 'What's going on? What are you and Nowak up to?'

'Nowak and I are up to nothing – I said I'd report the tour. But I am no friend of Nowak. He is, and always will be, a shit. Daisy knows everything about our past.'

Daisy's phone pinged. Six photos had arrived – she opened the email and attachments. They were perfect. She immediately forwarded them to Kelvin Edwards, inwardly thanking Elstree's ultra-fast in-house internet connection.

She showed the pictures to Rob Andrews and Danny. They were spot-on publicity pictures – almost certainly worthy of a front page.

'That's really not Martha?' questioned Andrews.

'Nope. Her twin sister Vikki.'

'That's amazing.'

'Yep. We know.'

Daisy's phone pinged again. Email from Kelvin Edwards. *'Front page on Sunday. Want an interview with Martha soon.'*

'Will sort it soon. Thanks – we must do lunch,' she replied.

Which roughly translates as, 'no chance – and I have no intention of eating with you'. *But let's hope he never finds out that he has been duped,* thought Daisy, *otherwise we'd all be on the front page for a different reason. But needs must.* The weekend circulation of the *Tribune* was three million. *Never let the truth get in the way of a good story. Bound to sell a load more tickets.*

'So, what is bloody well going on?' Rob Andrews was not a happy bunny. 'Have you any idea where Martha is? This is now getting very serious. She has been gone for over a week and no one has heard from her. And you are bloody well misleading me. You made a promise, no secrets.'

It was a good thing that Andrews couldn't read Danny's mind.

Daisy began. 'Only Vikki has heard from her – she had received a text message saying Martha would be away for "a week" and something about "being excited and secret pampering". That was last Thursday – so Vikki assumed Martha would be back here today when she visited. But why would Martha just disappear in the middle of rehearsals? Some artiste's behaviour can be weird, but even this is pushing the limits. But it could be true, she might just be taking a break. We don't know.'

'Nowak arrived about an hour ago. He admitted he didn't know where Martha was either. Without her he's screwed. I believe him too.' Danny surprised himself. 'Did you see the look on Nowak's face when he saw Vikki? Nowak knows something.'

'So, this is still a Missing Persons investigation. The question is, are we talking about kidnapping or worse? I'm going back to talk to, what's her sister called, Vikki and to Nowak.'

'Hang on,' said Daisy. 'Someone is leaking stories to the press. Kelvin Edwards at the *Tribune* found out that Martha was missing. That can only have come from someone here at Elstree. And how do we know they are not talking to other people, whoever they are?'

'You are leaving the studio doors open. Maybe time to keep them closed – anyone walking by can see what is going on.' Danny was well aware that a bung in an envelope would overcome any secrecy agreement and turn any itinerant passer-by on the Elstree site into a tout.

'On Sunday, when Kelvin is published, everyone will think the rehearsals are all going well, it's bound to go viral on social media, including to whoever has got Martha? It will confuse them – and could spook them. They will wonder whether or not they actually have the real Martha and who the other Martha is in the pictures.'

'It's not difficult to find out on the interweb that Martha has a twin sister,' offered Danny.

Rob Andrews was thinking. 'If we assume Martha is being held against her will, who benefits from her disappearance? And, where is she? I can't see how Nowak wants Martha gone – but he knows something he is not telling us. Let's hope we are not putting Martha in danger.'

Silence.

'Unless it's an insurance scam?' pondered Danny. 'No Martha. Insurance pays up, covers all costs and maybe loss of profit.'

'Who would I talk to about that?' Andrews asked Daisy.

'Jimmy or Nowak will know.' Daisy's phone went again. She looked at the caller display. 'Talk of the devil...' She slid answer. 'Hi Jimmy...'

'Where are you? I've got Vikki – she wants to go home.' Jimmy sounded exasperated.

'In the bar by the main gate, why don't you bring her down?'

Jimmy agreed.

'I'm going to talk to Bill. Nowak is still the centre of our investigations.' Rob Andrews got up, went outside and down one of the many private roadways where he could not be overheard. He waited while three storm-troopers, without headgear, walked past on their way to another studio chattering about how awful the actress playing the five-headed-monster was. 'Of course she's shagging the director.'

'He wouldn't be interested. I blew him off last week – #MeToo works both ways.' They laughed and disappeared into one of the buildings.

Bloody actors, thought Rob.

In the bar Daisy and Danny were alone. 'What are we going to do?'

'I really don't know. Yuliet messaged me. She wants to meet ASAP. I haven't responded yet.' Danny spoke quietly, although there was no one else nearby.

'We can't leave now – don't want our friend DS Andrews putting his foot in it. Think we need to control him if we can.' Daisy wasn't hopeful.

'I doubt it, he pretty well knows his mind – not our job and he is the police. Don't forget about Dick and Dom too – we said we'd wait?'

'Christ, this is complicated.' Daisy lent back into the comfortable sofa and rubbed her eyes.

They sat in silence. In the distance Rob Andrews paced up and down – the conversation was obviously robust. A couple of minutes later Jimmy and Vikki arrived with Dick and Dom in tow a few metres behind.

Andrews ended his call and beckoned Jimmy over outside. Vikki made a beeline for the bar.

'Look, I've really got to get back, will this take long?' Jimmy was impatient with Andrews.

'No, but this is important.' Andrews was insistent. 'Simple question – who benefits if Martha doesn't perform? What insurance have you taken out?'

Jimmy slowly sat down on the low wall. 'We have Public Liability and Employee Insurance, plus all the statutory insurances we need in each country. We couldn't afford production or key person insurance. If Martha doesn't or can't perform the fans may get some of their money back, minus booking fees, in theory. But most likely the production company would declare itself insolvent, call in the administrators and no one will get anything. One of the reasons I insist all wages are up to date. We have also paid the deposits on all the venues.'

'Where did the money come from? To put on a show like this costs millions.' Andrews made notes in his pocketbook.

'Nowak put up most of the seed money – plus we have advance sponsorship payments.'

'Where did Nowak get the money from?' Andrews needed to understand how it all worked, it might help get to the bottom of Nowak's involvement.

'I've no idea. A further two million arrived a few months ago into the production account from a bank in the Cayman Islands. Not my job to ask questions from who or where or how it came. There are plenty of angels out there who support the arts – sometimes in exchange for a good return. Ask Stanislaw.' Jimmy really didn't want to go there.

'He hasn't just been given the money. If the tour doesn't go ahead how is Nowak going to repay his benefactors? They will want something for their investment.'

'That's show business. It's touch and go whether any show makes anything. But when a show does make a profit, it's normally massive. You've got to kiss a lot of frogs.' Jimmy looked at his watch, 'I've really got to get back – have you any idea how much a live band costs if they go into overtime?'

'Stay in touch, I'll need to talk to you some more.' With that, Jimmy jogged back up the gentle hill to the George Lucas stage to oversee rehearsals. He waved at Vikki who was now sitting down inside the bar with Daisy and Danny.

Dick and Dom waited outside. Rob wandered over to them. 'These bloody luvvies are a nightmare.'

'Tell me about it. One of the wardrobe guys has just made a pass at me,' laughed Dick.

'Lucky for some.' Dom was jealous. Rob and Dick realised that Dom had just outed himself to them. It wouldn't go any further – it was none of their business.

Meanwhile in the bar, Vikki's eyes were shining. 'I understand now why Martha loves this business. What a buzz!'

Is she on something? thought Daisy. *Vikki's eyes dilated, over-excited.* Daisy knew the effects of cocaine.

'I need a drink. A caipirinha please.' Vikki wanted to continue the buzz – *no wonder after-show parties often became a den of iniquity,* she thought.

Danny went over to the bar. Daisy and Vikki remained silent. They looked out the window at the escorted crowd of pre-pubescent girls, with a few worried-looking boys, on their way up to the TV studio set up to record a teen quiz show. They were all far too young to recognise Alexander Armstrong and Richard Osman walking the other way, heading towards the bar for a pointless post-show lemonade.

Danny returned – Vikki didn't say thank you or acknowledge him. She just sipped, through the paper straw, the cocktail made with dark cachaça and muddled limes. No plastic straws here, the barman had told Danny.

'It's Brazil's national cocktail,' said Vikki as she finished off half the glass in one pull, 'always fancied a holiday there. To have a few more of these.'

'Do you know where Martha is?' demanded Daisy.

'Don't know anything more than that text message. Sorry. You seem worried – I was fine until I got here. Now I'm worried too. Where's my sis?'

'That's a good question.' Rob Andrews had returned. He looked at Vikki. 'I'll get a car and a WPC to take you to your house, pick up a few clothes and then I think a few nights in a safe house for your own protection.'

'Why? I'm not involved. Is Martha in danger?'

'We don't know. Better to be safe. Anyone could see those pictures on Sunday – some might even be online now?'

Daisy disagreed. 'Knowing Kelvin, he'll want to keep his powder dry. Nothing will be out until Saturday evening as a teaser to boost Sunday circulation. He gets a bigger bonus from sales on Sunday.'

'We must assume that someone is holding Martha against her will. When whoever has Martha sees the pictures, they'll know they cannot be of Martha on-stage – or alternatively they do not have the real Martha, which puts Vikki in danger.'

They all looked at Vikki; she didn't seem the least bit phased by the potential danger. Daisy thought she looked as if she was getting off on it.

'I'm fine until Saturday night then? That's good – have a party tonight.' Vikki fidgeted as the words tumbled out in a constant stream. 'I was going to ask Martha to come along too. I need another drink.'

She thrust her ice and mint filled empty glass at Danny. Danny made hand-gestures to the barman for another caipirinha for Vikki. DS Andrews made a note of all Vikki's contact details.

'As you say, Danny, it's not difficult for anyone to find out that Martha has a twin sister,' mused Daisy.

'You lot seemed to have missed it,' said Danny to Rob.

'We didn't. Our colleagues were going to talk to Vikki as part of the roll out of the Missing Persons investigation. We thought it wasn't immediately relevant to the main investigation.'

'What do you mean, main investigation? Isn't Martha missing the main one?' Vikki demanded.

Rob Andrews realised he had made a mistake. 'We are pursuing a number of lines of enquiry.' He left again to call a car, a WPC and to arrange a safe house, pleased to remove himself from what was going to become a difficult conversation.

Daisy decided to change the subject as well – diversionary tactics. 'You looked totally amazing on stage.'

'The lights are so bright. I don't know how Jenny, sorry Martha, can see the audience.'

It would help if your eyes weren't so dilated, Daisy thought. 'She can't really, unless the audience lights are fully up – even then she can only see the first twenty rows or so. It's all part of the game. The show is about making Martha look as amazing as possible.'

'I didn't hang around with her when she was famous the first time around. I was still in shock about the deaths of the rest of my family. I couldn't believe then that Jenny could use the accident to push her own career.' Vikki was rushing her words. 'I think I'd like to be more involved this time? What do you think? Can I come on some of the tour?'

'You'll have to speak with your sister.' Daisy was shocked how Vikki could move from criticism to craving favours all in the same breath.

'I'm sure she won't mind. I don't have any money though.' Vikki was almost aggressive.

Not surprising really if you put it all up your nose, Daisy thought.

'One more on the rooming and travel budget shouldn't make any difference. I'll speak to Jimmy. You might be useful as an additional PA to Martha.' Daisy resumed professional mode – she didn't see the point in arguing with Vikki.

'That's amazing. Thank you.'

'Nothing certain yet.' But Vikki didn't want to hear that part of the conversation. As far as she was concerned it was all yesses.

Rob Andrews returned. Looked at Vikki. 'Right we'll pick you up at your house in the morning about eleven – pack a bag for a week.'

'Really? No, really? Is that really necessary?' Vikki was inherently anti-police.

'Until we find Martha it's for the best, especially with those pictures out there. I don't want you to be seen leaving here.' A police car stopped outside the bar, one of the two WPCs got out. 'They'll take you home.'

Rob Andrews gave Vikki his card with the mobile number. 'Here's my number. Anything at all, call me. Anytime. I will see you at your house tomorrow morning, before you leave, to go through a few more things.' A visit to someone's home always revealed something. The unexpected always happened unexpectedly. Andrews was old school sometimes.

Vikki left with the WPCs and was ushered into the back seat of the police car, then out on Maxwell Road with a blanket over her, lying flat on the back seat.

'Going to a party tonight?' questioned Daisy.

'Hardly the worried sister?' Dan agreed.

'I thought that.' Rob gave Danny and Daisy a contrived smile. 'Right you two, offer of a lift rescinded! I want you to walk back up to the station and take the train to Blackfriars – act normally, don't try to hide. Then get the water taxi to Westminster. Some of my team will be at the pier head.'

They all finished their drinks. Just outside the main gates DS Andrews got into the front seat of a grey unmarked police car. Danny took Daisy's hand – reassurance or affection, he wasn't sure which – and departed through Elstree's main entrance. They turned left to walk up the high street. Two people left McDonalds on the other side of the road and followed them. A short while later Dick and Dom followed all four – they had the advantage of knowing where they were going to end up and what they all looked like.

As they approached Elstree and Borehamwood station at quarter past the hour, a Blackfriars train was pulling in. Normally they would have made a quick dash over the last 200 metres or so to catch it. On this occasion, bizarrely, they didn't want to lose their string of tails. Danny pointed at the station shop. 'I want to get some mints and a paper, the trains are every fifteen minutes, so we don't have to wait long.'

Daisy waited outside and nonchalantly looked around. She could see Dick and Dom in the far distance but wasn't sure if there was anyone else. She couldn't relax – she was a PR, not some sort of sleuth. Once Danny had his shopping, the two of them scanned their credit cards at the barrier and waited on the platform. Sod's law played its part, their next train was cancelled, so they had to wait over thirty minutes. They walked up to the front end of the platform where there was a solitary purple and pink metal bench. The paint worn away by too many bottoms – and Darren inscribing his love for Tina, whoever they may be.

Danny offered Daisy one of his mints, which she gladly accepted. Her mouth was dry. They sat in silence, occasionally looking at their watches in the vague hope it would speed up the arrival of the train.

At the other end of the platform Dick and Dom waited at what would be the back of the train so they could see who was getting on and off. In the middle were the other watchers, who seemed unaware of Dick and Dom, focusing solely on Danny and Daisy.

Eventually the Thameslink train arrived, not that full, before the schools turfed out their students. The six of them embarked on their journey, nine stops later off they all alighted. 'Why do these train companies have to use bloody silly railway language – next station stop, terminates and alight?' Danny demanded of Daisy, as if it were her fault. Daisy didn't bother to reply.

They walked along the underpasses, up into fresh air then onto Blackfriars pier, mingling with the crowd of happy tourists eager to see the Thames from the water. The 220-seat catamaran arrived, disgorged half a dozen passengers. Daisy and Danny swiped their credit cards and walked across the short gangway and down into the boat. The front seats were free, so they thought they might as well enjoy the view along the Thames.

Just over ten minutes later the good ship *Aurora* docked at Westminster Pier. Dick and Dom were among the first off. Inconspicuously they acknowledged their waiting plain-clothed colleagues. There was a sudden flurry of activity and the two extra watchers were bundled off the pier by four burly chaps and into the arms of four uniformed policemen. Without ceremony they were handcuffed, marched across the road and through the ne'er-do-well's entrance of New Scotland Yard.

In all the commotion Daisy and Danny used the opportunity to jump into a vacant taxi heading up the road towards Parliament Square, leaving Dick and Dom seriously embarrassed.

23
FRIDAY LATE AFTERNOON

'ST PANCRAS, EUROSTAR SIDE PLEASE.' THE cabbie acknowledged the request and went back to listening to Talk Sport.

Daisy cuddled up to Danny. 'That's glamorous – a dirty weekend in Paris?!'

'Passport not needed. Meeting Yuliet. This time on a Friday the station will be very crowded. Good place to meet.'

Daisy moved away in mock admonishment.

Danny opened WhatsApp on his iPhone. Clicked on the cog-like settings button, clicked on security and enabled security notifications. He always kept the app up to date – end-to-end security encryption meant, in theory, messages and calls can't be intercepted by anyone or any organisation as they travel between devices. As a precaution he always deleted messages and call logs straight away in case someone 'stole' his phone.

He WhatsApped Yuliet.

'*I wondered where you had got to*' she replied. No hellos or greetings.

'*Had an interesting afternoon*' Danny typed one-handed.

'*We need to meet*' was Yuliet's terse reply.

'*Champagne bar, St Pancras station. 18h30.*'

'*Okay. Have a bottle on ice. You owe me!*'

They disconnected. Danny and Yuliet both wiped their message logs.

Daisy cheered up with the thought of a glass of fizz in Europe's longest champagne bar – with its 'Press for Champagne' buttons on every table and heated leather seats on every banquette.

The traffic, as expected on a Friday evening, was awful. They struggled around Parliament Square, along Whitehall lined with its stone and steel protective barriers, past the heavily guarded entrance to Downing Street with its permanent bands of demonstrators opposite. They stopped and started in the pollution around the bottom of Trafalgar Square – making them both feel a bit nauseous. *The constant sounding of horns did nothing except increase stress levels,* thought Daisy. Cyclists and couriers weaved precariously in and out of the stationary traffic. Eventually they sprinted past St Martin-in-the-Field and then on for a whole 200 metres up Charing Cross Road, before returning to a stop-start snail's pace. Twenty-five minutes later the Euston Road was virtually at a standstill – more stop, start, horns and pollution. The 2.6-mile journey took a frustrating hour – the taximeter demanded £32.40. Danny gave the driver £40, asked for a fiver in change together with a receipt.

Relieved to be out of the taxi, they walked through the doors of the magnificently restored St Pancras station, past the international commuters manically jostling to join the Friday-night Eurostar queues, turned left and took the escalators to the crowded champagne bar. They found a table at the very far end – Dan ordered a bottle of Searcy's Selected Cuvée Brut Rosé, NV and three glasses. The time was twenty-five past six according to the massive, restored, ornate clock on the far wall of the station. The noisy environment of the station made eavesdropping almost impossible. The station announcer, in three languages, invited passengers to start to board Train 9050 to Paris. The yellow-nosed train with the white and blue carriages waited beside them, each protected from the other by thick glass.

Danny thought Daisy deserved a little light entertainment. 'The original station clock was sold to an American collector for two-hundred-and-fifty thousand pounds. When they were taking it down, they dropped it. Smashed into thousands of pieces. The American got his quarter of a mill back – and the pieces were sold for twenty-five pounds to a retired train driver. That clock is made from moulded replicas of the original clock.'

'Gosh, how jolly interesting.' Daisy could be sarcastic. 'Look at the time on that clock. I might have to leave!'

Danny could also be interesting about military aircraft, but the champagne arriving saved Daisy from further 'entertainment'. For the first time that day they sort-of-relaxed, clinked glasses, looked into each other's eyes, connected and smiled. Danny reached over and affectionately took Daisy's hand.

'How sweet? Sorry I'm late, wanted to check if I was being followed.' Yuliet had arrived in a swirl of multi-coloured coats, scarves and bags. She was a bit breathless after her brisk circuitous walk up Gray's Inn Road.

'No worries. Good to see you again. Your timing was perfect – Danny was just telling me all about the refurbishment of the station clock.'

Yuliet looked askance. She took a glass of the pink fizz from Danny. The bottle was empty – he hadn't realised they had drunk that much whilst waiting. He pressed the champagne button.

'What's so important?'

Yuliet explained how she had received the bundle of papers in St George's Gardens.

'Any idea who the woman was?'

'Not really – I have an idea, but not certain. I had sent out what I thought was a secure message to all our journalists and researchers, I suppose one of them could have triggered it. But it was a bit weird. The information in the file could only have come from confidential authority sources. Bill Kelly maybe?'

'Why would Bill Kelly send a confidential file to you?' Danny could see that Yuliet was hiding something from him.

Yuliet ignored the question. 'It is what it said that worried me.'

The second bottle of champagne arrived. They waited in silence while the waitress silently opened the bottle, put it in the ice bucket and left.

'It seems that Ali Baka has fingers in lots of serious organised crime pies. Human trafficking. Drugs. Guns. Cybercrime. Possibly even terrorism – not for faith or political reasons, simply for money. He has been associated directly or indirectly with the murder of at least twenty people, mostly former associates or competitors who the world is not going to miss. There's not enough concrete evidence to bring him in, it's all hearsay and conjecture. The way he operates it seems is to get someone else to do his dirty work – he reels them in innocuously and then springs a trap.'

'Could Stanislaw Nowak be one of Baka's intended traps?' Daisy was worried.

Danny too had his concerns. 'Maybe. We don't know. Nowak is twitchy and obviously hiding something.'

'But what has that got to do with Martha and the tour?'

'We know that Nowak and Baka have met, but we don't know why.'

'The tour schedule is weird – and going to places that no normal pop tour would consider.' Daisy frowned. 'We have more transport than we need from a company in Poland no one has heard of. The tour is a cover for something – could it be people or drug smuggling? Or what?'

'All good points, but that only works if there is a tour. Currently there isn't one with Martha missing – that puts the tour in jeopardy? Scuppering everyone's plans?' asked Danny. 'It doesn't make sense. Doesn't benefit either Nowak or Baka.'

They sipped their champagne while they contemplated. *Bit like a naff movie*, thought Daisy – *sipping champagne while discussing organised crime.*

'There's more. Apparently, Baka has pissed off the Russian *Vory* – something is developing.' Yuliet dropped the bombshell that had really knocked her back.

'Vory?'

'The Russian super-Mafia.' Yuliet didn't need notes. 'What makes the Vory distinct from other organised crime groups is their growing global influence, unlike the Mafia in Italy, the Sinaloa Cartel in Mexico or the Yamaguchi Gumi in Japan. The Vory are well organised and likely to have a portfolio of interests from legitimate to totally criminal. They could wear a Savile Row suit, stay in up-market hotels in Mayfair or even have houses and family here – difficult to differentiate from anyone else in wealthy society. They call themselves "*Vory v Zakone*" – "thieves following a codex". Vory culture is heavily connected with organised crime.'

Daisy put down her glass. Any thoughts of relaxation gone. 'Oh great. Not content with a tour funded by crime, now I'm involved with the nastiest super-Mafia in the world. My day just gets better and better.'

'Actually, if one had to come up with some kind of league table of global Mafias, the Italians are still the most powerful and the richest,' Yuliet said. 'But the Russians are the most international – mobsters to the world!'

'You're not making me feel any better.'

'The Vory have become very clever – they are now criminal wholesalers offering drugs, computer hacking, contract killing, human trafficking, money laundering, anything you like, to others around the world. Instead of trying to take over territory or criminal markets as they did, unsuccessfully, in the nineties they have refined their international approach. They work as brokers, but strictly on their terms. They say, "What do you need? Whatever you need, we've got it. But don't step out of line".'

'And is that what Baka has done?' asked Danny. 'Stepped out of line?'

'Maybe, once again we don't really know. An increasing number of individual criminal entrepreneurs offer crime-as-a-service – again could be Baka. The online trade in illicit goods and services enables individual criminals to operate their own criminal business without the need for the infrastructures maintained by "traditional" organised crime groups.'

'These Vory might have Martha?' asked Daisy. 'As a way of trying to control or blackmail Baka?'

'Seems logical. Many of these groups try to avoid outright violence as it can attract the attention of the authorities. However, some groups involved in migrant smuggling have been known to use the threat of kidnapping to extort debt payments – either from those being smuggled or the monasseks.'

'Monasseks?'

'The organisers of the smuggling routes – which again could include Baka.'

'So, we do think the tour could be used for people smuggling?'

'Maybe? But with Martha missing there is no tour. It's a dichotomy.'

They sipped their champagne. Danny caught the eye of a waiter and ordered some nuts, crisps and olives.

'Apart from his possible disagreement with the Russians, what about Baka himself – what else do we know about Baka from these files?'

'He was born in Kuala Lumpur, where he had a reputation as thug and a hired hand. According to some, he had to leave in a hurry aged about twenty-five when he forgot to hand over the proceeds of one bank robbery – the ring leaders were found dead a few days later. Nothing proven, but the word is that Baka disappeared with ten million Malaysian Ringgit – just under two million pounds – having removed any threat and leaving a bloody signal not to follow him.'

'So that's how he funded his activities. Do we know where he went?' Danny was now on a roll.

'The stories are various and not clear. Baka toured for a while before setting up business bases in Egypt and Syria. He has a place on the south-east coast of Spain in the hills above Calpe, about thirty minutes from Benidorm and also here in the UK, somewhere in the Wye Valley. He hasn't been seen in either of them for a long time.' Yuliet was surreptitiously using the file for reference.

'So, where does he live?'

'No one really knows. Seems to spend a lot of time chopping and changing between hotels and apartments. He keeps moving.'

'What do we know about his houses?' asked Danny. 'I know the Wye Valley quite well. Used to spend some of my summer holidays camping and kayaking near Symonds Yat. My parents used to rent a cottage near Tintern Abbey every year, until I was twenty-three or four, for family Christmas and Hogmanay.'

'He only bought the Wye Valley place two years ago. He spent a year doing it up, architect managed. Beyond that, the file doesn't say a lot – he has a couple of full-time staff there. And that's it.'

'And Marbella? The Costa del Crime?'

'It is not the organised crime hot spot it once was, but it still has ruthless gangs. Andalucía is one of the key entry points for immigrants, cocaine, heroin and, of course, marijuana grown just across the Med. The word is that Baka had teamed up with the O'Murchadha clan. The gang's leader Conor O'Murchadha is worth an estimated two hundred million euros, considered one of Ireland's wealthiest criminals. O'Murchadha spent some time in jail where he probably met some Vory. According to the file, he was released in 2017 – he is now back in action allegedly with a string of brutal murders settling scores with associates who fell out of line during his time behind bars. One particularly brutal retribution was in broad daylight at a bar in Marbella. Bullets sprayed all over a public square. No member of the public was hurt, but it was a close-run thing. Four former associates were killed. They had allegedly stolen over a quarter-of-a-mill from the O'Murchadha clan.'

Daisy and Danny sat in shocked silence. The nuts,

crisps and olives arrived. They declined a third bottle of champagne.

'What the bloody hell have we got ourselves involved in?' Daisy was pale. Not even the champagne could liven her up.

'There's only one person that knows what is going on – that's Nowak. I'm going to talk to him.' Danny couldn't believe what he was saying – his foot started throbbing. 'He won't or can't talk to the police. It might be a way in to find Martha? I don't like it, though.'

'Not on your own you're not. I'm coming as well. We share this story,' Yuliet demanded.

'Whoa! This isn't a story. This is about finding Martha.' Daisy was getting angry.

Yuliet and Danny said nothing, but both their journalistic juices were overflowing. The mutual look agreeing that they shared the story. Danny didn't feel the least bit guilty about Daisy's opinion. This time it would be publish and be damned – time for revenge, albeit ten years late.

'Maybe this is the reason you were given the file? Could be we can do more than Bill and his merry men? Nowak would never speak to the police,' Danny suggested.

'When and where and how do we see Nowak?' asked Yuliet.

'Where does he live?' asked Danny, looking at Daisy.

'No idea, Docklands somewhere, I have his business phone number.'

'How do we keep this away from Rob, Bill and their

team? We're being followed. Most of the time.' Danny looked around theatrically. 'They are also following Nowak and have bugged his home too.'

'How do you know?'

'I was in a meeting at Scotland Yard when it was announced.'

'That's high-level stuff,' said Yuliet. 'Only the Home Secretary can authorise that sort of thing.'

'We have to talk to him at Elstree then, somewhere it is expected we'd all be. In the studio – it's too big to easily bug.'

'It's Friday night and full rehearsals don't start again until Monday.'

'That might be too late for Martha?'

It was Daisy who had the solution. 'I can phone Nowak and arrange a production meeting for tomorrow morning at Elstree – something to do with a sponsorship deal.'

The other two nodded. With that she took out her mobile phone. 'Hi Stanislaw, it's Daisy. Sorry to disturb.'

The others could only hear one side of the conversation.

'Where are you? Are you alone?'

Daisy nodded at the other two – raising her eyebrows.

'On your way home. Don't blame you.'

Pause – Daisy had confirmed that he couldn't be overheard.

'Sorry about that. It's a bit noisy. I'm at St Pancras having a glass of champagne.'

Pause

'Looked fabulous didn't it.'

Pause

'Think we've got another sponsor.'

Pause

'Not sure yet. Been talking to a sponsorship agent, should be decent, but they want to see the stage and set – and to meet you before they say who their client is.'

Pause.

'No, they won't consider it without meeting you. I know it's Saturday. But I said Elstree tomorrow morning at ten. I'll speak to Jimmy to get the lights and sound up, so it looks at its best – he said he has a few of the crew in for tech checks. Shirley will be there too, so we can get a coffee or something.'

Pause – thumbs up.

'See you at ten somewhere near the stage. Okay. Thanks. Bye.'

Daisy put the phone back in her bag.

'Good job. But what is he going to say, or do, when he discovers we've lied?' asked Yuliet.

'He won't have a lot of choice. I am sure he wants to find Martha as much as we do and he needs to get the show on the road…' Danny hesitated, '…assuming she's still alive. We secretly record the meeting – if he steps out of line, we send the recording to Bill. But how do we get Yuliet into Elstree without her being seen? We really don't want Bill and his boys to know that Yuliet is any more involved than she is. We've shaken off Dick and Dom for now, but they'll be pretty pissed off – I imagine we'll be followed once we return home.'

'Stay at mine tonight – I assume you two are sharing a bed?' offered Yuliet. 'And we'll take my car up to Elstree first thing. We shouldn't be followed.'

Daisy's turn to take Danny's hand; no need to hide

anything. 'It's the weekend, so I can arrange parking out of sight in the underground car park – the one that's used to get celebrities in and out without being seen.'

'Where's your car now?'

'At home in the car park under my flat.'

'And home?'

'West Hampstead – one stop from here.'

Danny paid the bill and the three of them walked down to the St Pancras Thameslink platform. Half an hour later they were in Yuliet's flat having stopped off first at the Tesco Express opposite for the makings of spaghetti Bolognese together with a couple of bottles of organic Primitivo to wash it down.

They had a pleasant evening with an unspoken agreement not to talk about the current messy business. Yuliet amused Daisy with stories of investigations past – including her off-the-record dealings with Detective Chief Superintendent Bill Kelly – and the behaviour of some well-known people as they tried to deny the undeniable, despite the plethora of photographic evidence. Danny dozed off in the armchair; it was well past his bedtime. In the end the shared bed was used solely for sleeping.

24
SATURDAY—ELSTREE

SHIRLEY DELIVERED THREE STRONG CAPPUCCINOS AND three bacon butties in crusty bloomer bread – they hadn't had time for more than a mug of tea before they left Yuliet's house, in part due to the champagne and Primitivo.

Shirley, as ever, was in ebullient mood. 'Here you go. Put hairs on your chest. Too much booze was it?'

She cackled as she returned to her kitchen domain, wiping her hands on her branded white apron. Yuliet surprised Danny and Daisy by the huge volume of tomato ketchup she plastered onto her sandwich.

'So? I like ketchup.'

Danny's phone rang. Withheld number.

'Hello.' Danny was hesitant.

'Where are you?' came the cranky reply.

Danny mouthed the word 'Bill' to Yuliet and Daisy.

'Having a day off. Is something wrong?'

'You know what's wrong. You gave my guys the slip – deliberately.' Bill definitely wasn't happy.

'No, we didn't – Daisy and I were going for a night out. The taxi was there, so we took it.'

'You didn't go home last night.'

'You're my mother now are you? I'm a big boy. We stayed over at a friend's.'

'Bollocks.'

Danny decided to change tack. 'Who were those two following us, that you arrested?'

'None of your business.'

'What happened to sharing everything?'

'I could ask you the same? We've tracked your phone. You are at Elstree. Is Martha's sister with you?'

'Err, no. Why?' Danny was puzzled.

'Rob went around to her house to talk to her, before taking her off to the safe house. She wasn't there – like you, she hadn't been there all night.'

Out of the corner of his eye he saw Nowak arriving. It was nine forty-five.

'Gotta dash. Nowak's here. Talk to you later.' Danny disconnected, immediately switched the iPhone to airplane mode. He hit record and left the phone apparently randomly upside-down on the table.

Nowak looked at the half-eaten sarnies and shouted over at Shirley, 'Same for me, love.' No please, no thank you. Just a barked command.

He smiled at Yuliet, assuming she represented the new potential sponsors – he thrust out his hand, which Yuliet took.

'Stanislaw Nowak. Welcome to the world of Martha Movin' Out. No G.'

Before Yuliet could answer. Danny decided to take the lead. 'There is no sponsorship deal. We needed to talk to you in private. Here seemed as good a place as any. And we get a good breakfast.'

Nowak leapt up, jerking the table and spilling some of the cappuccinos. Daisy was alarmed by the sudden swing from jovial to threat.

Yuliet said quietly, 'We know about Ali Baka.'

Nowak stopped, turned towards Yuliet, who refused to look intimidated.

Yuliet repeated, 'We know about Ali Baka.'

'Who?' said Nowak.

'Ali Baka,' replied Yuliet, 'we know about him.'

Nowak slowly sat. 'What's going on?'

Yuliet lifted the blue tote bag from beside the table and wiped off the cappuccino that had spilled onto the fabric. She took out a slim file containing a few of the pages copied from the file she had been given. The original was locked in a safe, carefully hidden back at her office. On the top of the pile was a photograph.

'Ali Baka,' she said, handing over the picture to Nowak.

He pretended to study the picture, remaining silent.

'We know you two are involved with each other.'

'Who are you?'

'I could be your best friend or your worst enemy – that's up to you. Depends what you say now.'

She's got balls, thought Danny.

'Who are you?'

'Call me Yuliet.'

'Why?'

'Because that's my name.'

Daisy couldn't help but laugh. Nowak and Yuliet looked at her – the smile went.

'What do you know?'

'We know that Ali Baka is involved in people trafficking, slavery, prostitution, drugs, guns, extortion, terrorism, organised crime and more. He is also associated with the murder of at least twenty people – shall I go on?'

Shirley delivered Nowak's coffee and bacon butty – he ignored them all.

'You and Baka have met and have some sort of deal going. What's the million for?'

Now Yuliet really had Nowak's attention.

'Million?' Nowak was playing for time.

How did she know about that, thought Nowak?

'I overheard your conversation,' Danny interrupted, 'don't deny it. I was hiding in the quick-change area. You were just outside. You said to Baka that Martha was missing, and it had been reported to the police. You then said that he had changed the deal and you made an offer of one million. Final, I think you said?'

Nowak took a bite of his sandwich. He was thinking quickly – and chewing slowly.

'I borrowed some money from Ali Baka to fund the tour, that's all. He's a businessman concerned that he wouldn't get his money back because Martha was missing. He was trying to up the interest payments. Bigger risk, bigger return required.'

'You know the police are following you and your flat is being bugged? They will have followed you here. Tell us everything and we might be able to help you to get Martha back – that's all we are interested in.' Danny ignored Yuliet's hard stare; he was using the information as an olive branch. Something to show good faith. Bill Kelly would not be happy if he knew he had told Nowak – *but needs must*, thought Danny.

'All we're concerned with is getting Martha back safe and well,' Daisy emphasised. 'We don't care about anything else.'

Danny, Daisy and Yuliet stared at Nowak, challenging him.

'I want Martha back too. And I want the tour to go ahead – I'll be ruined if it doesn't happen.' *Financially and physically*, thought Nowak.

'Then what is going on?' asked Yuliet.

'Baka...' Nowak's speech slowed, '...has Martha.' Just speaking the words out loud had a cathartic effect on him.

'What? Why?' Yuliet demanded.

'He wants to change the deal we had,' Nowak admitted.

More silence. Nowak wasn't going to tell anyone about using the tour for people smuggling, and certainly not using the tour for trafficking.

'Where's Martha's sister?' Danny broke the silence.

'What do you mean?' This was the first any of them had heard of this.

'That was Bill on the phone, he wanted to know if I knew where Vikki was.'

'But we saw her go off with the police last night.'

Yuliet was getting confused. They had all been so obsessed with Ali Baka that neither Danny nor Daisy had mentioned Vikki. They'd talked about how fabulous the show was going to be – but somehow managed to avoid talking about Martha's twin, Vikki.

'How do you know the police are following me – and bugged my flat?' Nowak asked.

'What about Vikki?' Yuliet's turn.

'Both of them gone?' Daisy was distraught. Was it her fault? Had the photos of Vikki been released? Did the kidnappers, Baka, think they had the wrong person?

Daisy leapt to her feet and screamed, 'Oh for fuck's sake!'

Shirley, Jimmy and some of the crew rushed over at the screams.

Daisy slumped down, her head in her hands and let out great sobbing retches.

25
SATURDAY – THE WYE VALLEY, MONMOUTHSHIRE

MARTHA HAD BEEN LOCKED IN HER ROOM SINCE her involuntarily aborted attempt to escape for a walk on Wednesday.

The room was luxuriously well appointed – there was nothing for which she could have wished. But she hated being confined. Hated being a prisoner. Although polite, but guarded, none of the people Martha saw would talk to her other than to ask about day-to-day housekeeping and catering.

Martha was, if nothing else, a pragmatist. Her days, weeks and years in the ups and downs of the shitty music business had taught her to always cheer up, things could get worse. In this case a whole load worse. But she thought if she was going to be killed, raped, tortured or worse –

whatever worse was – 'they' would have done it by now. Her mind kept wandering to who would have imprisoned her; she didn't want to use the word kidnapped. The 'K'-word had far too sinister an implication and Martha had battled through life by always staying positive. But this was at the edge of reason and the edge of her ability to keep it together. She thought back to the endless counselling sessions after the death of her parents and her family – *if she could survive that and come out the other side, then this was a piece of cake. Yeah, right. Who was she kidding?* She realised she was talking to herself.

Mental health and physical health go hand in hand – she took to the running machine at a vicious pace. To keep her spirits up and stay sane, she thought that she might as well get fitter, nothing else to do – hopefully she had a gruelling tour in a few weeks. At her request a treadmill, a rowing machine and some securely tethered weights had been brought up from the gym and set up in the corner of her massive suite.

She also thought this was an opportunity to write a few songs – she couldn't complain about the peace, free from life's normal interruptions. Her hosts had provided her with a Mac and a colour laser printer, together with an eighty-eight key hammer action piano-type keyboard, a Focusrite microphone, drum pads, with sampler, synthesiser and Pro-Tools programmes plugged into her room's Genelec loudspeakers. As expected, no internet access. She was also given a couple of memory sticks and stacks of paper to save her work – some indication that she might be set free? *Hopefully, or am I being optimistic?*

'Write from experience,' she had been taught by Guy, her first producer. In an earlier life Guy had played the melodeon in a Ceilidh Band, not something many knew, but occasionally this influenced his collaborations – several of which had minor chart success. Not surprisingly the first few song scamps Martha was thinking about were rather melancholy, reminding her of Tom Jones and 'The Green, Green Grass of Home'; the prisoner awaiting execution longing for his family house and gardens. In Martha's case it was the drab grey streets of London; conversely the view from her luxurious prison's windows was glorious in the sunshine. *Always look on the bright side of life*' – Eric Idle popped into her head. She had just read his book, one of many stacked up on her bookshelf.

The enforced solitude and captivity broke the dam. For over six years her creative juices had all but dried up – she was aware, and eventually admitted that her work had not been up to standard. Her captivity had compelled her to some honest contemplation.

Suddenly she was writing and composing again. It seemed to come easily. Her mood lifted.

There was a knock and Martha's door immediately opened. No one waited before entering, potentially giving Martha the chance to prepare for escape or sometimes to put on clothes – she was expecting breakfast.

'You have a visitor.' It was 'Oliver Mellors' with someone folded over his shoulder.

He dumped the sleeping form onto the super king bed, with a bounce.

'You don't mind sharing a bed for a few days, do you?'

Martha was about to object when she realised she was looking at her sister. She was shocked at the state of her. 'What's wrong with her? What have you done to her? Why is she here?'

'She'll wake up soon – give her plenty of water,' advised Oliver, 'it'll help with the headache. She drank a lot last night. I was seriously impressed.'

'I'll bring you both your breakfasts in a few moments,' added Natalia. 'With some ibuprofen. Your sister might need them.'

The door closed with the normal heavy double clunk as the electronic deadlocks engaged.

Seeing her sister lying there prostrate on the bed upset Martha. Her earlier euphoria disintegrated – the emotional roller-coaster was too much to take. She felt crushed and cried properly for the first time since arriving at Piercefield, massive racking sobs.

The door opened again. Natalia ignored Martha's anguish. Breakfast for two was laid out on the wheeled trolley – with extra freshly squeezed orange juice.

Natalia put additional bathroom products, toothpaste and toothbrush on the sideboard, together with more towels, and a selection of fresh clothes, underwear and trainers. She left without a word. It was almost as if she cared.

Martha cradled Vikki, gently rocking her.

'What have they done to you?' she asked rhetorically. Martha stayed hugging her sister for over an hour.

Ever so slowly, Vikki opened her eyes – with the back of her hand she wiped the accumulated sleepy-dust away from the corners of her eyes. Her face brightened when she saw Martha.

'Sis, you're back. Where have you been? Fuck, my head hurts.'

'Stay still.' Martha went over to the trolley, poured a large orange juice, adding some ice, and took 600 mg of ibuprofen from the box. She gently helped Vikki to sit up – she gulped the tablets with the juice. Her face was ashen, blue bags under her eyes, her make-up smudged all over her face, her hair lank and greasy. Her breath stank of vomit.

'That's a bit better,' Vikki smiled. 'God, I was blasted last night. But what about you? Where have you been – we've all been worried about you.'

'I've been here since last week.'

'Fabulous room. And look at those views. Where are we? How did I get here? Can't remember a thing.' Vikki tried to stand up – and immediately crashed back down on the bed. 'Feel like a pile of shite.'

Vikki's eyes inexorably shut – she remained asleep for another three hours, a combination of the sedatives she had been forcefully given, the self-imposed alcohol and this morning's ibuprofen. She did not notice her sister gently pulling a blanket over her or clean her face with one of the luxurious face wipes. Martha sat in the armchair beside the bed watching Vikki's chest gently moving up and down in a deep, seemingly dreamless sleep; she envied her peace. But that would all change soon, when Martha would have to tell her sister that they were both prisoners.

26

SATURDAY – ELSTREE

'THE POLICE ARE BUGGING MY FLAT AND following me?' Nowak was not as outraged as Danny thought he should have been. Nowak looked around for any sign of his followers – made a big show of it.

Danny was rhetorical. 'Why are the police bugging and following you?'

Nowak didn't say anything, so Danny helped. 'Because you are a nasty piece of shit that no one trusts. And let's be clear, the police know about what you did to my foot and why. What everyone wants to know is why you are involved in this tour and with Martha?'

'So many questions. You don't really think I'm going to answer a fucking journo who was sacked because he was crap at his job? It's fuck all to do with you. I'm not having it.'

Yuliet, however, was having it. She was like a figurehead on a man o' war ploughing through the stormy seas. 'You know why Danny left his job. And, like Danny, I too am a bloody good journalist. I smell a great big story here – and you might become the star headline. So, stop swinging your tiny little cock and let's have a proper conversation.'

Nowak was partially aroused by Yuliet's direct approach – not a feeling he had expected. No one talked to him like that normally – especially a woman.

'Let's start with a simple question. Where is Martha?'

'Simple question?' Nowak paused. 'Difficult answer. I really have no idea.'

'Stop fucking around Nowak. This conversation can go one of two ways. One way we get Martha back and the tour goes ahead. The other way you are dead.'

Danny and Daisy were seriously impressed with Yuliet – and a little bit scared.

'Ooooh. Handbags at dawn is it sweetie-pie? Are you threatening to kill me then? Ooooh, I'm really scared!' Nowak shrugged up his shoulders and pursed his lips in mock terror.

'I'm not, but the Vory or Conor O'Murchadha might kill you.' Yuliet watched for a reaction.

And got it.

For the first time Nowak's bluster looked at risk. 'What has Conor or the Vory got to do with all this?'

'You don't think Baka used all his own money, do you? One million was it you renegotiated? And he isn't working alone.' Yuliet was busking it. In a room full of liars, the biggest one wins.

Nowak considered his future. He really didn't know what to do or how to retrieve himself from this increasingly impossible balls-up. He came to a decision – or maybe he made the decision a few days ago, and was now trying to justify it. The opportunity to come clean had just presented itself. In for a penny.

'Two plus interest.' He sat back into his chair, waiting for the reaction.

'Two what?'

'Two million plus one hundred thousand interest. Goes up to four million if I don't deliver the tour.'

'Jesus!' Danny was stunned. Yuliet and Daisy just stared. They didn't expect this.

'One word of this leaks and we are all in the shit. You'll wish for death if the Vory get hold of you.' Nowak was genuinely scared, probably for the first time in his life.

It was his old school mate and friend from childhood, Pietr Ostrodzko, who Nowak was most concerned about – he had unwittingly become the catalyst for Nowak's decision. Nowak had always led a life on the edge, he accepted the risks, but he had made a promise to Pietr that he would not involve him in people trafficking. *Pietr is a good, decent bloke with a family and children,* he thought – *and doesn't deserve to be embroiled in this mess.* The dam burst – Nowak had not been sleeping, worrying about what he could be doing to his oldest friend.

He simply couldn't think of a way of getting out of the shit storm of his own making. The tour was probably going to be a success without the need for less-than-legal sidelines – the problem he had was how he had borrowed the seed money and how he was going to return it without very personal and unpleasant sanctions.

If he was honest with himself – and there was the irony, being honest – he was fed up with life on the outside of society. He craved respect. He wanted to be able to hold his head up and not continue life looking over his shoulder. To sleep soundly at night. He was tired and getting older. He wanted to settle down with someone. Children and grandchildren maybe? Maybe, maybe, maybe. Maybe it was all too late. Is it possible to put your past behind you?

Daisy, Yuliet and Danny were dumbfounded by Nowak's transformation. It was as if he had aged ten years in front of their eyes. His face creased. The sparkle left his eyes. His shoulders dropped. His back curled. Daisy noticed the chewed nails and hands with the dry, peeling skin.

No one spoke – they all realised that Nowak needed to talk in his own time.

Nowak, with great care, finished the bacon sandwich and his tea. He got up, taking all the dirties with him, wandered the forty metres or so over to the catering truck and put everything in the washing pile.

'Thanks Shirley, that was delicious. You really are wonderful.' Shirley didn't know what to say. *Praise from Nowak, never heard such a thing. Whatever next?*

'Please can we have four more cappuccinos?'

'Yeah, right away,' Shirley stammered. 'I'll bring them over.'

'Thank you.'

Nowak stood for a while and looked back into the rehearsal studio. It was a masterpiece. One of the sound team was playing one of Martha's tracks at reduced volume. The lights synchronised. What a show it was going to be! He realised he was enormously proud of this – his – achievement.

Eventually he rejoined Daisy, Danny and Yuliet and wilted into his chair, the cappuccinos already waiting on the table with a pile of Shirley's hand-made ginger cookies. He dunked a biscuit into the creamy froth and took a bite before it went soggy. He wiped his palms down over his eyes and face, exhausted, then looked at his three unlikely companions. He was out of his depth and felt impotent. He began slowly, hesitatingly.

'I haven't known Baka long. We met in a bar last year while I was on vacation in Cairo. I overheard him talking to someone on the phone – threatening a monassek. A monassek is someone who—'

'We know what a monassek is. Go on.' Yuliet was impatient. Danny gave her a look to shut her up. Uninterrupted, encouraging listening was what was required. Best counselling techniques.

'Threatening a monassek?' Danny used his old interviewing technique taught to him by a specialist educator – repeat the last three most important words that were said. Nowak took his cue.

'Baka caught me listening to him on the phone. He came over to me a bit antsy – his bloody fault if he has a conversation at the top of his voice in a public place. I bought him a drink. He calmed down a bit and we started talking. Baka was bollocking someone about the monassek cocking up his travel business, not doing a very good job. We left it at that on the first night and agreed to meet again.'

Nowak dunked another cookie. Left it too long and part fell back into his coffee – he ate the biscuit and stirred the soggy detritus into the froth.

'The following day I did a bit of research. Talked to a few associates. I discovered amongst other things Baka was a people smuggler but his business was under pressure from the Russians. Muscling in. I thought he meant the Russian Mafia, not Vory. I had a big moment when I realised that the tour could make for a perfect cover to bring a few migrants into the UK – forty at a time camouflaged into three mobile generators. And, of course, safely – no risk of drowning. Hate water, I can't swim.'

Nowak omitted any information about his business supplying passports and identification documents.

'Rather than ask for a fee, I said I needed investment for Martha's tour. After a bit of haggling we agreed two million over two years at a cost of a hundred K repayable after two years. Simply in exchange for transporting two hundred people in five journeys.'

'So that explains the weird tour schedule?' Daisy's turn.

Nowak nodded. 'My condition was strictly voluntary migrants who wanted to get into the UK. We shook hands on it. After two weeks our briefs exchanged contracts and we both signed – strictly for the loan terms, nothing mentioned about our travel guests.'

'So that's how you raised the rest of the money for Martha's tour.' Yuliet again.

'The money came from a numbered account in the Cayman Islands. After a bit of digging I found out that the money arrived there via bearer bonds, totally untraceable. No CCTV and no one can remember what the woman looked like. Corporate amnesia – what the banks call discretion. Nobody here cared about where the money came from as the tour was now in business. We now have, more or less, all the cash we need. Advance ticket sales and sponsorship have exceeded our expectations in the business plans.' He looked at Daisy. 'Thanks largely to your efforts. Thank you.'

Daisy didn't know what to say. 'Martha's reputation really, my bit was easy.'

Danny simply didn't believe that Nowak could change like this – the jury was out for now.

'All was going well. The generators had been converted and are now on their way here from my friend Pietr. Then, last week, Baka changed the deal. His timing was awful for me and perfect for him. Fucking shit, too late for us to do anything. I went to his hotel in Soho – he was a changed man. Totally different to the man I met in Cairo. Very aggressive. Bombastic. Threatening. Evil – and I know evil. He told me he wanted to up the numbers from forty to one hundred people per trip. I said it wasn't possible, too risky. Of course, I realised he was then talking about people trafficking. Something I specifically said I would not get involved in.'

'What's the difference between people smuggling and people trafficking?' Daisy wanted to know.

'Not a lot I suppose. But as far as I am concerned, migrants want to come to the UK. Trafficked people are being forced into slave labour, sometimes in appalling conditions.'

'Don't tell me you have suddenly acquired a conscience?'

'It's Baka that has kidnapped Martha.' Nowak dropped the bombshell.

There was stunned silence, broken by Danny. 'That doesn't make sense – no tour means he doesn't traffic his people. You both lose.'

'Do you know where she is?' asked Daisy.

'No idea.' Nowak was even more deflated. 'Baka is blackmailing me. He offered me a choice. To get Martha back either we move his extra people, or I give him four million. I don't have that sort of money. There wouldn't be a tour because I'd be bankrupt. I signed the contract convinced all would be well, so like a twat I ignored the punitive cancellation terms. You overheard me agreeing to transport the extra people, but in exchange for a million quid – so I would only return a mill. But I'd promised Pietr we wouldn't get involved in trafficking. Pietr is one of my oldest friends.'

'And now we must assume Baka has taken Vikki too?'

'But why?'

It was Daisy who had the answer – it had been playing on her mind. 'Baka must have seen the rehearsal pictures of Vikki on stage – he wanted to ensure the tour couldn't go ahead. It's a testament to his warped mind that he thought we'd go ahead without the real Martha.'

'But those pictures aren't out there yet.'

'Yes, they are,' Yuliet held up her iPad, 'they went up on *The Daily Tribune*'s website yesterday, promoting star-reporter Kelvin's full story in *The Sunday Tribune*. They've gone viral too, over half a million shares, reposts, likes, comments and outright plagiarism.'

'Sorry, I was wrong about Kelvin.' Daisy was distraught that Vikki's kidnapping could have been down to her.

It was Shirley who broke up the introspection. 'Jimmy says they've all finished. He wants to lock up for the day and send everyone home. I promised my hubby I'd go with him this afternoon to watch Watford beat the Arsenal – can't stand football m'self. But we don't get the chance to do much together and we need to get over to Vicarage Road. Can I do you another coffee before I leave?'

'That would be great, thanks Shirley. Give us the take-away cups.' Nowak decided for them all.

Shirley cleaned up the table and returned five minutes later with the coffees in the Martha Movin' Out branded reusable beakers. They had, while waiting, not said a word – deep in thought.

'They won't you know,' said Nowak, looking at Shirley.

'Won't what?' Shirley was confused.

'Watford won't beat the Arsenal.'

They all laughed. Shirley happily scuttled off.

'What are we going to do then?' asked Danny.

'You do like that word "we" don't you?' Daisy wasn't laughing.

Nowak's phone rang.

'Yes, what do you want?' Nowak was straight to the point.

27

SATURDAY – SOUTH DEVON

'It'll all be fine. Nowak is on the edge of caving in. He's more or less agreed to a hundred per trip, we're just haggling about the fee – might well be able to make it a hundred and fifty.' Baka was speaking quietly on his iPhone, sitting on a bench overlooking the River Dart at Dittisham, about six miles up-river from Dartmouth in the Devon countryside.

He had just enjoyed a very good pasty lunch at the Ferry Boat Inn. He was waiting for the tide, so he could be picked up from the floating jetty by tender to take him to the luxury yacht with its deep draught only able to navigate this far up the River Dart two hours either side of high water. From there he would sail as a covert passenger to the north coast of France without troubling the UK or

French Border Forces. *It only seems fair to reduce their workload,* he thought, *as they are so busy trying to stop illegal immigrants.* He laughed out loud at the thought. A small boy, with three crabs dangling from the bacon on the end of his fishing line, stared at him. Baka glared back. The crabs let go, dropping themselves back into the water probably for the twentieth time that day – the boy gave him a hard stare; losing the crabs was obviously Baka's fault.

Once in France Baka could travel anywhere within the twenty-six states of the Schengen zone without being challenged to show one of his several passports – or, he hoped, being found or followed. He'd travelled down from Paddington by train first clas earlier that day on the GWR intercity express train, for once on time, more or less. The train was crowded with cooing grandparents and uncontrollable children all excited to be beside the seaside. Anyone who attempted to sit with him at 'his' table soon changed their minds when Baka gave them a hard stare.

Traffic fumes to fresh air in a little over three hours.

The view across the widest part of the river surrounded by the glorious countryside was a calming influence. He looked across to Greenway, the holiday home of Agatha Christie, where she had planned and penned many of her books; the woodland gardens running down to the expanse of the sparkling river. He gazed at the mighty green oaks, colourful bulbs, camellias, rhododendrons, magnolias and the boathouse, scene of the crime in *Dead Man's Folly*. Baka had read all Christie's books – there was a certain old-fashioned charm to crime, murder and punishment in her day. In the middle of the river sat the 'Scold Stone', where unfaithful wives were tied as the punishment for their sins. Up until the middle of the nineteenth century, Dittisham men were permitted to sell their sinful wives. *Serves them right for getting married in the first place – the men that is*, Baka thought.

Conor O'Murchadha was spoiling his reverie; he was shouting down his phone. 'On the edge and more or less won't do. We have clients and they want certainty. I've made promises. I don't break my promises. Do you?'

'As I said, it'll be fine.'

'It better be – we are charging a premium to make this work.'

'I am aware of that. No need to get irritated.'

'Really. You have a million of my money riding on this and I want it back, in full, on time, with the five per cent interest.'

'And you stand to make a lot of money – I'm only in this for the fees.'

'I'll see you at Róisín O'Mulligan's, nine o'clock Tuesday night to sort out the arrangements as planned. Don't be late.' O'Murchadha disconnected. Róisín O'Mulligan's is a well-known Irish pub in the back streets of La Cala de Mijas, halfway between Marbella and Fuengirola on the south coast of Spain – and a regular meeting point for O'Murchadha and his 'associates'.

Baka was uncomfortable for once. Conor O'Murchadha wasn't aware that he was going to do well out of this. He had falsely pleaded poverty when he did the original deal with O'Murchadha for transporting his 'goods' directly from Turkey and North Africa into the Republic of Ireland.

The pictures that appeared online late afternoon on Friday had worried Baka – they certainly looked like Martha. He had called his lads to investigate and, if necessary, bring this new Martha to Piercefield. He had the call that morning to say that Martha's sister, Vikki, was now safe and sound in their care.

Sneaky trick, he thought, *so time to ramp up the pressure on Nowak then*. He speed dialled the number via WhatsApp.

'Yes, what do you want?' Nowak was straight to the point.

'One point five and we have a deal,' offered Baka.

There was silence on the other end.

'Did you hear me, one point five, final offer.'

'No interest payments, that's it. Repayable on the same schedule.'

'Okay, deal. I'll send the revised paperwork.'

'And Martha and her sister returned unharmed?'

'That's the deal – when you've signed, and I have it in my stickies.'

'Do it quickly, we have to rehearse. And I want them back.'

'You piss me about, and it won't just be Martha and her sister dead. Your life will also linger to an end, exquisitely – watching them die first.'

Baka disconnected and immediately called O'Murchadha. 'Deal done, start getting the monasseks to put the goods together at the holding houses. Ready to go in three months, a hundred at a time at three- to four-week intervals. I'll let you know if we can manage more after the first batch.'

'Good,' said O'Murchadha and disconnected.

Baka called his solicitor, explained the need for the contract to be emailed as soon as possible with the minor amend. Tear up the old contract. The solicitor didn't see the accounts so had no idea exactly how much money had been exchanged, when or how. Not that she wanted to know, the less she knew the better. She knew that Nowak and Baka both had their fingers in many pies – some, well most, not altogether legitimate, but what the eye doesn't see?

The tender approached the jetty. *Sunspot*, the name of the yacht, sign-written upside down on the rear. Baka clambered over the gunwale, tripped on the transom and fell onto the wet decking. He didn't care. The deal was done, and everyone would be happy – he'd made half a mill plus his cut of the tickets. Always tickets, never people.

The boatman looked at Baka's land shoes in disgust, they would leave marks on the deck.

It would take all of the rest of the day and most of the night to sail across the English Channel to Le Port du Becquet, just to the east of Cherbourg. They would make land first thing in the morning – all the immigration, customs and passport nonsense avoided. The train journey from Cherbourg was to be a long one with an overnight stop in Barcelona. Baka always stayed in the hotel above the station, the Barceló Sants. It claimed to have a futuristic design and a cosmic atmosphere resembling a space station, allowing guests to imagine themselves on an intergalactic trip. *Just bloody weird,* he mused. *Even weirder looking out of a false porthole with imitation stars when having a piss in the middle of the night.*

Baka would be paying in cash separately for each leg of the journey and for the hotels. When needed, he had a selection of passports from which to choose – no one would be able to trace him.

SATURDAY 28

'That was Baka,' said Nowak.

'We guessed as much,' Danny harrumphed.

'The deal is done. Martha and Vikki should be returned soon. One and a half million to be repaid to Baka at the end of the loan term instead of the two point one.'

'What happened to your crisis of conscience? Or did six hundred thousand buy it?' accused Yuliet.

'We have more or less ten weeks before that becomes an issue, it's only after Casablanca and then Istanbul that the extra guests are on board. I still don't want to get involved in trafficking. What are we going to do?'

'Not we. That's not our problem – it's yours.' None of them were going to get involved in all this.

'And there I was thinking you cared about Martha.' Nowak didn't mention his own possible – probable – unpleasant death if this went wrong.

They were now all involved. Elation at the prospect of the return of Martha turned.

'There's no more we can do today. Let's see what the new week brings.' Yuliet was ever the pragmatist. 'Let's see what happens on Monday.'

The four got up. The studio was locked so they walked around the side and up to the main drag.

Nowak went up to the Martha production office in the administration block to await the new contract that was going to arrive sometime by email.

Daisy, Danny and Yuliet slowly walked back towards the main gate and entrance to the underground car park, deep in thought. As they approached, they saw Dick and Dom.

'You got us into deep shit,' said Dick. 'Bill was pretty pissed.'

Danny did look a little sheepish.

'We are here as much for your protection as to know what you are up to.' Dick gently revealed part of the brown leather straps of the shoulder holster holding the fifth-generation Glock 17 pistol.

'Are you SO1?' asked Yuliet.

Dick and Dom both knew who Yuliet was, so there was no point in concealing their purpose – but neither did they answer the question. 'Where's Nowak? We know he is here, this place is like a maze.'

'He's in the production office over there, waiting for

a couple of emails. He could be there a while,' answered
Daisy, pointing.

Dom walked away from them all. He appeared to be
talking to himself, but was in contact with Bill, Rob and
Nowak's watchers.

'You two can't be with us twenty-four seven though?'

'They'll be someone near you at all times.'

'Who were the two you arrested at Westminster Pier?'
No answer.

Dom returned. 'Bill suggests you need a chat.'

Yuliet was about to speak when Dom interrupted.
'Don't worry, not you two. This is a Danny-only
invitation.'

'Looks like I am not wanted.' Yuliet turned to Daisy.
'Do you want a lift then?'

Daisy nodded and departed with Yuliet down into the
underground car park. Dick and Dom followed – their
silver-grey Audi A4 Quattro was parked there too.

Out of the corner of his eye Danny saw Rob Andrews
striding towards him, ready to take him to New Scotland
Yard. 'You're beginning to annoy us.'

They walked to Rob's red, five-year-old perfectly
maintained VW Golf, parked in one of the few spaces
by the main gate. The studios were just beginning to get
busy as the audiences arrived for the Saturday TV shows,
both live and recorded. Several looked inside Rob's car
hoping some celebrity or other would be in there. The
silence on the journey from Elstree down to the Yard
was not companionable. Although only fifteen miles, the
journey took an hour and a half. There was the normal

hold-up outside Abbey Road Studios as crowds waited to take selfies on the famous Beatles' zebra crossing.

Eventually Rob broke the silence. 'So what did Nowak want?'

'We called him.'

'I thought you two weren't friends?'

'Ali Baka has Martha and Vikki.'

No more was said until they passed through the rigmarole of New Scotland Yard's security.

'You'll have to hand your phone over until you leave.'

'I have the recording of this morning's meeting with Nowak on it. Too big to email.'

'I'll take the phone, you will have it back when you leave.' Danny reluctantly agreed.

There was nothing other than tense, stilted professional small talk.

Danny and Rob took the guest lift once again to the fourth-floor meeting suites. Bill was the only person waiting.

'Danny how lovely to see you.' Bill did not offer his hand. 'What's going on?'

Rob answered for Danny. 'Daisy, Yuliet and Danny met with Nowak this morning. Baka has Martha and Vikki. There's a recording of the meeting on Danny's phone.'

Rob held up the phone with two fingers – as if it was infected. Bill took out his iPhone. 'Airdrop it to me.' A few moments later the file was on Bill's phone.

Bill turned to Rob. 'Would you mind taking Danny's phone down to the reception lockers, we won't be long.'

Unbeknown to Danny, Rob had watched him as he typed his PIN. Five minutes later specialist IT had added a couple of very secret apps to Danny's iPhone. One which enabled him to be tracked wherever he went, even if the phone was switched off. The other relayed all email, SMS and WhatsApp messages to Bill and the team. Danny would not be aware, unless he suspected the battery was running down quicker than normal.

Bill and Danny were alone. 'We have a leak – someone is sharing information with Nowak. He seems always one step ahead. Files and evidence have disappeared too.'

'What a fuck-up. Do you know who it is or how Nowak receives the information?'

Bill shook his head. This possibly explained why Nowak wasn't surprised when Danny had said his flat was being bugged. Danny couldn't tell Bill that he had revealed all this.

'Is that how he got away with the Blue Badge investigation?'

'Almost certainly.'

'So, this has been going on for years?'

'We have to be careful. When I catch the bastard, I'll make sure the key is thrown away. No one knows I know or suspect.'

'Why are you telling me?'

'You might be a slippery sod, but I trust you.'

Danny put on a cod American accent. 'Gee, you say the sweetest things.'

However, he was touched.

'We overheard one end of a phone conversation from Nowak's flat Tuesday evening, we don't know who the call was from. But from what Nowak said it could only have come from someone with inside information – and on the inside.'

'What else was said?'

'I'm not answering that.' Bill continued, 'If you get the chance please record all future encounters with our friend Nowak.'

'I'll try.'

'Right let's have a listen.'

Bill hooked up his iPhone to the meeting room's speakers. He tapped 'play' on the app – the recording wasn't perfect, but they could hear the words. Bill made notes.

If Nowak's reaction at the mention of the Vory and Conor O'Murchadha was one of shock, Bill's was even greater. He stopped the playback. 'How does Yuliet know so much?'

'Yuliet was handed a file by a mysterious woman when she was having lunch on a park bench. All very secret squirrel – she doesn't know who or why. The file was a photocopy of what looked like official records, deep background. It could have only come from an official source. I thought it was from you?' Danny countered.

'Not from us.' Bill frowned at Danny. After some thought he suggested, 'Perhaps up the Thames?'

'Why would they be involved?' Danny was curious. 'Why?'

'Our friends in Five and Six have been trying to understand organised crime for years but they don't share information they don't want to. They suspect our leak too.'

Bill thought for a while. 'I have always thought that some of the worker bees don't agree with keeping secrets with the home teams. Maybe this is a way of sending a message to us – they do seem to have their own set of clandestine rules.'

'That's daft. Surely you are all on the same side? Why use a third party – especially a journalist?' Danny marvelled at the bureaucracy and Chinese walls of the intelligence and investigative services.

Bill ignored the question. 'They know Yuliet and I have covertly collaborated in the past. We would never rat on each other – it was a win-win. Yuliet has proved herself to be responsible. She understands public interest, and selling a great story, but she doesn't put the source at risk.'

Bill lent over to restart the recording. He stopped. Looked Danny straight in the eye. 'Can you get a copy of the file please – strictly for my eyes only. No one else must know.'

'I can try. It's up to Yuliet.'

'She hands over a copy voluntarily, or we'll raid her offices with a search warrant and everyone will know.' Bill was fidgety. 'But it does explain something. This time do you really promise to keep a secret?'

Danny nodded his agreement. 'Scouts' honour.'

He'd never been a Scout, but it was the best he could do.

'Your followers were Russian. Undeclared FSB with diplomatic immunity. Very few people here know this.'

'Bloody hell. How did they get involved? Why us? Why me? Why FSB?' Danny knew a little about the FSB –

the Federal Security Service of the Russian Federation, the main security agency of Russia and the successor to the USSR's KGB, Committee of State Security. 'I thought the FSB was internal only?'

'True,' replied Bill. 'Normally. But lately they have been involved in the fight against organised crime, terrorism, and drug smuggling – and this led them to the Vory's activities outside of the homeland. The Vory seem to be inside everywhere at all levels of government and state. We've been liaising with the Spanish and Russian police via Interpol, our focus has been the proliferation of Russian and European organised crime's involvement in people smuggling. There are over one hundred and eighty thousand offenders linked to serious and organised crime in the UK alone. That's more than twice the strength of the regular British Army.'

Danny was stunned. 'Are these figures public?'

'Oh yes,' replied Bill. 'We've been trying unsuccessfully for more funding for years. Serious and organised crime in the UK is chronic and corrosive, its scale is truly staggering. It kills more people every year than terrorism, war and natural disasters combined. It affects more UK citizens, more frequently than any other national security threat. And it costs the UK at least thirty-seven billion a year – that's nearly two grand for every family.'

'Bloody hell.' Danny was appalled. 'Can I write this story? It has to be told.'

'It's all in the public domain, so that's up to you,' Bill agreed. 'The issue is the professional enablers such as accountants, solicitors and those working in money service businesses – they are the ones increasingly facilitating crimes with their expertise. Nowak and Baka are some of many, the tip of the iceberg, but we have to do something.'

'Are Interpol investigating, too, then?' Danny thought this was all getting out of hand.

'Interpol is not an international police force. It has no actual police or warrant powers of its own but is an information clearing house for its one-hundred-and-ninety-two members including Russia – any of whom can issue notices to all the others that someone is wanted. There is an encrypted internet-based worldwide communications network known as I-24/7 that gives constant access to Interpol's databases at their HQ in Lyon. Member countries can also access each other's criminal databases via the I-24/7 system.'

'Why undeclared FSB?'

'Interpol protocol demands that any state declares if they have sent investigators to another state. The Russians hadn't mentioned they had sent some people here. When we spoke to each other they confirmed that we were leaking and we couldn't be trusted to remain secure. Rather embarrassing for us – and how the hell did they know we were leaking?'

Bill made no mention of the second set of surveillance in Nowak's apartment. He restarted playback of Danny's recording.

Nowak's voice. 'What has Conor or the Vory got to do with all this?'

Bill paused the playback again. 'So he didn't know about their involvement?'

'I don't think so, he looked genuinely shocked.'

Bill tapped play again. They listened to Nowak talking about how he had raised the money for the tour from Ali Baka. The tour's travel schedule. Nowak's insistence that they only transported voluntary migrants. The generators. And then Baka changing the deal at the Soho meeting.

'We know about that meeting. It was the first time we had picked up on Nowak and Baka being involved with each other. Baka blackmailing Nowak explains Martha's disappearance.'

'At the moment we don't really have proof that Nowak is using the tour for trafficking – Casablanca will be a turning point. Where is the next gig after then?'

'Istanbul, I think, then no idea – have a look at the ticketing website.'

After a bit of googling, the Martha Movin' Out tour page came up. Dublin followed Casablanca six days later.

'So, where are Martha and Vikki? And where is Baka?' asked Danny.

'You realise we can't use this recording as evidence, don't you?' Bill was a little dismayed by the UK's archaic laws. 'But it's useful in our investigations to know what is going on. We'll have to get the proof by other means.'

Danny surprised Bill. 'It's not a crime to record a conversation without telling someone – okay, it could be considered a breach of their privacy. Nowak won't go for that. However, journalists can publish secret recordings without a legal backlash, provided they can prove the released recording is in the public interest. I'm a journalist.'

'Not yet you don't. This must stay secret – we don't just want Nowak and Baka, we want the whole chain. Shut them down. We're not trying to stop genuine asylum seekers but we have to take organised crime out of smuggling and trafficking.'

'You still haven't answered why or how the FSB were following Daisy and me?'

'Sorry, can't answer that.'

'Can't or won't?'

'Bit of both.' Bill was cagey.

Rob Andrews re-entered the meeting room without knocking. The meeting came to an abrupt stop.

'That'll do for today. Thanks Danny. Rob will take you back down. Remember to collect your phone.'

SUNDAY

SUNDAY WAS A FRUSTRATING DAY FOR EVERYONE.
Martha and Vikki were locked in their room with
no obvious sign of release. Martha tried to break it as
gently as possible to Vikki about their predicament – not
surprisingly she hadn't taken it well, especially the removal
of her mobile phone and no access to social media. Or no
bottle of wine with their Sunday lunch of roast lamb and
all the trimmings. Martha had spent two hours solidly
working out in her personally appointed gym while Vikki
made the most of the Sunday papers, especially *The Sunday
Tribune* – she was rather pleased with her pictures on the
front page with the massive headline in 196-point block
capitals, 'MARTHA'S RETURN'. Allegedly Kelvin Edwards
had been given 'exclusive' access to the rehearsals and had

even quoted Martha from his 'exclusive' interview. Martha herself was impressed with his ability to 'exclusively' mind-read. Vikki couldn't wait to show her mates her pictures, then had a panic attack thinking they would never be released alive. Martha's stoicism calmed her a little. The day continued in endless circuitous reflection, worry, blame, anger, tears and frustration – mainly from Vikki.

Daisy and Danny had spent Saturday evening together at the Donmar Warehouse. Danny had to review the first night of yet another revival of *Measure for Measure*. He was struck by the play's central themes – its hypocrisy and the answer to the life-long question who sins most, the seducer or the seduced? By the time Danny had finished post-performance interviews and they had both quaffed as much free champagne and small plates as was politely possible, they had returned to Danny's flat and quickly fallen asleep. The following morning after a restorative Sunday brunch at Danny's favourite, HOB on Balham High Road, they returned to the flat for an afternoon of recreational activities. He had made no mention of the FSB or Bill's leak. Both were slightly on-edge waiting to hear if Martha and Vikki had been released – there was a fair amount of post-coital introspection. After an hour or two they were distracted again. Later Danny had looked out the window; there was the inevitable Audi A4, this time with a man and a woman sitting inside, both looked bored yet alert. He wondered what they would do when he left his house at five tomorrow morning, leaving Daisy peacefully asleep?

Yuliet spent the day at work investigating the Vory, Conor O'Murchadha, Baka and Nowak. The deeper she dug, the more appalled she had become, but certain here was a great story waiting to be told. She had a couple of replies from her sources about Baka – the consensus was to stay away from him. No new information, but independent corroboration of some of the facts she already knew from the files. The reports of Baka's house in the Wye Valley intrigued Yuliet and she made a note to follow this up. Baka was a pussycat compared to O'Murchadha. Here was a malevolent organised crime mega-boss on a European if not global scale. She wasn't sure if either Baka or O'Murchadha was a psychopath or a sociopath. They both seemed to break the laws and make impulsive decisions without feeling guilt for anyone else. She felt sorry in some ways for the naïve Nowak. Yuliet decided that Nowak was a moderately successful UK gangland boss not really respected by his peers, but good enough to be left alone. All three could be both charming and charismatic when required. She sent out a confidential enquiry to her sources about O'Murchadha and the Vory.

Bill Kelly was going through files trying to find a connection to the internal leaks. It was difficult; he was now certain that one of his long-term supposedly trusted colleagues was going to be exposed. He hated the thought that he had been let down by someone close. He didn't leave the Yard all day – he nipped down for a sandwich and a nice cup of tea for lunch in the canteen. He sat on his own, no one joined him as they could see he was in a filthy mood. He was sure that dogged good-old-fashioned police work would uncover a small mistake and lead him to his bastard. He also laid a couple of traps. But it was

Danny's original Blue Badge article and accompanying pictures that made him sit up and take notice, if only he could put his finger on it. Tomorrow, Monday, he would talk to his Secret Intelligence Service liaison contact about the files Yuliet had received.

Nowak sat at a computer terminal for the rest of Saturday logged into his email account. Nothing had arrived from Baka's solicitor, which worried him. Baka's phone wasn't responding either. Nowak did respond to quite a few emails that had been festering for a week about his other business enterprises. By the time it was dark his inbox was almost empty – he felt surprisingly good about it. He had already given his driver the rest of the weekend off and Saturday night he had booked himself into the Ibis hotel across the road from the studios. He knew he was being followed but couldn't stand the thought of being listened to in his own home – his nerves were jangling. Sunday morning, he ate what the hotel called a hearty full English breakfast. No black pudding, which annoyed him. He read the celebrity pages of *The Sunday Tribune* – with 'Martha' on the main front cover. *Well done Daisy*, he thought, *that's another three million who know about the tour.* He did wonder how Kelvin Edwards had the audacity to say he had interviewed Martha – don't let the truth get in the way of a good story. He returned at eleven to the production offices with the rest of the Sunday papers and waited for the email, which never came. Still no contact from Baka. Late afternoon he went back to his hotel room across the road having made telephone arrangements for a visit from two professional ladies – he hoped it would relieve his stress. The anxiety had got to him for the first time in his life, leaving him frustrated, the professional ladies quite relieved, but claiming they 'understood', and his watchers giggling like schoolchildren. They had bugged his hotel room when they discovered he was staying for at least a second night.

Baka had been bored senseless on the trains from Cherbourg to Barcelona via Paris. The crossing from Dittisham had gone well, a stiff breeze and relatively calm seas meant he had a good night's sleep, despite not being a natural sailor. No one bothered him as he left the yacht and took a taxi to Cherbourg's train station. After four hours on the first train, temporary relief came in Paris where he had to change stations by taxi from St-Lazare to Gare de Lyon. He paid cash for his next first-class ticket to Barcelona, reserving a single seat upstairs in the carriage next to the bar. He then went for an old-school lunch in the ridiculously ornate, palatial surroundings of Le Train Bleu on Gare de Lyon station – *Volaille de Bresse à la crème d'estragon frais* with *riz basmati grillé* washed down with a couple of large glasses of *Crozes-Hermitage*. He didn't have as much time to luxuriate as he would have wished, declining dessert and coffee. With minutes to spare he boarded the TGV, took his seat and dozed. Early that evening he arrived in Barcelona Sants Estació a little bit pissed from several more glasses of wine and a couple of brandies from the bar on the train. He wobbled up the escalators to the hotel, which he had booked in the name of one of his aliases – he paid in cash at the absurd spaceship-inspired reception desk. He went up to his room, ordered a burger from room service and within an hour was sound asleep. His had switched off his phone. It was Sunday, the day of rest despite his discarded religion.

MONDAY

AT FOUR-THIRTY IN THE MORNING DANNY'S iPhone yet again sang 'Another Day of Sunshine' from *La La Land* – Daisy tucked her head under her pillow and wrapped the duvet around her.

'What time is it? It's still dark,' came the muffled voice.

'Four-thirty.'

'Oh, for fuck's sake. And you've ruined *La La Land* for me.' More muffled voice, followed by duvet pulling.

Danny leapt straight into the shower. He shut the bathroom door before switching on the lights. Daisy was already back gently snoring. He really didn't know how much longer he could continue this pre-dawn malarkey – his body and brain attacking him relentlessly, and that ignored the feelings of any companions who didn't seem to last long under the assault of the pre-dawn alarm either.

He arrived in Starshine's Leicester Square studios as usual at ten to six. He did not notice that he had been followed by two new watchers even in the relative quiet of 'that time of the morning'. He was reassured that the Audi had remained outside his home when he left for the Tube station – at least Daisy would be reasonably protected, he thought.

As usual there were the normal DJ Gordon Monday-morning mood reports. As usual on a Monday morning he was in a foul mood. As usual they were professionally on-air at six-thirty all bright and shiny. Unusually the talk was of Martha and the pictures in yesterday's *Sunday Tribune* and online everywhere.

Gordon was joyously animated that 'his' celebrity and music reporter had been at Elstree to witness the first full rehearsals of the Martha Movin' Out tour – anyone would think that Gordon had personally sent Danny to deliver an exclusive radio report. Kelvin had reluctantly quoted Danny in his Sunday special report cross-linking Starshine at his editor's 'request' – the group owned both the paper and a string of radio stations, which included Starshine. Danny, as ever the professional, did not disabuse the listeners. Enthusiastically he told Londoners how wonderful the show was going to be, and how glorious the wardrobe was. He did not lie. Well, maybe a little.

'The set, stage and sound is awesome… Martha's opening wardrobe will be the centre of attention as the golden beams reflect around the auditorium… Her vocals were better than ever… There will be a mix of new and old familiar songs that the audience will want... It's going to be amazing... Tickets are selling fast with more dates being released almost every day... And you can win four tickets by going to the Starshine webpage and clicking on the Martha Returns page...'

There were some advantages of having a girlfriend in Martha's PR department.

Girlfriend? thought Danny. *Where did that come from?* He rather liked the idea. Delete that – he really liked that idea. She could be 'the one'. Introspection of his love life was interrupted off-air by Gordon schmoozing Danny. 'Can we go up together to Elstree after the show one morning this week and meet Martha please? Always loved her work.'

Danny was non-committal. 'Let me have a word with Daisy, the tour's PR, when I see her next. I'll see what I can do.'

Danny didn't admit to how often he had been at rehearsals or how well he knew Daisy, in every sense. If the truth were known, he had let his contribution to the morning show slide a little, but he did have a backlog of stories that would fill. But this couldn't go on for long.

At nine-thirty the show finished with jovial banter between Danny and Gordon pushing the competition for tickets to see Martha. Danny didn't hang around long.

He left the studios and found a quiet-ish spot to call Daisy, down Orange Street, a side street off Leicester Square. The phone rang five times before Daisy answered it.

'Good morning, you left early?'

'Did I wake you?'

'A bit, but I went back. I don't know how you do it.'

'A day in the life of a breakfast broadcaster.'

She laughed. 'I've just had a shower. Going up to Elstree for eleven via my house for some fresh clothes. I didn't listen to you – you were off-air by the time I came around.'

'That's one less listener. The ratings will go to pot.' Laughter. Danny then became serious. 'Have you spoken to Nowak?'

'I tried his number. No reply – left a message. I assume if Martha had returned, he would have emailed me.'

'Let me know if you hear anything. I have a few things to do. Hopefully I'll come up for mid-afternoon.'

'I may not be there. Have meetings. Let's work out what we do later.' Daisy paused. 'Can I stay tonight please?'

Danny wasn't expecting the question. 'Yes, of course.' There was a pause while he considered his feelings. 'I'd really like that. Can you stand being disturbed at four-thirty again?'

'I'll manage. Don't promise to be polite though.'

'Humph!'

A pause.

'Would you mind if I brought over some things to keep at yours – if this is going to be a regular event?'

He hesitated; he hoped this wasn't going too fast. 'That would be lovely.'

The conversation didn't go further. The phone was knocked out of Danny's hand – he turned to shout at the bloody idiot who had bumped into him. He felt a cloth close over his mouth and nose, he tried not to breathe in the sweet-smelling scent. He feinted backwards and with all his strength elbowed the person who was attacking him. It was pointless, like hitting a brick wall. He began to feel dizzy and nauseous. He wasn't unconscious, but not focused either – he was vaguely aware of a scuffle around him and a shout of, 'Armed police, stand still.'

As his head cleared, he realised he was staring into the face of Dom. Dick was on the phone.

'Are you okay?'

'I think so. What happened?'

'You were attacked by a couple of thugs, lucky we weren't far behind.'

Danny noticed that Dom was developing a prize-winning black eye and his hands were grazed.

'Are you okay?' asked Danny. As is often the case the attacked are as concerned about their helpers as themselves.

'Don't worry about me. All in a day's work – a couple of obvious bruises always good for team morale.' Dom grinned, it reminded him of his club rugby days in Rickmansworth. He became serious. 'Had a bit of a to-do, hence the shiner. What about you? They got away sorry to say but Dick is on the phone giving descriptions, also getting Bill's team and the control room onto the CCTV. We should be able to follow them with any luck.'

Dick disconnected and came over to check on Dom and Danny. 'You're looking a bit better.'

'No real damage apart from my phone.' Danny was now standing. 'What was it they put on the cloth? Stinking headache.'

'Some sort of sedative – might even have been good old-fashioned chloroform?' suggested Dom. 'It takes four or five minutes to knock you out, but a few sniffs will sedate you enough to make you easier to overcome, make you feel drunk, leaving you with a hangover too.'

'Certainly does.' Danny rubbed his forehead.

'The control room tell me they have a good frontal pictures of them both that they are putting through the automated facial recognition system.' Dick was optimistic. 'Hopefully they will be on our watch list. We're following them on CCTV too – they are on the Piccadilly Line westbound from Leicester Square. We can't see them on the trains but facial recognition should be able to pick them up when they exit at a station.'

'Any idea who they were?'

'Not really,' Dick lied. 'Professionals probably. I pulled my gun and shouted "armed police" – they just coolly carried on running, taking cover in the crowds. They knew I couldn't get a shot off. Scared a few tourists though.'

Dick was making light of the enormous amount of paperwork he now had to complete. Drawing a weapon in public had to be recorded and investigated.

'I chased them, bloody tripped on the kerb,' Dom held up his hands, 'and that was the end of that.'

'They cannot have been on their own – they must have had a vehicle very nearby. They would have planned to put you in there and get away and no one would have been any the wiser. You would have simply disappeared. That's why they got rid of your phone – you could have been tracked.'

'We are looking at the CCTV in the area to see if we can find any suspicious vehicles waiting.'

'Thanks guys.' Danny was feeling a bit better, nothing that a load of water, paracetamol, strong coffee and breakfast wouldn't sort. 'I was on my way to Francisco's. Least I could do is to buy you breakfast? You can take my statement there.'

'We're not allowed to accept gifts. But on this occasion, it'd be rude not to.' Dick and Dom nodded in agreement. 'Our job is to keep an eye on you, so doesn't look as if we have a choice. We'll have to file a report.'

Danny found the remains of his phone a few metres away, smashed in the melee and then run over by a taxi. He rescued, he hoped, the SIM. He would try and trade in the wreck when he visited the Apple Store in Covent Garden after a proper brekky.

The sudden disappearance of Danny's iPhone had alerted Bill's team – only destruction of the phone or removing the battery would shut down the tracking app.

Ten minutes later Francisco welcomed Danny with his normal effusiveness, full English breakfasts with all the options including black pudding were ordered for them all, together with three cappuccinos, fresh orange juices and lots of water for Danny. No Mediterranean diet this time. They sat in the far corner away from the door, so they could see everyone arriving and departing. The two banquettes either side of the table had room for six – Dick and Dom sat one side and Danny the other.

'You've all had a busy morning?' Bill Kelly accompanied by Rob Andrews squeezed in next to Danny. 'I heard it called in. I guessed where you would be going next.'

No mention of the now useless iPhone apps.

'You two will be paying for your own meals I assume?' Bill was feeling mischievous.

As were Dick and Dom. 'We assumed you'd come here to pay for us all?'

'Get outta here!' Bill got down to business. 'Right, any ideas?'

They sipped their coffees personally delivered by Francisco – this morning leaving them alone. He knew when customers wanted their space.

Danny was first to speak. 'Someone must think I know something. The question is who? And, I suppose, what?'

'The question is – do you?' asked Dom.

Normally Dick and Dom weren't involved in discussions about the finer detail of on-going investigations, their job was to follow and protect. Do as they were told. But this time Bill was happy to discuss everything, well, some things with them. They were clean – no chance of being tainted by the past or leaking, not that Bill was going to admit this.

'You are not exactly keeping a low profile. I listened to you on the radio this morning talking about Martha. That Gordon chap is a bit thick, isn't he?' asked Bill.

'I'll introduce you.'

'Thanks, but no thanks.'

Dom was inquisitive. 'Who were the two you picked up – following Daisy and Danny?'

'This must remain absolutely secret. No mention outside of here – you don't even speak about it, including you, Rob, to any of the team.' Bill looked serious. Danny, Rob, Dick and Dom nodded their assent.

'Russians. Undeclared FSB. They've been sent home. But nothing to say they haven't been replaced.'

'Bloody hell – didn't realise we were playing with the big boys,' exhaled Dom.

'Not that big, or we wouldn't have caught them. They didn't spot you two. We know that Baka has Martha.'

'But why the Russian involvement?' Dom was a little worried.

'Perhaps they thought Danny is closely involved with Nowak? Or thinking Danny knows what is going on?' Rob asked.

'That's daft. I wouldn't do anything with that shit,' Danny complained.

'You know that, and we know that, but not everyone is in the loop,' suggested Rob.

'We know Baka is directly or indirectly associated with the Vory – and also Conor O'Murchadha? So, we must assume that Nowak is connected as well. This is getting more serious by the day. Conor O'Murchadha has a reputation for offing anyone that crosses him.' Bill's blood pressure was ramping up.

'Have you forgotten about Martha?' Danny was getting frustrated. 'According to Daisy she still hasn't showed up. Nowak did the deal with Baka – we thought we'd see Martha on Saturday. Still nothing. Where is she?'

'I suppose she's safe wherever she is – she is collateral. Without Martha no one gets their money back and everything will come falling like a pack of cards.'

'We have no idea how she is, she's been held for well over a week. No idea what conditions. Whether or not she'll be fit to perform – physically or mentally.'

'It's in Baka's interest to keep her fit and well too.'

'But does that apply to Vikki?'

'Martha has already lost two brothers and two sisters – if Vikki dies or isn't released, she won't be in any fit state to perform – and everyone loses.'

'But they could be anywhere. Where's Baka?'

'His phone popped up at eight this morning in Madrid, nine their time. We're trying to get the Spanish police via Interpol to triangulate his position. Their mobile phone networks are very good – better than the UK. If he is in Madrid, with the number of masts in the city, we should know where he is to within about a hundred metres, maybe closer.'

'But we can't just arrest him. We have no proof so it's going to be difficult. He's a slippery sod.'

'We don't want to arrest him. We want to know what he is up to, tail him.'

'Spanish already on it.' Bill's phone had just vibrated to indicate an email had arrived. 'We'd stick out like a sore thumb in Spain.'

'How did he get from London to Madrid? I thought we had an all-ports warning on him – and he hasn't shown up anywhere?'

'Get on to UK Border Force.'

'The problem is that exit checks are still a bit haphazard. And for the right bung it's pretty easy for someone to stay under the radar.'

'Baka is at the heart of all this – find Baka and we find Martha and probably Vikki.'

Rob looked at the wreckage of Danny's phone. 'What happened to that?'

'Run over in the disagreement. Going to get a new one after breakfast.'

Five breakfasts arrived. The conversation ceased whilst they all concentrated on their first-class breakfast – with black pudding and doorsteps of thick white toast, preloaded with dollops of butter accompanied by thick-cut marmalade with added whisky.

Danny's headache slowly disappeared. *But how safe is Daisy?*

31
BAKA–SPAIN

BAKA'S SOLICITOR HAD BEEN TRYING TO CONTACT him all weekend. She wasn't prepared to send the revised contract to Nowak without her client's signature together with a formal email instructing her to proceed – no matter what he had said on the telephone. There was simply too much money involved and she didn't trust either Baka or Nowak – it was also her job to act in the best interests of her client.

Baka switched on his phone and iPad at nine Monday morning while he was still lying in bed trying to avoid the spaceship and intergalactic decorations. He logged onto the hotel's WiFi. As expected, he faced a barrage of messages and emails. While everything poured in, he got up, went to the bathroom and then made a coffee with several sugars.

He sat at the desk in the lounge of his suite at the Barceló Barcelona Sants Estació Hotel and opened his iPad. From the massive picture windows, he could see the magnificent, Disneyesque Temple Expiatori del Sagrat Cor, The Church of the Sacred Heart perched at the top of Tibidabo, the mountain to the north overlooking the city. The sun was well up, the reflections glistening across the azure sea. Normally Baka would have found the view calming and peaceful.

He had seventeen emails waiting and five WhatsApp messages.

The email from his solicitor annoyed him. His reply was terse. *'I told you to send the contract. Bloody send it to Nowak now.'*

A few minutes later his solicitor replied. *'Please print the contract, sign, scan and return. Cannot send until signed.'*

Baka swore out loud. 'What the fuck do I pay these half-wits for?'

No point in arguing he thought, he found it difficult to retain solicitors that were prepared to work for him for more than a few months – a combination of his temper and what they were asked to do conspired against a lengthy relationship.

Baka levered himself up from the desk, stripped off the hotel's monogrammed dressing gown and showered – five minutes of hot and a minute of as cold as he could stand. Twenty minutes later he was in the hotel's business centre next to the coffee shop on the ground floor. He parted with twenty-six euros for a printout of the contract;

he initialled each page, signed on the dotted line getting the business centre manager to witness his signature. He then paid a further twenty for the contract to be scanned and sent to his personal email address so he could forward back again. *Forty-six bloody euros for what?* thought Baka – he paid in cash and didn't leave a tip.

Everything was watched by a man and woman drinking coffee. Couples hanging around in hotel lobbies apparently attract less attention.

Baka returned to his room. He sent the signed contract now on his iPad to his solicitor. The email accompanying the attachment was to the point: *'To be forwarded to Nowak immediately.'*

The two Spanish police left their coffee and crossed over to the business centre, closed the door and pulled the blinds. They showed the business centre manager their IDs.

'¿Quién era ese hombre?' asked the policewoman.

'Señor Adam Megat desde la habitación 706,' replied the worried business centre manager. She didn't want to be difficult due to the personal stash in her desk drawer.

'Necesitamos ver una copia del correo electrónico.'

The manager hit print without argument. A few seconds later the Spanish police had a hard copy of what they needed.

'Por favor reenvíe a esta dirección de correo electrónico.' The policeman gave the contract a quick once-over – he understood most of it. The names Nowak and Baka confirming what he needed to know. He gave the office manager his email address and told her to forward everything.

The contract had been signed by Ali Baka, not Adam Megat, the name Baka had used to register at the hotel. Now they had proof that Baka was using a false name. They had one of Baka's email addresses. They had physical proof of a business relationship between Baka and Nowak. That was a good morning's work. The information was sent to Interpol who forwarded it to Bill Kelly.

The two Spanish police returned to their now cold coffee – the cups hadn't been cleared away. They ordered two fresh ones from a passing waiter, who was trying to avoid their attention. The white circular monstrosity where they sat in the reception café area gave an unobstructed view of everyone coming and going. The alleged space-age lighting above them looked anything but space-age. The coffee arriving distracted them; they almost missed Baka as he took the elevator down to the train station immediately below the hotel – more unfinished coffee. They followed, watched him buy a ticket, cash. A moment later they showed their warrant cards to the ticket office assistant, who immediately gave then the information they needed – Baka had bought a first-class ticket to Madrid.

Baka's plan was to catch the lunchtime train from Barcelona, change at Madrid Atocha onto the Málaga train, arriving early evening. It was circuitous route, but the only sensible option travelling by train. He hoped the several changes would make him less easily followed. The plan was to stay in Málaga for a couple of nights – he had meetings with some of his business associates Tuesday during the day.

The meeting with Conor O'Murchadha at Róisín O'Mulligan's in La Cala de Mijas wasn't until Tuesday evening. The taxi would take about forty minutes each way. He had plenty of time. It had all fitted together rather well, he thought.

He had booked a deluxe suite at the Barceló Málaga attached to the high-speed AVE train station. He had stayed there in the past and was rather looking forward to it – he checked the name he had used then, in case he was recognised. Silly mistakes like not using the correct *nom de guerre* had nearly caused his downfall in previous times. He remembered that the rooftop bar and swimming pool had fantastic views across the city and to the sparkling Mediterranean. He also remembered the avant-garde steel slide from the first floor. He had never seen anyone but children use it despite the bullshit name – Sliding Structure for Daring Humans.

He was rather looking forward to Wednesday, when he planned to bus to Algeciras and from there by ferry to Tangier, where he knew passport and identity checks could be circumvented at both ends as easily as at Dittisham and Le Port du Becquet. Once in Tangier he had pre-booked his normal driver to take him to Bni Wassine, the summer retreat a few kilometres to the south. He had arranged to meet his North African team of monasseks to discuss current and forthcoming travel arrangements. At least one of them was going to feel Baka's wrath – ten lashes should concentrate his wandering mind and *pour encourager les autres*.

Today's journey went well for everyone. Baka changed trains in Madrid and arrived at his hotel in Málaga on time. His two followers were not spotted, and they looked forward to the overtime payments at the end of the month.

Neither Baka nor his followers spotted the team of four who were also watching every move.

32

MONDAY – UK

By the time Baka's solicitor had received, processed and forwarded the signed contract to Nowak it was mid-afternoon. Nowak initialled each page and signed at the bottom having carefully read through the eleven pages – he wasn't going to be caught out a second time, no matter how quickly he wanted Martha back. Everything was as agreed. He persuaded a passing techie to witness his signature without letting her see the contents of the contract.

Two hours later the re-scanned contract was returned to Baka's solicitor. Nowak received an out-of-office message by return – his frustration mounted.

Rehearsals without their star were equally frustrating, despite everything going smoothly. The crew and band were pretty much going through the motions, but without Martha was it all academic?

Bill Kelly was inspired with the evidence just received from the Spanish police via Interpol. At last everything was beginning to come together. He received authorisation to intercept Baka's email account – he forwarded the details to GCHQ.

The conversation with his SIS liaison officer was exasperating. Nobody was available with any information but there was a promise to 'get back to you as soon as possible'. *Fucking spooks.* Bill was not a fan.

He returned to looking for his mole. Something had been bugging him about Danny's Blue Badge piece; he took it out of the file. Separately he took out the photographs – and there it was. He couldn't see the whole man, but he could see the very recognisable tie worn by the person just behind Stanislaw Nowak. It could be anyone, of course, but he knew of only one person on his team who wore the 5th Inniskilling Dragoon Guards striped tie.

Yuliet had been researching Baka, Nowak, Conor and the Vory with the help of her associates and Google. She had sent Chris Robinson, a stringer from south-east Wales, to have a look at Baka's mansion in the Wye Valley. Mid-morning, she had a phone call.

'Doesn't seem like there is a lot of activity. But it seems heavily protected for what it is.'

'Any chance you can observe for a while?'

'Shouldn't be an issue – problems here with wild boar. I have a license, it's as good a cover as any if I am challenged. There are a couple of hides I could use in sight of the house. Don't have night vision equipment – so can only usefully observe during daylight – but I have my camera and twelve-hundred millimetre lens.'

'That would be great, thanks. NUJ fee plus twenty-five per cent okay?' offered Yuliet.

'That'll do, *diolch yn fawr cariad* – I retain rights to the photographs?'

'Seems fair,' agreed Yuliet.

'I'll report back if or when I have news.'

33
TUESDAY

AFTER A VERY LEISURELY BREAKFAST BAKA HAD met with a couple of his associates in the cafés hidden in backstreets of Málaga. Nothing of importance was discussed but he had found that the occasional, apparently social meetings kept everyone's minds focused. He thought of himself as the admiral in charge of a fleet of ships – a suggestion here, a nod there, occasional praise, more often a stern word. Nothing definitive, more a hint, a slight touch on the rudder – unless someone was out of line, then disciplinary action would be taken. The punishment was set according to the misdeed, anything from a simple beating to a finger or toe being amputated by a bolt cutter without the benefit of anaesthetic. His team rarely strayed, especially if they were forced to bear witness. He issued detailed instructions to be passed to his monasseks.

Baka had tried to contact his lawyer several times to check if Nowak had signed the contract. Her assistant said she was out, and could she take a message? She said she couldn't do anything without the permission of her boss. Baka tried to phone his solicitor directly – it went to voicemail. The email he sent auto-responded with an out-of-office message – back first thing Wednesday morning. Once the contract was sent, time for a new lawyer, thought Baka, and this one wasn't going to get paid.

He called Nowak.

'Stan, my old friend. How are you?'

'Where's Martha?'

'You're beginning to sound like a stuck record. You're old enough to remember records, aren't you?'

'Where's Martha? I've signed the contract and returned it. You said she would be released immediately.'

'These things take time – the law works slowly.'

'Then I've got nothing to say to you.'

'Now don't be like that. We're friends, aren't we? This is just a bit of local difficulty – all will be well in a day or two.'

'It better be, or you'll regret it.'

'Don't be silly, Stan,' Baka was at his contemptuous best. 'Please email me your detailed tour schedule. I need it for a meeting tonight – we need to make the arrangements for the smooth transit of our guests.'

'You'll get the tour schedule when I have Martha back – and her sister.'

Nowak disconnected, leaving Baka in a terrible rage. Baka tried to call Nowak a few more times – not answering. Baka emailed Nowak. *'I need the tour schedule by 6pm tonight.'*

Nowak answered. *'Then I need Martha and her sister back by 6pm tonight.'*

Baka was getting increasingly nervous about the meeting set for nine, eight UK time, with Conor O'Murchadha at Róisín O'Mulligan's. The problem with Conor was his erratic mood swings and terrible temper. Baka had promised that everything was ready to go – Conor liked detail, everything crossed and dotted.

Baka had booked a taxi through the hotel's concierge to arrive at seven forty-five, take him to Cala de Mijas, wait and then return him after the meeting. Baka didn't want to rely on a local taxi to bring him back.

Dead on time, the pale-yellow Mercedes arrived. The driver didn't want to make conversation – he was more interested in the phone he had permanently pressed to his ear. Baka wasn't sure of the language – Albanian maybe? The driving was one-handed and erratic as they careered at well over the speed limit along the coastal motorway.

The Spanish police following didn't have trouble keeping up, but made notes to review the taxi driver's licence at some time in the future.

Róisín O'Mulligan's was a typical pseudo-Irish pub sat in a row of other restaurants, cafés and bars designed to attract a certain sort of tourist looking for a good time. Garish menus with photographs of the meals they allegedly served were posted outside, well made-up ladies with exposed décolletages and men with tight black trousers and unbuttoned shirts revealing hairy chests touted their establishments' wares. Music throbbed from every door – the cacophony was ear-challenging. The neon signs, LED screens and bright lights made the sky appear darker, the light pollution ensuring the glorious stars in the night sky remained unseen.

Baka entered Róisín O'Mulligan's – The Chieftains' music played, the animated chatter struggling to overcome the music. It was a pastiche of everything he hated about 'traditional' Irish pubs – rows and rows of bottles of Irish whiskey, beer pumps covered with condensation, dark wood panelling, football scarves, faux stained-glass windows, several TVs showing sports that no one was watching and beer-bellied boozers leaning on the bar or tall poseur tables raucously talking bollocks over pints of 'the black stuff'.

One of the bar staff in sexed-up 'traditional' dress exhausted her entire Irish vocabulary, '*Fáilte*, what'll you be having?'

'Conor O'Murchadha.' Baka said no more – he was tense.

Her smile faded and without a word, tilted her head towards the rear room. Baka threaded through the drinkers towards the back – he noticed a couple of Conor's lookouts following him. Baka, no stranger to street fighting, felt reassuringly for the knife in his belt – be prepared. Without knocking he opened the door into the back room. The beams from the low-hanging lights over each table highlighted the acrid blue haze of cigarettes and cigars. The walls and ceiling were discoloured from too many nicotine-infused evenings. Two men in the far corner were chalking their cues beside a pool table that had seen better days. Conversation ceased as Baka entered and the drinkers turned to stare at him.

'Ali, my friend, there you are. What'll you be having?' Conor's soft Irish accent was all bonhomie – the sign for everyone to resume conversation. The loud crack of the cue ball breaking the rack made Baka jump, followed reassuringly by the patter of balls distributing themselves around the table.

Conor O'Murchadha looked like many ex-pats in this part of the world – overweight, puffy, rheumy eyes; and long, combed-back grey hair balding on top. His skin was brown leather. He wore the de rigueur fuller cut Under Armour polo shirt with mock collar in Irish green. The shirt was tucked into Royal & Awesome Plaid-a-Blinder golf trousers, allegedly great for golfers looking to add some fun and colour to their round and the drinks at the ninteenth hole. The over-tightened Hugo embossed leather belt bought at the local Sunday market helped maintain the trousers at slightly half-mast, semi-holding back his flopping gut. The heavy gold chain around his neck matched the massive Rolex watch on his wrist. No one had the courage to tell him that it was less than a picture of sartorial elegance.

'Jameson's. Large. No ice.'

They shook hands – Conor smiled. He pointed at a seat at his round table in the corner. Baka looked around, assessing escape routes should they be needed. Conor waved away his associates to another table. It was to be just the two of them.

Conor, taking elaborate care, relit his half-smoked Romeo Y Julieta Wide Churchill Gran Reserva cigar. He threw the expired match into the ashtray and blew a blue smoke ring into the air over Baka's head. Conversation was hesitant.

'Did you have a good journey?'

'Long one. Came down by train from near Cherbourg.'

'Cherbourg?'

'Got a lift over on a yacht from Devon. Didn't trouble border controls.'

They both laughed. Conor took a long draw of his cigar, savoured the buzz and exhaled.

'No one knows you are here then?'

The whiskey arrived. They clinked glasses.

'¡Salud!'

'Sláinte.'

How could such an innocent question sound so threatening, thought Baka? He was becoming tenser – a bead of perspiration started to run down his back. It wasn't that hot.

'Four trains – all paid for with cash. Two hotels using two different passports. Trains and buses are still the only transport that don't require ID. Can't do more?'

'Have you met anyone else?'

'Had a few meetings today with my associates in Málaga – sorting out a few things. All trusted. No one knows we are meeting if that's what you are asking?'

'And Nowak? How is he?'

'Nowak is behaving. I'll return Martha tomorrow when I have his signed contract. He has agreed to the extra travellers – the transport is not far off ready. Sign-written with steel reinforced cut-outs to confuse the scanners at the ports. First consignment after Casablanca. Then Istanbul. The exact schedule will be up on the Martha website in a day or two – these luvvie tours seem to be flexible.'

'My money safe?'

'Fourteen months is the agreed time-scale, plus five per cent interest. More than you'd get in the bank.'

They both laughed.

'You're certain you weren't followed?'

'Nah! Would have noticed.' Baka began to relax.

Conor nodded to one of his associates. Baka was as certain as he could be that no one knew he was here. The taxi had dropped him off 400 metres away. The door flew open and the woman, struggling to free herself from the grips of two of Conor's men, was pushed onto the floor.

'Then who is this?'

Baka was temporarily tongue-tied. 'No idea.'

The woman's arms were forced painfully behind her back and cable tied. Same with her feet – a rope was passed between the two, hog-tying her. One of the heavies searched her clothes and pulled out a Spanish police ID card. He handed it to Conor.

'Ali, let me introduce you to…' he looked at the police ID, '… ah yes, Valentina. Valentina meet Ali Baka. She has been following you all day.'

Outside, every word could be heard by the *Grupo Especial de Operaciones* team – the GEO – concealed in the filthy, apparently abandoned van parked just around the corner. The room had been bugged several days ago when it was discovered that Conor O'Murchadha used it as his informal meeting place and temporary office.

'No one has been following me – I am certain I would have seen them,' Baka insisted. 'I'm not a bloody amateur.'

'Ali, my friend, you are wrong – and now you have led the police to me.'

Valentina had *cojones*. She spoke in heavily accented English. 'We know what you are up to – people smuggling. It's over. We're shutting you down.'

Without knowing it, Valentina had absolutely condemned Baka. Now there was no doubt about Baka's involvement.

The room was silent, apart from Conor's throaty laughter. 'We have done nothing wrong. This scum bag, Ali Baka, has been trying to persuade me to use Martha's tour to traffic people – I wouldn't want to get involved in such despicable behaviour.'

More laughter.

Baka was beginning to feel uncomfortably dizzy – Conor's face was a picture of malicious joy. Gamma-hydroxybutyric acid, GHB, causes amnesia, impairs movement and speech. It can be added to drinks with no trace or taste apart from a little saltiness, missed by most people. Its effect can be felt in as little as five minutes, especially at the dose that Baka had been given. He was now feeling light-headed and nauseous.

'Youf shirt. Wasst you've giffen meeee?' Baka then remembered nothing more.

Conor decided it was time to leave. He looked at the two who had dragged Valentina into the room. 'Wait five minutes after we have left, then take her away. Kill her. Not here. Check you are not seen leaving – she can have an accident.'

Two of Conor's other associates grabbed the comatose Baka under the arms and dragged him out of the back door of the bar to Conor's parked car. Once outside in the dark back alley his pockets were searched – wallet, keys, the knife, phone, everything removed and handed to Conor. The key to Baka's hotel in Málaga, in its wallet with room number conveniently scrawled inside, was handed to one of the heavies.

'Go there now, hurry before the police arrive. Clear out his room – make it seem he checked out. Pay his outstanding bill in cash. Use the room number only, he is staying there under another name.' Conor's associate disappeared into the night.

Baka's hands and feet were cable-tied, and he was unceremoniously dumped into the capacious boot of the black Mercedes S-Class.

Conor O'Murchadha was gloomy – he wouldn't be able to use Róisín O'Mulligan's again. *Oh well*, he thought, *onward and upward.*

Cock-up or conspiracy – no one saw them leave.

The three Spanish policemen following Baka stayed seated at the outside tables. They had watched Valentina as she went inside the bar – no one would suspect a single woman, they thought. After five minutes or so they began to feel anxious, they had no idea what Baka was doing in there. They assumed meeting someone, but who? She should be out by now.

They also had no knowledge of the *Grupo Especial de Operaciones* team, the GEO, watching Conor O'Murchadha.

Peace was broken by aggressive shouting designed to shock everyone into temporary submission. *'Policia armada. Bajar. Quédate abajo'* – armed police, get down, stay down. There were screams. Some ducked, some stood up. People react differently when scared. Six special forces GEO with their faces covered by balaclavas stormed the bar – Heckler & Koch HK G36 assault rifles to their shoulders, the red targeting lasers dancing in the smoke. They crashed through the front bar, knocking over tables and drinks. They barged down the unlocked door to the back room. It was all over in ten seconds, probably less; no one was timing it. Conor's remaining associates realised that it was pointless to resist such force. They put their hands up.

'¿Estás bien?' One of the team cut the cable ties to free Valentina's hands and feet. She rubbed her wrists – the circulation was painfully beginning to return. *'Estaré bien. ¿Quién te llamó tan rápido?'*

Valentina was confused; how did the GEO get here so quickly? Her three erstwhile colleagues rushed through the bar, IDs held high. *'Gracias chicos. Estaré aquí para ti también.'*

'¿Dónde está Conor?'

'Quitado.'

Conor had gone.

Half an hour later, unaware of what was happening in the bar, Conor's driver stopped the car in the deserted forests above the town. It was pitch black. Conor ordered the driver to drag the unconscious Baka out of the boot and prop him against a tree. He threw him a shovel and told him to dig – the soil was soft and it was relatively easy to prepare a makeshift grave.

'You can go now. Take the torch – walk that way.' Conor pointed. 'It's six kilometres to the bus stop downhill. You'll be there in an hour and a half. Call me tomorrow.'

Conor lit a new cigar and waited – just him and the trussed Baka. He was a patient man and he luxuriated over the opportunity to finish the cigar without being interrupted. Two hours later Baka started to show signs of coming around.

'Welcome back, my friend.'

Baka struggled to break free of his bonds. After a minute or two he gave up, realising it was futile.

'What did you give me, you shit?' Baka's speech was still slurred.

'GHB – gamma-hydroxybutyric acid.' Conor was at his malevolent best. 'Created by Alexander Zaytsev in 1874. Dr Henri Laborit used GHB to drop people's temperature during surgery, to reverse the symptoms of shock caused by their injuries. In four hours, it will disappear from your system. But, by then, you'll be dead.'

Conor snuffled a minor laugh.

Baka struggled. 'Let me go.'

'You've screwed my business. The police know about our plans.'

'How? I didn't tell them.'

Conor stood up and slowly walked over to the prostrate Baka. He sat beside him, using the trunk of the tree as support for his aching spine. He drew heavily on a newly lit cigar, savoured it and blew the smoke into Baka's face. Baka coughed.

'Our Vory friends are also going to be pissed off – you've put us all in danger. You have been under surveillance by the Spanish police. Nowak has been under surveillance by the British police. The FSB are also involved. You have created a shit storm that has led them all to me.'

Baka was struggling. 'We'll work something out. Blame Nowak.'

'The trouble is that Nowak knows nearly everything. If he disappears, I won't get my money back. We need a fall guy, a scapegoat – and I'm sorry to say that's going to be you.'

Conor O'Murchadha's methods were not pleasant. 'I like you Ali, but this is business. Your death will not be as painful as some over which I have presided. I'm not going to cut off your balls and stuff them in your mouth – well, not before you die anyway.'

'Come on, Conor, I'm sure we can work something out?' Baka was seriously scared and begging. 'Please, don't do this.'

'Sorry, my friend. It's all too late for that.'

Conor stubbed out his cigar on Baka's chest and stood up. Baka whimpered.

He returned to his car and from the front storage box, carefully donned a pair of leather driving gloves – he went to the boot to retrieve a thick carrier bag.

'Goodbye, Ali, no regrets now.' Conor carefully pulled the bag over Baka's head – there was nothing he could do.

Baka thrashed about. 'No, please Conor. Come on. We're friends.' He began to cry, then pissed himself.

'Come on now, don't make it any more difficult for yourself than it has to be.' It was as if Conor cared.

Conor took a roll of gaffer tape, so loved by the entertainment industry; he tightly wrapped it around the carrier bag and Baka's neck, ensuring a good seal. It took Baka twenty minutes to painfully asphyxiate – as he gasped his last waking breath, his final memory before he passed out was seeing 'Tesco at El Corte Inglés Bag for Life'.

Conor took the cigar from Baka's chest and relit it, ignoring the burn marks and the smell of burning flesh combined with piss. He allowed himself the luxury of half an hour to finish it, admiring the night-time view over the town and out to the ships in the far distance. From his pocket he drank deeply from his silver flask, a present from his late mother – he was particularly fond of Fundador Solera Reserva, the Spanish brandy.

'Let's get this done,' he said out loud.

He cut the cable ties, unravelled the gaffer tape from around Baka's neck and then removed the Bag for Life from Baka's lifeless form. He carefully put them all in a black sack in the boot of his car. Conor was a powerful man; despite that, Baka was heavy lump. He dragged him into the grave, already dug. With the shovel he covered the corpse with soil, which he carefully trod down, smoothing as he went. He arranged the leaves and undergrowth, so the newly dug grave would not be immediately noticed. He changed his shoes putting the old ones in the black bag, followed by the cigar stubs. He took another drink from his hip flask and drove off into the night.

An hour later the black bag, together with its contents, were in the Marbella Hospital's incinerator – 100 euros and the threat to kill his children ensured the silence of the operator. Always carrot, always stick was Conor's mantra.

WEDNESDAY

AT SEVEN-THIRTY NOWAK'S IPHONE RANG – HE was back home in his own bed. Number unavailable. He nearly didn't answer it but then thought it could be news of Martha.

'Whoever it is fuck off, it's too early.'

'That's not a very nice thing to say. I'm only trying to help.'

'Who is this?'

'Why it's your old mate Conor O'Murchadha.'

Nowak's blood ran cold – not literally, of course, but his body gave a cold shudder. He thought. His flat was bugged. What to do?

'Cynthia, how lovely to hear from you. We must meet again soon – best blow job I've ever had. Haven't got my diary here, it's at the office. Send me your number and I'll call you back as soon as.'

'What the feck are you talking about?'

'Hugs and kisses. Got to get to the office. Bye Cynthia.'

Nowak disconnected. Conor got it. He sent a phone number to Nowak by WhatsApp – he had been told that WhatsApp was uncrackable, but he still used a Spanish burner phone. Nowak's phone dinged – he didn't hear it as he was already in the shower.

By eight-fifteen Nowak was walking out of the flat – how to escape his tails was the issue. He deliberately left his normal mobile phone at home, he would go back and get it later. He hailed a black cab to Liverpool Street station where he bought a pay-as-you go phone, adding fifty pounds credit. He dived down into the busy Tube to the Central Line to Bank, doubled back to Mile End and then to West Ham to get the above ground DLR to Canning Town, where he changed to Beckton. The Tubes and trains were crowded until he got onto the DLR, away from the rush-hour commuters aiming for the City. He sat at the very front of the driverless carriage looking at the tracks off into the distance. No one was near him – even if he was still being tailed, he couldn't be overheard. He called Conor.

'Hello, who is this?'

'My flat is being bugged – didn't want them to know who I was speaking to.'

'Thank you, they know too much already.'

'How are you, Conor? Long time and all that. What do you want?'

'Baka has died in unfortunate circumstances.'

Nowak was silent for a moment – he was trying to think through the consequences. There were simply too many variables.

'Are you there?'

'Yes. You don't beat about the bloody bush, do you? Do I assume you were somehow involved in his demise?' Nowak didn't know how to react. Good news or bad?

'The police found out about Baka's, your, travel activities – he led them to me, put me at risk. Sorry to say our little arrangement is cancelled.'

'What do you mean cancelled?'

'You're on your own – don't need your tour. Can't risk it. But I do want my million back plus five per cent – you have a month.'

'My arrangement is with Baka, not you.'

'Shall we say that I have inherited his interests? One month – one point oh five million.'

'Where the hell am I going to get that sort of money at such short notice?'

'That's not my problem.'

'Where's Martha?'

'Ask Baka.' A snigger. 'Oh, of course, you can't.'

Conor disconnected. Nowak's mind was galloping. It might just be possible to return the cash. Ticket sales after the weekend's papers and Monday radio with Danny had rocketed. He was almost euphoric. No people smuggling. No trafficking. He wasn't going to let down his best friend. He had funded the tour and now it was self-supporting.

It was short lived. Before he died, had Baka given instructions to release Martha, and Vikki, he begrudgingly considered as an afterthought? Back to square one. No Martha, no tour – and this time he was dealing with Conor O'Murchadha. And what of the Vory?

The DLR terminated at Beckton. He left the station, turned right and walked the short distance to the Winsor House Brewers Fayre – not his normal choice for breakfast, but it would do. At least they had black pudding.

Several cups of tea later he had formulated a plan. He called Daisy – she didn't recognise the number.

'Stanislaw here, sorry, different phone. Can I meet with you, Danny and Yuliet as soon as possible please? Say Elstree at one?'

Daisy was surprised by the request. 'Let me see what I can do. I'll get back to you. This number?'

'No, use the normal one.'

He removed the SIM from his burner phone, bent and crushed it, surreptitiously hiding the remains in the leftover beans on his plate. The phone itself disappeared down a road drain as he bent down to tie up a shoelace.

Although he had taken a roundabout route, Nowak's flat was only a couple of hundred metres from Prince Albert station, a few stops down the DLR from Beckton – he was home in less than fifteen minutes. He collected his normal phone and called his driver to take him to Elstree.

35

WEDNESDAY

'BAKA'S DISAPPEARED.' BILL KELLY HAD assembled his team at short notice. Everyone was there in the basement meeting room of New Scotland Yard.

'Weren't the Spaniards following him?' asked Rob Andrews.

'They were. He was picked up in Barcelona and followed on the train to Málaga. He spent most of the day there meeting with a succession of hoods. In the evening he met with Conor O'Murchadha in some dodgy Irish bar between Marbella and Málaga. And this is where it becomes confused. It seems the Spanish police were already interested in Conor O'Murchadha – which is just as well. Conor's mob spotted one of our Spanish followers and captured her. To everyone's surprise, five minutes later

315

the GEO, the equivalent of our SCO19, stormed the bar to rescue her. They were listening – Conor had told his lot to kill her. I'm waiting to receive the surveillance recordings, but I am told Baka sounded either pissed or drugged. When the GEO got there Conor and Baka were gone, but they did save the life of the Spanish policewoman. No lasting damage, just a bit shaken and bruised. An hour later Baka checked out of his hotel room in Málaga. No one has seen or heard of either Conor or Baka since.'

'Do we assume that Conor and Baka are together?'

'No idea but seems likely I suppose. The question is how did they get away before the raid? Were they tipped off?'

'Do we know where Nowak is?'

'He is on his way to Elstree to meet with Daisy, Danny and Yuliet. Rob, get up there now. He knows we are following him, and his house is bugged – he led us a merry dance earlier, playing ducks and drakes on the Tube and the DLR. He then returned to his flat. We heard him order his car to take him up to Elstree. However, he bought a pay-as-you-go phone and fifty quid of credit at Liverpool Street station on his outing – it's gone now we must assume.' Bill was in command.

'Since Danny's mugging incident we can't track or intercept calls to and from his phone anymore. He bought a new one but is using his old SIM. The app we placed on the phone has obviously gone.'

'Nothing can be done about that now. Our priority is to locate Baka and Conor – we need solid evidence about their trafficking plans. This is the first time we have ever got close.' The team was excited.

'And find Martha and Vikki too,' Rob added. 'Was Nowak followed by our FSB friends?'

Bill nodded disappointedly. 'Our lot lost Nowak, we simply didn't have the manpower – but they did spot extra followers before it went to rat shit. See if you can turn Nowak, Rob. It's Baka and Conor we want, they are at the top of the tree. Right, go – we'll meet again here same time tomorrow. Earlier if any developments.'

Everyone stood, collected their papers and departed.

'Detective Sergeant Maguire, would you stay behind please.' For Bill Kelly to use his formal title meant it was serious. The others leaving the room wondered what was going on. Maguire felt sick – he knew what this was going to be about.

Maguire resignedly sat back down opposite Bill Kelly.

Bill took out the photograph of Nowak from ten years ago – with the unidentified person wearing the 5th Inniskilling Dragoon Guards tie in the back of shot. He passed it to Maguire.

'Well?'

'Well what?'

'Is that you?'

Maguire knew who it was. He carefully considered his reply.

'No.'

Bill Kelly looked straight into Maguire's eyes – and held the stare.

'No,' he sighed. 'It's my uncle. We were both in the same regiment, at different times of course. He was job too – Commander Barry Fitzpatrick.'

'What! He died a few years ago, took early retirement. Cancer or something wasn't it? What was he doing with Nowak?'

Maguire stood up, went over to the coffee jug on the sideboard, held a cup up and gesticulated to Bill Kelly. Bill nodded. Maguire poured two cups, added milk to both. Neither took sugar. He passed one cup to Bill Kelly and sat down again. They each drank. Bill nodded for Maguire to carry on.

'My mother, his sister, was very ill – she found walking any long distance painful. Most of the time she was fine but the pain would come on suddenly leaving her totally immobile. Stuck. Her GP wouldn't sign the application for a disabled badge as he said she didn't fit the parameters. My dad was beside himself, tried everything. One day I had a call to say that my mother had been stranded, stuck, just sitting on a low wall outside the shopping centre. She'd been there for five hours in the cold and damp. Couldn't move. Legs wouldn't support her.' Maguire exhaled a long sigh. 'She said she didn't like to make a fuss – you know how they are. She thought she'd be fine in a wee while.'

They both drank some coffee. Maguire was emotional but somehow letting go was cathartic.

'She didn't have a mobile phone. Didn't hold with them.' Maguire gave a short ironic laugh. 'Eventually my father found her – he'd been out looking for two hours. He drove his car into the pedestrian precinct to take her home. Some bloody local plod decided to book him. Anyhow, they got her home somehow. If she hadn't had to walk so far from the car park, she would not have been in the situation she was. The irony was that the nearby disabled bays were full – delivery lorries, bloody four-by-fours and posh motors, none with badges. The plod didn't book any of them. I thought then something had to be done.'

'Too much paperwork?'

'We all went and saw the GP – but he wouldn't budge. My mother wasn't disabled enough to have a Blue Badge, he said. Which was bollocks.'

'What happened?' Bill thought he knew what was coming.

'We'd just started investigating disabled badge fraud. And I wasn't prepared to see my mother in that situation again. I gave my father Nowak's contact details. He went and saw him. We're not rich. No way we could have afforded Nowak's prices. M'dad tried everything, appealing to Nowak's better nature – which we know he doesn't have. He got stroppy and threatened Nowak with me and my uncle. You know, the "my-son's-a-policeman" routine. My dad said that Nowak wasn't threatened – he told him to get me to contact him.'

'And did you?'

'A few days later my uncle and I spoke to Nowak face-to-face, just the three of us. Nowak offered us a deal. My mother would get a Blue Badge if I occasionally helped Nowak, keep an eye out for him. I told him to fuck off. But he said I had no choice – if I didn't help, he said he would end both our careers. I'd only just joined your team.'

'What about Commander Fitzpatrick, Barry? What did he say? What did he do?' Bill was disappointed that one of his heroes had possibly been turned.

'Once he scared the shit out of Nowak, he stayed out of it. On the way home he told me he was taking early retirement. He didn't say why – but, of course, we now know he was stage four cancer.' Maguire realised how much he missed his uncle and his sage counsel.

'Why didn't you come straight to me with this?' Bill was stroppy – he felt let down that Maguire hadn't trusted him enough to come clean.

'Oh, come on. Nowak said he'd do for my mum and dad if I told anyone. I believed him. Three days later the Blue Badge arrived at my parents' house. They were both ecstatic – couldn't thank me enough. They didn't know I'd sold my soul to Nowak.'

They both sat in silence. Bill Kelly was contemplating what to do.

Maguire had reached a decision to tell all. 'Nowak threatened to ruin my uncle's reputation even after his death. I wasn't having that. I just had to keep going. It was me that put Nowak onto Danny. It was me that removed the evidence. I warned Nowak that he was being bugged. I warned Nowak about other things – I'll write a full statement. Only Nowak, no one else. And not everything, generally low-level stuff. Just enough to keep him off our backs.'

Maguire finished his coffee and with ultimate, exaggerated care replaced the cup back onto the saucer. He used a napkin to wipe up some spilled drops from the table. He looked straight at Bill Kelly, having taken a decision.

'My mother doesn't need the badge anymore – she died six weeks ago. There is no other family now.'

Maguire took his warrant card from his inside jacket pocket to hand it to Bill Kelly. Kelly ignored it, stood and walked to the door. 'Go home Mike. Just go home.'

Kelly knew what he should do. But sometimes? He wondered why he wasn't as angry as he should be. If anything, he was completely devoid of feelings. His phone interrupted his reflections – he left the room.

Maguire sat there sobbing, not out of self-pity or relief, but for his mother. The first time he had properly cried for her. Stress often manifested itself as grumpiness. *I owe the team an apology. My team. The team I have grown to respect and admire*, he thought, *I have let them down.*

He slowly got up to make his way home – relief and a release from the stress he had been under for years.

WEDNESDAY–ELSTREE

'WHAT DOES NOWAK WANT?' ASKED YULIET.

Danny waved at Shirley and made the universal gesture for three coffees – Shirley, by now, knew their needs.

They were sitting at their regular table in the midday spring sunshine, away from the others. Shirley delivered in person. 'Morning everyone.'

'Morning Shirley,' in unison.

'Mr Nowak was wrong – Watford did beat Arsenal. We had a nice afternoon. Hubby took me out for a slap-up meal after too. To celebrate.'

Danny, Daisy and Yuliet smiled at Shirley, but added nothing. She took her cue, looked over to the queue forming at the catering truck. 'Can't stand here all day nattering, have lunch to serve. Can't leave the team on their own.'

'Thanks, Shirley.'

When Shirley was out of earshot Daisy continued, 'Nowak called me. He sounded distracted – he simply said could he meet with us all as soon as possible please? Here at one. And here we are.' Daisy looked at her watch. 'Twenty minutes early. Aren't we good little sheep?'

Yuliet ignored Daisy's vitriol. 'I've continued researching the Vory, Conor O'Murchadha, Baka and Nowak. Baka and O'Murchadha are the fully finished pieces – nasty shits, both psychopaths and sociopaths if they can be combined?'

None of them laughed.

Yuliet continued, 'Baka is a pussycat compared to O'Murchadha. By all accounts he is the most malevolent organised crime mega-boss in Europe, if not the world. And one of the richest. I doubt whether Nowak fully comprehends what he has got himself involved in.'

Nowak arrived via Shirley – he brought over four more coffees on a tray with Danish pastries.

'Thanks for coming.' He put the tray carefully on the table and handed around the Danishes.

'Wouldn't have missed it for the world,' lied Danny. He wondered if Nowak understood irony. He took a bite from the cinnamon swirl he had selected.

'Baka's dead. Conor killed him.'

'What?' Crumbs everywhere.

Yuliet was disgusted by the shower of sticky flakes now all over her.

'Why?'

'How?'

'When?'

'How do you know?'

'Fuck!'

'Conor called me this morning. He didn't say he had killed him – but it was pretty clear that he had.' Nowak didn't bother to mention his antics shaking off his tails to take and make the calls. 'He told me that the police had been tailing Baka and he led them to Conor. He said that everything was cancelled, and he wanted his million plus interest back – in a month.'

'But why kill Baka?'

'Don't know a lot more. All Conor cared about was getting his money back.'

'Can you get hold of that sort of money at such short notice?'

'I probably could if we get Martha back and the tour goes ahead – we would be cash positive. I asked Conor if he knew where Martha was. He told me to ask Baka. Bastard laughed.' Nowak didn't.

'I think I know where she is.' Everyone turned to Yuliet.

'What? Where?'

'Baka has a house in the Wye Valley – bottom right-hand corner of Wales. I have someone watching it. He has just sent me this picture.' Yuliet had been fiddling with her iPad Pro – she turned it to face the other three. Obviously taken from a long way away was the picture of a window; just behind the pushed-back net curtains was a woman. Yuliet zoomed in and enhanced the picture – and there was Martha, or was it Vikki?

'Bloody hell. You are a fucking genius.' Danny was seriously impressed.

'That's her. Wonderful. What now?' asked Daisy.

Rob Andrews' arrival solved that problem. He peered over Yuliet's shoulder to see the screen of her iPad. 'That's Martha!'

'Or Vikki?'

'Either way, where is this?' Rob Andrews was intrigued.

'Baka has a house in the Wye Valley about ten miles north of Chepstow.' Yuliet was triumphant. One up on the police.

'How the hell didn't we know about that?' Rob's intrigue was turning to annoyance.

'Ask Bill.' Danny enjoyed the irony.

'Send me the pictures and the contact information for your man on the ground.' Yuliet gave Rob the email address and mobile number. Rob forwarded it all to Bill.

'Back soon.' Rob walked off to somewhere private.

'Let's not count our lucky chickens.' Yuliet was a fan of the mixed metaphor. 'We don't know yet how Martha and Vikki are. They could well be traumatised, even injured. We don't know what conditions they have been kept in.'

They contemplated.

'If they are safe and well and Martha can perform, then we are in the clear. We haven't done anything illegal.' Nowak felt as if he was grasping at straws.

'Why do you insist on saying "we" – this is your bloody mess not ours. All "we" want is Martha and Vikki back safe and well. If you can't pay back the million then that is your problem.' Daisy stood and stormed off.

Danny and Yuliet turned to Nowak.

'She's right you know.' Yuliet felt for Daisy – she went off to find her, leaving Danny and Nowak alone.

Nowak was deflated. 'Oh fuck. I can't take this anymore. Bloody roller-coaster ride. I'm going straight from now on – not getting involved in anything illegal ever again.'

Danny was scathing. 'What like you mean never drinking again, the morning after the night before?'

Danny was getting fed up with Nowak trying to hang on for a bit of sympathy. The brewing row was defused by the arrival of Rob.

'Where's Yuliet and Daisy?' Rob asked.

The tense silence and looks between Nowak and Danny partly answered the question.

'Yuliet's looking for Daisy,' Danny answered.

'Bill is on the case. We should know something in about an hour.' Rob thought he'd get more of a reaction from Nowak.

'Baka's dead. Murdered,' Nowak announced.

'What? How do you know?' Rob was nonplussed.

'Conor O'Murchadha called me this morning to tell me.' Nowak didn't care that he had essentially admitted to his connection with organised crime.

'Why did he tell you?'

'He thought I'd be interested.'

'What happened? Who did it?'

'No idea. Conor didn't say.' Nowak had enough sense not to offer an opinion.

Rob went off again to phone Bill – information was coming in thick and fast. The pieces of the jigsaw falling into place.

It is said that waiting is the worst part of it.

Yuliet and Daisy walked up to the remains of the Big Brother house – the series over, it had been de-rigged and stripped, a forlorn skeleton never to be used again. It would be flattened when another production needed the outdoor space.

Back in the studio, Danny sat in the chairs where the front row of the audience would be on the night, watching the fine tuning.

Nowak went to the production office to check on ticket sales and answer a few emails. He was fizzing with a combination of excitement and dread. Could it all be over?

37
WEDNESDAY AFTERNOON –NEW SCOTLAND YARD

NO ONE ASKED WHERE DETECTIVE SERGEANT Michael Maguire was – and Bill didn't offer to tell them. Thirty people were crowded into one of the larger meeting rooms normally reserved for senior management on the top floor of New Scotland Yard. Bill's team wondered what they had done to deserve the sudden attention.

The door opened. Bill Kelly ushered in the Assistant Commissioner, Specialist Operations ahead of him. Everyone stood – the AC waved them to sit down. A couple of moments later the Director of Communications rushed in and saw the crowded room. 'Sorry I'm late.'

No one cared. Glances were exchanged – obviously something big, communicated by raised eyebrows.

Everyone ignored the top brass as the live video feed sprang to life – projected onto the screen on the far wall. There was no audio, but it wasn't needed. The pictures spoke for themselves.

Two helicopters could be seen circling Piercefield House – the pictures must have been taken from a third. The first of the two 'Blue Thunder' Dauphins landed to the rear. Eight figures in black, assault weapons to their shoulders, leapt out. The team could see smoke and large flashes as they approached the rear doors – two smashed windows as they threw in objects. Smoked billowed from the holes in the broken glass.

It was a little weird, almost normal – unlike watching a movie. If this had been an action film, there would have been dramatic music, shouts, gunfire, close-ups and the thunder of helicopter blades. Instead, silent voyeurism.

From the front of the house three people emerged and ran towards the black Mercedes. A futile decision. The second helicopter landed on the drive just behind the front gates – four figures emerged and deployed onto the ground, legs akimbo, assault weapons facing the direction of the approaching car.

The car stopped, the three got out and raised their hands. Their positions exchanged, the troops stood and the four car passengers laid down.

The rear assault team entered the house. Nothing seemed to happen for ten minutes. Then from the front door came the unmistakable figures of the twin sisters Martha and Vikki – both dressed in identical track suits. Unlike in US movies the room did not burst into spontaneous applause, hugging and back-slapping as everyone competitively tried to out-celebrate the other. Instead there was just excited, jubilant chatter as everyone enjoyed the moment.

Bill sipped his tea in quiet jubilation.

'Whoa, what's happening?' shouted one of them. They turned back to the screen to see one of the sisters run back into the building, followed by two of the troops.

The helicopter taking the video landed on the lawns twenty metres away. The camera remained focused on the front door – one of the sisters and the two troops re-emerged to join the others. She brandished a carrier bag.

The two sisters were helped into the third helicopter. Both looked well enough with enormous smiles on their faces.

Bill Kelly spoke for the first time. 'Right everyone. That appears to be Martha and Vikki safe and sound. Thanks to AC, Specialist Operations who contacted Hereford who are less than twenty-five miles away from Piercefield. They have an immediate action special forces unit there just waiting for the call.' Bill didn't need to explain who Hereford are.

A phone rang. The AC answered it. 'Thank you.'

A pause.

'Any shots fired? Injuries?'

Another pause.

'All's well. Good. Please pass on our thanks to the team.'

He spoke to the room. 'Martha and Vikki are on their way back to London by helicopter. They'll be picked up by car from the heliport and brought here to be debriefed. They are both very well and seem completely unfazed. We'll be able to confirm this when they get here in about two hours. The hiatus was Martha going back into the building to collect a memory stick and some of her printing – she said there was important stuff on it. We'll look at it when they get here. You'll be delighted to know no shots fired, no injuries. The assault team will stay on-site until the local police arrive – Piercefield is in the middle of nowhere, so it may take a while.'

WEDNESDAY LATE AFTERNOON – IN THE AIR AND LONDON

Vikki had never ridden in a helicopter before. 'This is wicked, sis.'

The two sisters sat as close together as the seat straps allowed.

'It's been good seeing you. On our own.' Vikki was contemplative. 'I hadn't really understood what you did. I just saw the fame and fortune almost as an outsider. I guess we talked for the first time properly since we were in school?'

Martha realised that she had sometimes been a shit to her sister. The death of their parents and siblings drove them apart. Celebrity ensured neither of them really had the opportunity to grieve together or become close as sisters. Martha's 'people' deliberately distanced her from

Vikki – they didn't want Vikki's lifestyle to infect Martha's reputation.

'It's an ill-wind and all that,' Martha snorted. She turned to her sister and gently held her face with both hands. 'Thank you. It was my fault. I know you didn't want to be there, but between us we kept our shit together. I am not sure how much longer I could have stayed on top of it on my own.'

'We'll always be sisters,' was all Vikki could manage before they both let the emotion of release wash over them.

Martha had been in helicopters many times back in the day when she was a global star – she hated them. She didn't understand how something with such flimsy blades could keep them all in the air. But she wasn't going to let down her sister. 'Great views.'

Vikki looked out the window and smiled, *I have family.*

Ninety minutes later it was over – the sisters feeling different emotions. But they were free. They landed at the London Heliport, one of the most advanced heliports in Europe located on the south bank of the River Thames opposite Chelsea Harbour. An unmarked police car was waiting for them – the news hadn't reached the press, not that they knew what was going on.

Martha and Vikki spent Wednesday evening at what the police later described as a secure location, the Royal Horseguards Hotel, just around the corner from New Scotland Yard. The bustling view from their rooms overlooking the Thames was a far cry from the tranquillity of the Wye Valley. Earlier Sergeant Martha-lover had been sent to both Martha's and Vikki's homes to collect clothes and a few personal items, the hotel had supplied everything else. It wasn't a lot different to Piercefield – luxurious. Supposedly free, but with armed police outside their doors.

Daisy and Danny had both met with police counsellors before their visit. They had been told, 'Freedom often brings a sense of elation and relief – adjusting back to the real world after being held hostage can be just as difficult as abruptly leaving it. Some find the transition from captivity to freedom often results in significant adjustment difficulties. But everyone is different – people's reactions vary from one individual to another.'

Daisy and Danny accompanied by Bill Kelly were the only ones permitted to visit Martha and Vikki at the hotel that evening. The door to the two-bedroomed suite was opened by the authorised firearms officer carefully cradling his Heckler and Koch MP5SF – and there they were.

Danny hugged Martha. 'Jenny, how are you?'

'There's not many that use that name now,' laughed the reply.

Danny did the introductions. Martha could see that Daisy and Danny were close – Martha was surprised how this affected her. Not jealously, but the sense that 'her' Danny was in a good place. *Maybe the demons of the acrimonious break-up finally laid to rest?*

Danny visibly relaxed. He was concerned how this first face-to-face would go. He needn't have worried.

Vikki was sitting in the armchair drinking a large white wine. 'You have no idea how I missed this.' She held up a glass.

Unbeknown to Vikki it was agreed by Martha, Daisy and Bill that she wouldn't have internet access until she had been fully prepared and formally debriefed – the orchestrated world of celebrity had started to return.

'They looked after us very well – the room was gorgeous. Good healthy food. In all honesty it wasn't that much of a hardship. Got a bit stir crazy once they locked me in.' Martha was matter of fact. 'No different to a long tour with close protection I suppose. I worked out for several hours each day – I am probably fitter than I have been for years.'

Vikki was less enthusiastic. 'It wasn't prison, but I missed everyone on Facebook.'

Bill was intrigued. 'Why did you go back into the house? What did you fetch?'

Martha held up the USB stick. 'They gave me recording equipment. I wrote most of my new album – and it's all on there. Thinking of calling it "Captivity".'

'Don't forget my credit,' shouted Vikki from her glass of wine. 'Equal billing on the lyrics.'

'Vikki helped me – she became my muse.' Martha smiled over at her sister. 'She still can't bloody sing though.'

There was laughter.

'I think it's my best work ever. Sometimes the weirdest things set you free.'

Everyone was stunned how well the two girls were at their first informal interview that evening. Each finishing the others' sentences – they were closer than they had ever been since school.

Then Danny asked the question that had been bugging him for days. 'Why me?'

'Why you what?'

'Why did you contact me to be your first exclusive interview? You could have asked anyone?'

Martha considered her answer. 'I knew something wasn't right. Shirley in catering tipped me off. She said she had heard Nowak speaking on the phone. You were the only person I hoped I could trust? You didn't let me down.'

Martha walked over to Danny and delivered a tender, chaste kiss. 'Thank you.'

'Right that's enough soppiness.' Bill was back on duty. 'See you in the morning. Sleep well.'

They all left. Danny and Daisy hand-in-hand – Martha smiled at them both.

THURSDAY

THURSDAY MORNING WAS SPENT IN FORMAL interviews and taking statements – everyone at the Yard seemed to be aware of what was going on. There was a sense of pleasure all around – a job well done? Bill Kelly wasn't so sure; he still wanted Conor O'Murchadha. Get him back behind bars.

The personal trainer, chef and the kitchen assistants had been taken to Gwent's Police HQ in Croesyceiliog – they claimed they had no idea that anyone was being held against their will. All of them shocked when the balaclava-clad figures crashed into their domains.

Natalia, Williams and 'Oliver Mellors' had been driven to New Scotland Yard in a high-speed blue-lit convoy. 'Oliver Mellors' had served with a couple of the guys who had captured them. There was subtle acknowledgement, but all accepted that secrets had to be kept – no quarter given or taken. Their night in the police cells was a lot less comfortable than their former captives.

Daisy had been trained to take control of the story – always be on the front foot. She went round to the headquarters of *The Daily Tribune* to meet Kelvin Edwards face-to-face – the meeting at first could only be described as difficult. He was fuming; Daisy had deceived him, lied to him. Martha had been missing, his sources were right. After a heated discussion, Kelvin, ever the pragmatist, soon realised he had the exclusive scoop of his career. Daisy had spun it wonderfully. She said she would publicly thank Kelvin Edwards for helping to ensure the safe return of Martha. And give him exclusive access – the words every journalist wants to hear.

Nowak's careful inspection of the contract with Baka was worth it, there was a standard fourteen-day cooling off period. Nowak emailed Baka's solicitor indicating that he no longer wished to borrow the money and that he was exercising his option to cancel the contract. The solicitor was surprised but had to accept that Nowak had properly served notice and there had been no consideration. She had, as instructed by Baka, also destroyed the previous, original contract, about the only thing she did do as requested in a timely manner. She hadn't been able to contact Baka. The two million that had arrived many months before into Nowak's account was now untraceable – deliberately with no connection to Baka. And he was dead. Nowak had two million pounds and no traceable source.

Thursday afternoon, the police had hastily arranged a press conference. After a bit of bartering between Daisy and the Met's Director of Communications it was agreed that neither Martha nor Vikki would appear. Daisy was in full PR control – this is what she lived for. She insisted it was important that *The Daily Tribune* had their exclusive. The conference was a dry affair with no advance notice of what was to be said and as a result, most media sent lowly reporters and interns. Bill Kelly walked into the press briefing room and sat in front of the blue background with the familiar Metropolitan Police logo. He smiled at everyone.

It had been suggested to Kelvin Edwards that it was best if a junior reporter and a snapper only were sent by *The Daily Tribune*.

'I'll start in five seconds.' This was for the benefit of the two TV news cameras and half a dozen radio journalists who started recording. He looked straight ahead – a few flashes went off.

'I have a short statement but will not be taking questions. Further information will be released in due course.'

Bill took a drink of water – he wasn't nervous, he'd done many of these. He wondered to himself what the reaction would be when the pack realised what it was all about.

'Good afternoon. I'm Detective Chief Superintendent Bill Kelly. At three-thirty yesterday afternoon as a result of detailed investigations by the National Crime Agency involving Interpol, the Spanish and Russian police, the

Gwent police, and with the assistance of the military, Jenny and her sister Vikki Jones were released from enforced captivity. Jenny will be familiar to many as the pop-singer Martha.'

The room went wild – questions started being thrown at Bill. He held up his hand to silence everyone. Once he had restored calm, ever the professional he went back a sentence or two, so the TV news teams could seamlessly edit.

'Jenny and her sister Vikki Jones were released from enforced captivity. Jenny will be familiar to many as the pop-singer Martha. They were being held against their will in a blackmail attempt by European organised crime syndicates to disrupt Martha's forthcoming tour. Both Jenny and Vikki are unharmed and in excellent health. We would like to thank the Ministry of Defence and Gwent Police for their help in expediting their safe release. We would also like to thank Kelvin Edwards of *The Daily Tribune*. His unselfish action in not publishing the news that Martha had been kidnapped probably helped to save her life. That is all for now.'

There was more chaos – despite Bill saying he would not be taking questions, they came thick and fast. Bill left the room.

Two hours later, *The Daily Tribune* hurriedly rushed out radio and TV commercials pushing their part in Martha and her sister's release and advertising tomorrow's headlines with exclusive interviews and pictures. Martha had recorded a short video clip on her iPhone. 'Read how I was held captive for two weeks and about my amazing rescue by Special Forces – only in tomorrow's *Daily Tribune*.'

Daisy and Kelvin were thrilled. Twenty-two words, eight seconds that would guarantee maximum publicity.

Kelvin had the exclusive newspaper and social media rights to the story. Danny had the exclusive broadcast TV and radio rights – the weekend would be spent with Martha on the set at Elstree with a three-camera crew.

40 FRIDAY

'MARTHA RETURNS – EXCLUSIVE' screamed the headline of Friday's *The Daily Tribune*. The rest of the page was filled with a picture of Martha and Vikki hugging by the front door of a mansion – they were escorted by four heavily armed, balaclava-clad figures in black. In the foreground, an unmarked helicopter. At the bottom – 'see pages 2, 3, 4, 5, 7, 8 and 10 for more details – and to read about the exclusive *Daily Tribune* Martha Movin' Out ticket offer'. The by-line acknowledged Kelvin Edwards, Danny Owen and Yuliet Spooner with exclusive photographs by Chris Robinson. Danny's first front-page by-line for ten years at the insistence of Starshine's and *The Daily Tribune*'s owners.

Chris had taken over 300 pictures of the entire

rescue plus some HD video – he was syndicating them to everyone and anyone prepared to pay the price. His retirement was sorted.

For Danny and Daisy, the rest of Thursday and Friday was chaotic – their phones didn't stop ringing as media outlets tried to play catch-up.

Jimmy negotiated with Elstree to extend the rehearsals by a week.

DJ Gordon called Danny from six that Friday morning – it wasn't Danny's day to appear and he wasn't going to change that. It could all wait until Monday.

The stories and trolls on social media became more and more outrageous in their claims, redefining fake news.

Kelvin appeared on radio and TV at first in the UK and then throughout Europe as the story developed. Kelvin's editor was thrilled – circulation rocketed.

Not surprisingly ticket sales exceeded Nowak's wildest expectations – he had more money in the bank than he ever thought possible. The Martha Movin' Out tour sold out time and again as fast as Jimmy and the team could book extra venues and additional dates. The North African gigs were quietly cancelled, freeing up more dates in the UK and Europe – ticket sales there were very low anyway, everyone received a full refund.

With Nowak's approval Daisy recruited two PRs to assist her manage Martha's time. Every TV station in every city and country where the tour was going to appear were bidding for interview slots.

THE AFTERMATH

WITHIN TWO WEEKS NOWAK HAD ENOUGH CASH to be able to pay off Conor, if only Nowak could locate him. Emails and phone calls went unanswered.

In many breaking major news stories, dog owners are credited with finding the body. Normally the dogs do the work, but never seem to get the praise they deserve. 'Alonzo' was a Perro de Presa Canario – a breed with origins in the Canary Islands as a result of the crossbreeding between the Mastiff and the cattle dogs. Alonzo's strong, massive, square-shaped head was buried deep in the undergrowth with its wagging tail and arse in the air – its head came up with a jubilant shake to show to its master the human hand attached to the human arm.

Bill received an email via Interpol from the Spanish police that a body had been found in the hills above La Cala de Mijas – later identified as Baka via fingerprints. Initial assessments – blue face and frothy lips – indicated that he had been asphyxiated. There were the sticky remnants of gaffer tape around his neck.

The large burn mark on the chest, administered pre-mortem and almost certainly by a cigar was what did for Conor. It was well known that Conor continuously smoked large, fat cigars – the starting point. Forensics were able to obtain DNA from the saliva on the remains of the stubbed ash – it didn't take long to definitively identify the smoker. A global arrest warrant was issued. Two days later the Spanish police arrested Conor as he returned to his home in the hills above Marbella.

He was taken to the duty court in Fuengirola for a behind-closed-doors hearing – he was rushed into the courtroom out-of-sight of waiting press amid tight security. That evening he was moved to the maximum security Alhaurin de la Torre prison, which has housed the likes of killer Eric 'Lucky' Wilson, the wife killer Dermot McArdle, and Christy Kinahan with his two sons Daniel and Christopher after their arrests for drugs trafficking and money laundering.

A few days later Conor O'Murchadha's boat, moored at the luxurious Puerto Banus, was searched by armed officers, along with his villa in the hills above Marbella. Underground secret storage facilities were uncovered, and computers taken. The volume of incriminating evidence was overwhelming. The probe into his alleged crimes, co-ordinated by the investigating judge was expected to last for several months. Under Spanish law, suspects can be held for a maximum of four years without charge. The British police and Irish Gardai had to wait their turn.

Conor had issues of his own. He had been working with the Vory on a number of 'projects' – his return to prison scuppered those plans. Overwhelming evidence of his connection with the Vory was found on Conor's computers, voicemail and phones. The Vory were owed money by Conor that they were unlikely to see – a message had to be sent.

Two days after his incarceration Conor O'Murchadha was killed in the showers by a single knife wound straight through the heart.

No one saw who did it or the barbed wire tattoo across the forehead of the killer – Vory symbolism for a sentence of life imprisonment without a possibility of parole.

Nowak couldn't believe what he was reading on the BBC World News website – Conor dead. Baka dead. No one connected the deaths to Nowak.

Unbelievably he had become a millionaire almost overnight – the two million was his to keep, he thought. There was simply no one to return it to and no paper trail.

Nowak called Danny. 'Please can I take you, Daisy and Yuliet to dinner to say thank you?'

Danny was surprised, but said, 'Yes'.

Nowak hesitated, 'I've never been to anywhere really posh – any chance you can get us into the Ivy?'

Danny laughed. 'I'll do better than that, I'll get a table at The Ivy Club – more exclusive. More private – we won't be bothered.'

The same day Bill met up with Detective Sergeant Michael Maguire in a café around the corner from the Yard. 'Right Mike, consider yourself fucking lucky. I should arrest you and throw away the key. But I'm not going to – I could be done for aiding and abetting, so we are both going to keep schtum. I'm not doing this for you – this is for your uncle. He was my mentor and I owe him.'

Maguire sagged, the relief palpable.

'If you ever, ever get into a situation like that again you come to me straight away.'

Maguire's emotions were all over the place – relief mainly. 'Thank you, Bill. I don't know what to say. Thank you.'

'In future I want one hundred per cent honesty – it's a two-way street. Understand?'

'Understood!'

'Is there anything else you want to tell me? This is your one-time opportunity. Who else have you betrayed?' Bill stared hard into Maguire's eyes.

'Nothing. No one. I promise. Only Nowak. I'm not bent – I just couldn't stand seeing what happened to my mother. I was only trying to help.'

Bill was convinced. 'We will get him, you know. Nowak. He's a crook with too much luck.'

'He deserves everything.' Maguire was ready for it. 'I'm the only one left in the family.'

Bill Kelly now had the most loyal sergeant he could have wished for.

THE O2

THE HOUSE LIGHTS DIMMED, THE AUDIENCE started to cheer and applaud. In the dark the band took their places.

Nowak paced backstage – Jimmy gave him the thumbs up with an immense smile.

The anonymous text message Nowak had received earlier that week was to the point: *'You owe us a million pounds.'* His reply was equally to the point: *'Fuck off'*. His euphoria and misplaced arrogance convinced him that he had got away with it. He forgot all about it and made his way up to the VIP seats.

Danny squeezed Daisy's hand. Alongside them Kelvin and his wife; Yuliet; Bill and the team; even Gordon with an over-made-up girlfriend – all given VIP tickets seated

348

in the block immediately to the left looking from the enormous stage. Each with a VIP golden circle ticket to the after-show party.

Nowak sat heavily into the vacant aisle seat beside Daisy – the seating creaked ominously but held. There was nothing more he or any of them could do. The show would be a fabulous success.

Deep-blue lights circled, the audience ramped up the excitement drowned by the heart-stopping ultra-bass. The brass kicked in with a tower-of-power rock fanfare. A single guitarist spot lit up-stage-right joined in with an E minor 9 funky vamp. The risers either side of the stage, with the rest of the musicians on board, smoothly lifted and rotated into position, the ultra-bass joined by an ostentatious tympani player up-stage-left building the tension. Fog and dry ice poured on and around the stage. The Vari-Lites circled.

The ten banks of 5x5 Par30 light matrixes illuminated the audience at full brightness, 'blinding' them so they couldn't see the stage. Suddenly dead black out, synchronised with the snare roll. More colossal cheering.

In perfect synchronicity, the massive Mitrix screens displayed a glorious cascade of gold discs behind bulging prison bars. As the words 'Martha Returns' resolved, Alan Dedicoat's pre-recorded voice-over boomed out in a rising cadence, 'It's time. It's time. It's time for the return of… Martha.' The bars broke under the pressure from the gold discs.

The O2 had never heard anything like it – the audience reached new levels of excitement.

Stage centre, there she was wearing a long, gold evening dress – the gold discs sewn into the fabric sparkled like personal mirror balls from the six follow spots illuminating her from back, front and sides.

The sniper, high above the crowds hidden in the catwalk, carefully prepared his shot – he didn't have to wait until the final pyrotechnic display to conceal the sound of his single suppressed shot, but he would. Patience and calm were a virtue, but he thrived on theatre. And, after all, this was the business of show, to send a clear, unequivocal message to anyone that betrayed the Vory. The Spetsnaz-issued Vintorez rifle was loaded with a heavy subsonic 9×39mm SP5 cartridge. In the indoors of the O2, windage was not a factor.

The massive O2 danced to the reflected sparkling gold. The ten-metre ultra-high-resolution video screens showed Martha's laughing face in ultra close-up – in glorious high resolution. The music kicked into the opening of one of her most high-energy songs, the perfect show-starter.

'Hello London. I... have... returned!' Ear-shattering cheer. 'And it's great to be back.'

Danny and Daisy will return in *Red Light and Bell*.

ACKNOWLEDGEMENTS

AS USUAL A NOVEL CANNOT BE WRITTEN WITHOUT the knowledge and help of many people – all of whom must be thanked for their kind and generous support.

Many very well-known TV, radio, music and personal friends have helped me with deep background to ensure the tittle-tattle of real life, show business and the law are accurately portrayed – including Spice Girl, singer, songwriter, entrepreneur, actress and television personality, Melanie Chisholm; broadcaster and voice-artist, Alan Dedicoat; former Police Superintendent Andy Pullan; Guy and Sarah Bowden for their creativity, fabulous suggestions and for reading early manuscripts; author and screenwriter Matthew Hall for his wise counsel; Alison King, my former business partner, for her freely-given critique; and the team at The Ivy Club led by Fernando Peire.

A very big thank you to my editor Sara Starbuck – who has helped me at every stage of this journey to bring this, my debut novel to you, dear reader!

Thank you also to the many other friends, too many to mention here, for their encouragement and for putting up with my ramblings as the plot thickened.

And last but certainly not least, to my wife, Sue, for her backing, support and love – and for forcing me down to my sh'office at the bottom of the garden in all weathers to write.

Any errors are mine – this is totally a work of fiction, a story.

Nothing, absolutely nothing is true…

Richard Cobourne
March 2020
Bandwagon@RichardCobourne.com

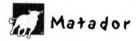

Matador